THE EIGHTEENTH FONTANA BOOK OF GREAT GHOST STORIES

Also in Fontana

The 3rd Fontana Book of Great Ghost Stories
The 5th Fontana Book of Great Ghost Stories
The 6th Fontana Book of Great Ghost Stories
The 7th Fontana Book of Great Ghost Stories
The 8th Fontana Book of Great Ghost Stories
Ed. Robert Aickman

The 9th Fontana Book of Great Ghost Stories
The 12th Fontana Book of Great Ghost Stories
The 15th Fontana Book of Great Ghost Stories
The 16th Fontana Book of Great Ghost Stories
The 17th Fontana Book of Great Ghost Stories
Ed. R. Chetwynd-Hayes

Lord Halifax's Ghost Book
Lord Halifax

and many others

THE EIGHTEENTH
FONTANA BOOK OF GREAT

Ghost Stories

Selected by R. Chetwynd-Hayes

FONTANA PAPERBACKS

First published by Fontana Paperbacks in 1982

Made and printed in Great Britain by
William Collins Sons & Co. Ltd, Glasgow

CONTENTS

ACKNOWLEDGEMENTS

The Editor gratefully acknowledges permission to reprint copyright material to the following:

The author for EYE TO EYE by Roger F. Dunkley. © 1982.
The author for HOUSEWARMING by Steve Rasnic Tem. © 1982.
The author for OFF THE DEEP END by Rick Kennett. © 1982.
The author and J. M. Dent & Sons Ltd for THE ANKARDYNE PEW by W. F. Harvey from *The Beast with Five Fingers & Other Midnight Tales*.
The author for OUTSIDE AGENCY by Daphne Froome. © 1982.
Curtis Brown Ltd on behalf of the Executors of Pamela Hansford Johnson for THE EMPTY SCHOOLROOM.
The author for OFF THE DEEP END by Phillip C. Heath. © 1982.
The author for THE SUMMER HOUSE by Heather Vineham. © 1982.
The author for THE FERRIES by Ramsey Campbell. © 1982.
The author for THE NEW OLD HOUSE by R. C. Solomon. © 1982.
The Literary Trustees of Walter de la Mare and The Society of Authors as their representative for BAD COMPANY.
The author for THE OLD RECTORY WELL by Patricia Moynehan. © 1982.
The author for STREETS OF THE CITY by Tony Richards. © 1982.
Stella Jonckjeere for KECKSIES by Marjorie Bowen.
The author for ABOVE AND BEYOND by Charles Brameld. © 1982.
The author for THE CHAIR by R. Chetwynd-Hayes. © 1982.

EDITOR'S NOTE

INTRODUCTION

Having re-read my introduction to the *17th Fontana Book of Great Ghost Stories*, I find that I wrote a learned discourse on the types of ghosts one may encounter in this haunted vale of tears. I classified them as: a disembodied spirit, a personality residue, a time image: I missed one out: the fear ghost. The most common I suspect.

Let us take a hypothetical example. You move into a house that has the reputation of being haunted by an old man carrying a lighted candle. While the sun shines through the nylon curtains you can afford to laugh at this nonsensical idea and even talk bravely of blowing his candle out, should he put in an appearance. But when long shadows creep across the garden and strange shapes appear in obscure corners, a little grey snake uncoils in your brain. You may possibly remember that someone (me) once said that every house harbours at least one ghost, even if the living inhabitants are too blind to see it. It is conceivable that you will recollect that the same person maintained that few people can boast of mounting the stairs without *something* walking very close behind them. Such reflections are not comforting when you are seated in an empty house that has the reputation of being haunted by an old man carrying a lighted candle – and the chances are that sooner or later you will see him.

Why? The answer is simple. Atmosphere, plus a generous helping of fear, will make your brain project the image it expects to see. Now, I am going to take this blood-curdling conjecture one stage further. Is it not possible that one or more people can create a fear ghost that becomes part of the surroundings and is later seen by someone who is – at first – not particularly frightened? Imagine – you may be on the receiving end of someone else's fear.

Roger F. Dunkley is a well established pillar of supernatural fiction, specializing in plots that usually have an ironic twist. *Eye to Eye* is no exception and contains as many chuckles as chills, a combination that is becoming increasingly popular. A haunted car is not a unique vehicle, but I venture to suggest that one inhabited by a ghost from the future is.

Steve Rasnic Tem has made quite a name for himself on both sides of the Atlantic and now enjoys the reputation of being a fantasy writer of merit. *Housewarming* is a subtle study of mounting terror. Poor Judith undoubtedly creates her own fear-ghost – and one that will be around for a long time. I can offer no comfort to the reader. This kind of situation could happen to anyone – and probably will. *Housewarming* is a plot I would dearly have liked to have thought of first, and now I can only gnash my teeth in pure envy.

Kindred Spirits by Rick Kennett is – as far as I can remember – the first science-fiction ghost story I have ever accepted. Normally ghosts and space ships just won't mix, possibly because authors of the two genres have completely different outlooks. One tends to concentrate on *what was* and the other *what will be*. But Mr Kennett – of Coburg, Victoria, Australia – has contrived a neat, if mind-boggling, plot that actually works. Imagine if you can a portion of earth being towed across space with the intention of making it part of a *jig-saw* planet that will eventually exist far out in the galaxy. Then add a ghost for good measure. Wonderful stuff.

The Ankardyne Pew by W. F. Harvey is a no-nonsense, spine-chilling ghost story, guaranteed to raise any amount of fear-ghosts and to murder sleep. The reader will note that a church is involved again, which might be one reason that such hallowed establishments are not as well attended as they used to be. My advice is as follows: read this story, then follow the narrator's example: . . . *I went to bed early with a volume of Trollope and a long candle*.

Daphne Froome has written quite a few stories for my various collections, the last being *The Last Innings*, which appeared in *The 17th Fontana Book of Great Ghost Stories*. This dealt with the bizarre happenings that ended a cricket match. Now Miss Froome has turned her attention to an equally disturbing game of golf. Is nothing sacred? Poor old Mr Grant ventures out onto the snow-covered golf course with the praiseworthy intention of improving his handicap and then . . . Precisely. And then! *A faint rustle . . . a cough . . . the muffled clapping of gloved hands*. I can only hope that Ms Froome will leave snooker alone. The idea of a haunted snooker table would be the very end.

Those who have read *The 16th Fontana Book of Great Ghost Stories* will remember I included a neat little story called *The Swan* by Pamela Hansford Johnson. Now I have pleasure in reprinting *The Empty Schoolroom* by the same author. Beautifully written, subtle and entirely convincing, this little masterpiece chills rather than frightens. I believe the narrator sums up the situation in the last paragraph, when she says . . . *but even now I cannot endure to awaken suddenly on moonlit nights, and I fling my arms about my husband and beg him to rouse up and speak with me until dawn.*

Phillip C. Heath lives in Grand Saline, Texas, U.S.A., and therefore naturally writes a story with an American background. *Off the Deep End* has a drowsy, countryside setting, where Bittercrest Lake nestles in a wide hollow of tree-clad hills, and the nearest community is Myrtle Springs, about seven miles to the south down Shady Hill Road. Sounds nice and peaceful. But it's not. Not when a young boy called Jeffrey goes fishing. Another sport bites the spectral dust. Anyway, this is a well-written and enjoyable story.

Heather Vineham has contributed several stories to my collections and now comes up with *The Summer House*, which in my opinion is well up to her usual high standard. Strange how children – like churches – seem to be perpetually involved in ghostly goings-on. Sylvie will persist in disappearing over the next door neighbour's garden wall, the mystery being: where does she disappear to? You will have to read *The Summer House* to find out. I suppose we must be thankful the little wretch did not play tennis.

I do not know if Ramsey Campbell had in mind the thought of receiving someone else's fear when he wrote *The Ferries*. Possibly not, but it is one explanation as to why Berry experienced what he did, after being in close proximity with a very frightened uncle. Let me state without reservation that *The Ferries* is a brilliant, imaginative slab of macabre, guaranteed to arrest your interest from the very first word, while making you extremely wary of shadows, unexplained pools of water and ships in bottles, for the rest of your life.

And as for that matter I cannot swear on my heart and soul that you can afford to ignore the warning depicted in *The New Old House* by Robert Solomon, not if you are the father of a small boy and becoming more than friendly with his form mistress. Mr Solomon has a flair for giving his readers a very nasty jolt, after leading them down a commonplace path. For sanity's sake, if you have an obnoxious young son, keep him out of the disused basement.

I never met Walter de la Mare, although as a very old man he lived but a short distance from me. I have often regretted this lapse, for I dearly would have liked to have – respectfully – questioned him about the source of some of his ghost stories. The one I have included here, *Bad Company*, seems to me to be at least three parts true. I quote:

The old man seated opposite – knee to knee – the only sign of life secreted in his eyes – hazed and dully glistening, as a snail in winter is fixed to the wall.

I am willing to bet that was based on an actual experience, even if what followed owed a debt to imagination.

I cannot understand why churches and adjacent buildings seem to be an ideal background for ghost stories, unless it is because their inhabitants are mainly concerned with the hereafter. It is reasonable to suppose that an earthbound ghost would make a beeline for the nearest place, where she or he (or it) might expect to receive expert advice. However, those beings who made life miserable for Nerissa in *The Old Rectory Well* by Patricia Moynehan, appear to be beyond advice – and are far from holy. Ms Moynehan has an uncanny knack of writing about very modern people who somehow become involved in what I can only describe as historical unpleasantness.

Those readers who expressed their admiration of Tony Richard's *After Dark* in *The 17th Fontana Book of Great Ghost Stories*, will not be disappointed with his latest offering, *Streets Of The City*, which has another unique plot set against the background of New York City. I would like to think that Marshall Harris was haunted by a fear ghost, but the macabre events suggest a much more tangible enmity. I regard Mr Richards as a very welcome addition to my growing stable of authors and hope he will continue to turn out such excellent tales.

In *Kecksies* by Marjorie Bowen we are back in Gothic Country again, that wind-swept realm where young esquires come riding from Canterbury, jolly and drunk, rolling in their saddles as they follow the winding road across the downs. I am inclined to believe that swopping places with a dead man is not a healthy pastime, and the practice of tossing the corpse into a dark bed of Kecksies (hemlock) should be avoided. My word, this is a nasty, shivering, sweat-producing, nightmare-creating, comfort-bereft story.

Above and Beyond by Charles Brameld is very much down-to-earth. Told in a slightly hair-raising, black comedy style, we are entertained by the reported haunting of a high-rise block of council flats. I have often considered this an excellent idea, but could never decide which haunting angle to take. One could of course have our old man with the lighted candle wandering down the stairs and doing dreadful things to a plumber who was too drunk to get into the lift. Or have a phantom charwoman clanging her bucket on the roof and crying out: 'Where's me soap?' You may be relieved to learn that Mr Brameld's ghost is not quite so obvious.

Lastly my own contribution, *The Chair*. What can I say about it? It is true? Could be. Someone is almost certain to write in and say they have such a chair and would like to dispose of it. My advice will be – hang on to it. Haunted chairs will soon be the vogue and worth their weight in postage stamps.

So – sixteen stories, every one written by a well established and in some cases world famous author. All written with the deliberate intention of scaring the living daylights out of the reader. I sincerely hope and pray this intention is realized.

May black angels keep watch around your bed.

R. Chetwynd-Hayes.

EYE TO EYE

ROGER F. DUNKLEY

The moment he pulled the car door shut, Myers knew something was not right with his latest acquisition. Had the garage delivered the wrong car? Did the cool leatherwork of twenty-year-old Daimlers always induce that strange flicker of unease? He straightened his tie, felt for the courtesy light, and clicked the switch. Nothing happened. Myers frowned in the darkness. The headache that had nagged at him all day returned. He was already late for the party; he was tempted to abandon the idea altogether. At least he wouldn't run the risk of colliding with the daunting Felicity Farr again. Ignoble and unprofitable thought. He dismissed it. Besides, he wanted to try out the car.

He placed the cigars and road maps on the seat beside him as if to establish his identity in, his ownership of, the new vehicle, then fumbled with the keys, cursed, fumbled again, and inserted the right one in the ignition switch.

But the sensation persisted, redoubled. The distant street light slanted cold shadows across the car's interior, leaving the back seat a wall of darkness. Myers wanted to turn round and check, but an obscure, a distinct misgiving held him back. Check what, for heaven's sake? He sat stiffly, staring ahead into the winter's night, angry and bewildered by this sudden foolishness. He recalled lying in bed as a child, cringing his toes in dreadful expectation of those gnarled, chilling fingers reaching up for him under the blankets. Why the hell should he be afraid to turn round *now*, afraid even to glance into the driving mirror? What atavistic impulse restrained him? Who – or what – was he scared of seeing? A masked hijacker, perhaps, sitting, silent and alone on the back seat, waiting? The glint of a knife? The eye of a gun?

The pain in Myers' head grew worse. He held his breath and listened. The air in the car seemed thick and oppressive, but he could hear nothing beyond the pounding of his own pulse; nothing stirred or breathed in the stillness behind him.

He put down his right hand to feel for the seat belt, which had evidently dropped to his side and, despite himself, hesitated before reaching behind him into the blackness of the rear seat. His fingers tentatively groped along the leatherwork, encountered a patch on the seat that was moist and tacky, and abruptly closed around something hard and cold. With a gasp he snatched back his hand. Then laughed drily. The seat buckle! He muttered to himself out loud to dispel his anger and to break the tense silence of the car. 'Afraid of groping the alien shoe now, are we? Afraid of a smear of oil?'

Darkness swallowed the words.

He fired the engine, revved aggressively, lurched forward onto the road with a roar, and drove out of town into the winding lanes of the Surrey countryside. 'There,' he told himself, 'confront a fear and it evaporates!' He descended the hill and swept round the yawning bend lined with towering oaks.

Abruptly, without warning, an access of fear rushed in upon him.

In that moment Myers Bainton knew. He knew he was not alone in the car. He knew what he would see if he were to lift his eyes to his driving mirror.

He could feel them quite distinctly: a pair of eyes, shining wide and wild. They were glaring into the back of his head out of the darkness of his new car.

Appalled, desperate for company, he held the car on the road and drove the last mile through the howling night into Gibbet's Corner.

The heart of the party was the lounge, which throbbed with noise, lights and people. Myers was thrust into it, introduced cursorily to several people who required him to repeat the pronunciation of his name, then to spell it, and then promptly forgot both it and him, all with much merriment. A bottle of tonic and a glass were pressed into his hands and he was propelled towards a girl in blue feathers and tight, sequined pants who was hugging the last bottle of gin between her knees. She raised her head and stared into his eyes. 'I'm looking,' she said, 'for love.'

'I'm looking for gin,' confessed Myers. He reached out a hand.

'Don't touch me,' said the girl. 'Men!' Her feathers nodded savagely. 'One thing: that's all you're after.'

'Gin, actually,' said Myers. He introduced the tonic bottle into her line of vision and waved it about. She screamed. Myers retreated to a corner and wondered where Ronnie and Angela hid their bottle opener.

He watched the party.

It was loud and in high spirits; so was Felicity Farr. He pressed himself flat against the wall. But she found him. 'It's Myers!' she said.

'So it is,' said Myers. 'Still.'

'You're hiding again.'

'Yes,' said Myers.

People looked up curiously.

'Everyone's having fun,' giggled Felicity.

'Or having someone else.'

'Especially those two by the foliage. No one likes to ask who they are – but what a floor show! It's all happening. Ronnie and Angela and Geoff are battling it out as usual in the kitchen. Come out and play.' Felicity tugged at his arm and saw his face in the light for the first time. 'Are you all right?' she exclaimed. 'My dear, you look positively grey. It's so unfashionable. Has something happened?'

'No,' he said. But he felt the warmth of human contact and saw concern in her look. He realized he was still trembling. 'Yes,' he said. 'Well, yes and no. Actually, it's the car.'

'Big end or tiny tappets, darling?' said Felicity. 'Sit down. Move that hand; she's not using it. Have a sip of this. That dreadful girl with the feathers – she looks like something predatory that just escaped from a zoo – is hoarding the gin. Now, tell Felicity all about it.' She beamed comfortingly and wove curls of his hair around her forefinger.

Myers sat back and began to unwind. 'It's a new car,' he said. 'I picked it up only tonight.'

'New-old or new-new?'

'Daimler; nineteen-sixty,' said Myers.

'Nearly vintage,' said Felicity, delight emerging in a squeal. 'How gorgeous! Bags of atmosphere.'

Myers shuddered. 'That's the problem,' he whispered. He felt himself back in the car, felt a dark shadow moving in the blackness behind him. He sensed those eyes. 'Bags of atmosphere,' he said. And relaxing in the attentive warmth of Felicity's caresses, he confessed to her, blundering through words in his attempts to convey experiences at once so intangible and so distressing, what he had felt earlier in the car.

'A tall dark stranger in your back seat. You should be so lucky,' she interpolated. But by the end of the story she was hugging her knees, rapt with attention.

'And when you stopped, there was really no one there?' Felicity was enthralled.

'No one,' said Myers. 'Nothing.'

'My dear Myers,' said Felicity Farr, her voice tremulous with excitement, 'how simply awful!' Her dramatic whisper penetrated the farthest reaches of the room. 'Your car's *haunted*! Something Very Nasty's happened in that back seat. What a pity Lucy isn't here.'

'Haunted,' said Myers gloomily. He drained the glass with a gulp. 'A ghost in my machine!'

'Something very sinister.' Felicity's eyes gleamed. 'We'll put ads in the paper,' she said. 'Won't it be fun finding out!'

But after the second owner had been traced, visited and found depressingly uninformed and uninformative, her enthusiasm evaporated. Myers' zeal correspondingly increased.

'You're obsessed,' said Felicity.

'I want to know,' said Myers.

'It's an obsession,' said Felicity.

Myers supposed she was right. But *she* had never actually experienced those eyes staring over her shoulder. Certainly their researches had produced little profit. One owner, a man with five children, a small wife and a large sheep dog, had used the Daimler to tow them all repeatedly in a caravan across Europe and back; he showed Myers and Felicity endless slides to verify these feats. An old lady with no children and a parrot called Piers had never allowed her chauffeur to let the car out of its garage in eight years of proud but stationary ownership. It was unpromising material, not redolent of the spectral nastiness that Felicity had set her heart on. The only sinister item they uncovered, as Felicity remarked, was 'that bloody parrot' – but that was because she was prejudiced; the bird, out of obscure motives of envy or revenge, had dismembered with its beak a rather chic hat she was sporting, concocted, they surmised, from parrot plumage.

'If you insist on pursuing this ghost hunt,' said Felicity, 'there's only one solution: Lucy.'

'Lucy,' said Myers.

Felicity tutted, and reminded him. 'Lucy has the vibrations.'

Thus Lucy was invited to Myers' house, flattered, dined, rested, and then taken outside to be sat in the Daimler.

'I'm not very good at this,' she repeated.

'Nonsense – darling.' Felicity's impatience sometimes travelled ahead of her manners.

'Honestly.' Lucy subsided tentatively into the driver's seat. They watched. She pressed a palm to her forehead.

Felicity leaned forward. 'What is it?' she said.

'My head . . . aches.'

'So does mine,' said Myers. He closed his eyes, swaying unsteadily.

When he opened them again, he saw Lucy, her head thrown back, shaking helplessly. A distraught Felicity stooped over her attempting simultaneously to soothe her and extricate her from the car. 'Help me, for heaven's sake,' she was saying. Lucy's voice was choked with sobs, but her words were as clear as her distress.

'Blood,' she moaned. 'Blood. I see rope, a knife.' Her body writhed in the seat. Her voice dropped to a frightened whisper. 'There's death in the car . . . It's black and twisted. A tree, a tree . . .!'

Her voice rose shrilly. She raised a finger and pointed at the driving mirror, shielding her eyes from the sight.

'Look. Look there . . .!' she gasped.

They manoeuvred her body back into the house.

'Brandy!' said Felicity urgently.

But Lucy opened her eyes, sat up, straightened her dress and gave an embarrassed giggle.

'Honestly, I told you. I'm not very good at this,' she said. 'Did anything happen?'

'The police,' said Felicity, when they met over a hurried lunch the following day. 'We should go to the police and leave it all to them.'

Myers sipped morosely. 'To tell them what? That my car's haunted by a murderer who strangled or stabbed his victim with a rope or a knife under some unspecified arboreal abortion that passes for a tree! Can you see their faces?' He essayed a wry chuckle and inadvertently blew bubbles in his coffee.

'I can see *your* face,' said Felicity, offering him a handkerchief.

Myers erased the coffee moustache. 'Evidence,' he said. 'We've got no proof.'

Felicity picked up her handbag, smiled brightly, said: 'Well, you've got only one option, haven't you? Sell the wretched car and forget the whole squalid business. Must rush, darling. I'm having a plumber at two. Delicious. 'Bye,' pecked him on the cheek, dropped the bill on his plate, and headed for the door.

Mysteries teased Myers; he could no more heed Felicity's advice than leave a crossword or jigsaw puzzle unfinished. As he watched her departing with her customary panache, he resolved to hunt down and confront for himself the one previous owner who had failed to respond to their advert.

He had formulated a plan.

Felicity reappeared at the table. 'No plans, Myers dear,' she said. 'Give up the Hercule Poirot bit. It'll only bring on your headaches.' She tinkled her fingers in farewell. At the door she turned and called, 'I meant to ask: are you coming to Whatsit's Corner tonight? Ronnie and Angela seem to do nothing but throw parties. I promise not to ravish you . . . without due warning.'

Myers hunched his shoulders over his coffee, groaned, and tried to look as anonymous as possible.

The plan worked.

Myers visited the local police, spun an increasingly elaborate yarn to a variety of increasingly mystified officers about his claim to have a valuable item left in his car by a previous owner, and finally managed to take note of a computer print-out of their names and addresses before slipping out of the room. He popped his head back round the door. 'I may be returning,' he told an officer at the desk. 'Citizen's Arrest.' He tapped his nose, nodding sagely. The officer gazed quizzically at Myers' retreating back. He shook his head. Then he picked up a phone.

Myers climbed into the car, smiling inwardly at his skill and cunning. He decided not to contact Felicity but, overcoming his reluctance to use the Daimler, drove across the town to seek out Mr Sidney Mortimer of 13A, Beaumont Buildings. He climbed the stairs ignoring, after the first flight, the graffiti that, he decided, were more colourful than witty, and resorting to the rusted railings to help him up the fourth flight. He had even rapped briskly on the dolphin door knocker before realizing that he had no clear idea of how he intended to tackle his most promising suspect. He pressed a hand against his forehead to dispel a lurking headache, and had a sudden nightmarish glimpse of a large, dark shadow of a man appearing in the doorway looming over him, winding a rope round simian knuckles and gazing down at him out of lunatic eyes. He turned to flee, and at that moment, after much clanking and shunting of bolts, the door opened. Myers hesitated, and turned back.

'Yes?'

'Ah, yes,' said Myers.

'Yes?' repeated the man. He peered to his left and right into the gloom of the corridor.

'Mr Mortimer,' Myers said, confidence returning, for the man was built on a human scale after all and was, furthermore, balding. 'Mr *Sidney* Mortimer,' he added. It felt the right thing to add.

'Police?' said Sidney Mortimer.

Myers stepped forward. 'Might I be?' he asked.

'Or you might be the owner of my old Daimler,' said the man. He investigated Myers' face more closely. 'I've been expecting you.'

Myers stepped back, his face pale.

'You look like a man in need of a chair,' said Sidney Mortimer, gripping his arm and guiding him firmly through a narrow hallway into a small, crowded room. 'Turf the cat and the newspapers off that settee. And the thriller. Do you like murder mysteries? Agatha Christie? I'm a fanatic myself.' He waved an arm vaguely. 'Tea? I would offer you whisky but – you understand, Mr – er – . The days of Daimlers and roses are over. Times change . . .' An unconvincing chuckle failed to escape his throat.

'No tea,' said Myers.

'Still we keep cheerful,' said the man, 'back in the old trade.'

'Trade?' said Myers.

'Butchering,' said Sidney Mortimer.

Myers leaned forward. His eye twitched.

'With the Co-op,' added the man. 'Life's not all bad is it!' He sighed. 'And we keep fit. Work-outs down the gym every night. It all helps.' He clenched his fist under Myers' nose and flexed his biceps.

Myers withdrew his nose, impressed.

'Helps you forget things.'

Myers' eyebrows lifted.

'The past.' The man stared ahead, lapped about with melancholy.

Myers cleared his throat – a brisk, business-like noise. 'About the car . . .' he began.

'She had a thing about that car,' said Sidney Mortimer. 'You married?'

Myers shook his head. The man echoed the movement sadly.

'My wife,' he said, 'of blessed memory . . .'

'Ah,' said Myers.

'Down under,' said the man.

'How did it happen?' said Myers.

'Painful. Very sudden. Very cruel.'

'Was it – natural?' said Myers. He pictured the car, the rope, the helpless victim.

'Never,' said Sidney Mortimer. He tore at the arm of his chair and thumped it with a savage fist. Beads of sweat stood upon his forehead. 'Never!'

'Murder?' whispered Myers.

'Wagga Wagga,' said the man.

'Pardon?' said Myers.

'Australia. Down under. She wanted to leave. Just like that. One morning. My best mate and her. Start life again, they said. Painful, Mr – er – . It hurts still. Five years after.'

'Yes,' said Myers. 'But they went? To Wagga Whatsit?'

'Never. She stayed with me. Died last winter. With her kidneys.'

'Ah,' said Myers. 'I'm sorry. And her mate – your mate – the other man . . .?'

Sidney stared abstractedly into the empty fireplace.

'You – dealt with him, I imagine.'

'I dealt with him all right.' He continued to stir amongst the embers of memory.

Myers stood up. He had heard enough. His suspicions congealed into a decision.

'Yes. That old Daimler. She developed quite a thing about it, the wife,' said the man. 'It reached the point where she wouldn't get in it. Even talked about it with Father Mulkerrins. Exorcism and such! Once she got an idea in her head . . . well.'

Myers stared at him. 'Well?'

'One of her fancies. One of her ways of getting at me, I suppose. After. It's just – she always said there was a smell of death about that car. Do you believe in ghosts, Mr –'

Myers drew himself up. 'I believe in justice,' he said. He jingled his car keys. 'I was wondering, Mr Mortimer, whether you'd enjoy a ride in the Daimler – for old times' sake?'

The man's eyes brightened. 'Are you serious? I was trying to think of a way of asking – without causing offence. Just lead the way. Tell you what. Take me to The Oak – Gibbet's Oak. It's not far.'

'Half my friends live there,' murmured Myers.

'There's something there might interest us both . . .'

Myers turned in the doorway. He looked at the man sharply.

'A drink!' said Sidney Mortimer.

'If you're sitting up front being chauffeur, I'll sit in the rear: Lord Muck, eh?'

Myers, quietly triumphant, pulled away from the kerb with his prime suspect safely ensconced on the back seat. The car purred comfortably.

Then the man tapped him on the shoulder. 'Hey,' said Myers, 'that hurt.'

'It was meant to,' said the man. 'OK. Where is it?'

Myers shot a grimace of bewilderment over his shoulder.

'This valuable you told them you'd found left in the car.'

The Daimler swerved.

'Don't worry. The police got in touch. Told me to expect a nutter. I didn't realize I was in for a three-star loony. Why the excuses? The prying? What are you really after? What's the mystery?'

Myers kept his head. 'It's a murder mystery, isn't it, Mr Mortimer? You're the Agatha Christie fanatic. Self-confessed.' He glanced in the driving mirror, repressing a brief resonance of unease. The man's eyes were half-closed, averted.

'Murder?'

'The man you "dealt with" so efficiently,' said Myers.

Amused indignation flushed the man's face. 'Jim?' he laughed. 'Jim's all set up in Bermondsey. Or was, last we heard. Car repairs. After he got repaired himself. This car was his first customer . . .'

Myers negotiated a bend, and drove on. 'Ghosts,' he said, 'talk. They leave memories. This car's like a travelling recorder, waiting for full playback.'

Sidney Mortimer produced a hybrid of snort and grunt, eloquent of disgust and incredulity.

'It's haunted with your crime, Mr Mortimer. We know it all. The knife, the smear of blood down the leatherwork, the rope for trussing up your victim, the staring eyes of the fanatic. It's all here. Vibrations. Printed into the fabric of the car.'

The Daimler veered dangerously into the side of the road as Myers' voice rose breathlessly.

'Stop the car,' said the man. Fingers dug into Myers' shoulders.

Myers slowed down. 'We've got your address now,' he said. 'It's too late to run.' He drew into a mud-furrowed lay-by. The late grey afternoon filled the car with thickening shadows. 'You're frightened,' he said.

'You're bloody right,' said the man. 'I've never been on a joy ride with a lunatic before. Get out.'

'I don't see . . .' said Myers.

The knife flicked close to his ear.

'I see . . .' said Myers.

'Keys!'

Myers flung them to the ground. The man retrieved them and led Myers at knife-point to the back of the car. He unlocked the boot, wrenched at the spare wheel, groped about in the dark interior muttering angrily, gave a muffled cry and hauled forth his trophy, like a triumphant midwife.

Myers' temple pulsed with pain.

'The rope!' he said.

'Tow rope,' said Sidney Mortimer. 'Still here! I always kept a length handy. After we broke down. Just in case. Come here.'

'There's blood on this rope,' said Myers, as the man coiled it round his arms and shoulders for the fifth time.

'Oil,' said Sidney Mortimer. 'Grease. You're obsessed, aren't you?'

'I want to know,' said Myers.

'Obsessed. And scared.'

A car, its headlights splashing a nightmare kaleidoscope of branches and shadows, swept past them into the twilight of country lanes. Myers shivered. He wished he'd phoned Felicity. Phoned anyone. The blind folly of his scheme began to oppress him.

The man trussed his feet.

'The police have got your number,' said Myers, staggering against the car.

'And yours, mate.'

'They're expecting me at the station. Citizen's arrest.'

'I'm saving them a ride,' said the man. 'And a dangerous loony hunt.'

Deftly, he flexed his arms, picked Myers up and moved to deposit him in the back seat.

'No!' Myers panicked. The vein throbbed painfully in his forehead. Intimations threatened at the back of his mind. His scalp prickled. Not there, dear heavens!

A tracery of trees flickered into light ahead of an oncoming car. The vehicle roared into sight down the hill. 'Help!' yelled Myers. The car rushed past. 'Felicity! Lucy!' he groaned into the gathering night.

Roughly he was thrust into the back of the car. He struck out with his legs; he crashed his shoulders against the doorway. Then, lungs straining for air, he subsided onto the seat.

Blood dripped from a cut in his hand. The leatherwork by his feet grew moist and sticky.

The driver's door slammed, and with a skid and a guttural roar, the car pulled out into the night.

In the rear where Myers sat, hunched upright, trussed and helpless, the shadows closed about him.

'Lucy!' said Felicity, pouting her lips to breathe on freshly painted nails. She grimaced at the receiver. 'Look, I'm just off to the party . . .'

'Pick me up,' said Lucy.

'Darling . . . Are you all right?'

'No,' said Lucy. 'It's Myers. We got it wrong. I – feel it. You know that tree . . . The tree I saw. I've just realized; I recognise it. It's down the road. We pass it every day . . .'

'Give me two minutes,' said Felicity.

'Make it one. We've got to change things . . .'

Myers struggled ineffectually. The rope bit into his arms, coiled about him as tight and implacable as fate.

He leaned forward. 'Listen!' he said.

His eyes grew wide in the darkness. He peered across the man's shoulder and caught a glimpse in the driving mirror.

His lips parted. Shivers of ice played at the base of his skull. Those eyes. Once before he had felt them, glaring into the back of his head. Now he saw them, shining wide and wild with fear, face to face.

Déjà vu; the moment of horror, its shadow cast before it, was locking into focus, now. Time was ticking inevitably towards place.

Myers stared at his terrified eyes, his mind tangling with impossible mysteries.

'Listen!' he repeated. His voice was choked by the shades that hung thick and stifling about the car. An awareness of mortality whelmed over him.

'Everything's changed,' he said. 'No, nothing's changed,' he said. 'But . . .'

'Save it for the shrink,' said the man.

'For heaven's sake. It's not too late, after all,' shouted Myers. 'I was wrong. Accusing you.' He wrenched himself to the edge of the seat. 'The whole business: *it hasn't happened yet.*'

His eyes opened wide.

'No one need be killed,' he said.

The man gave a dry laugh.

Myers butted the driver's shoulders with his head. 'Stop the car,' he growled. 'For Christ's sake.'

'Maniac!' The man regained control of the car. He hurled obscenities over his back.

The shadows pressed closer. Myers' head throbbed. The car tyres squealed. Trees rose up, flared into momentary light, and hurtled into the blackness of the past.

Then, in the distance, Myers saw the tree, picked out in the headlights of an approaching car. Its black branches were distinctively gaunt and twisted in the shifting light.

Panic seized him.

'Gibbet's Oak!' he said hoarsely. 'Death. Of course: all those hangings.'

'Black spot,' said Sidney Mortimer drily. 'That's as far as friend Jim got. When he ran off in my Daimler. The bastard. I rearranged the steering for him. Very untidy. An experience he's never forgotten...'

'Stop, now. Stop the car before it's too late,' cried Myers. Powerless, enraged and terrified, he launched himself against the driving seat.

Eyes dilated with horror, he watched the oncoming car sweep down the hill and approach the bend.

'Save Myers? Save him from what?' said Felicity to her distressed passenger.

Lucy pointed. 'There's the tree. Just ahead.' Then she screamed and pressed herself back in her seat. 'That car. It's gone crazy. Felicity –'

'Myers!' gasped Felicity.

The Daimler's wheel spun from the man's grip. There was a shrieking of tyres, the world revolved impossibly about Myers, time and the darkness of the shadow conjoined in one howling moment, and the ancient oak jarred at the twofold impact. Beneath its black boughs, the surrounding earth took the seeping blood and the pain and mystery of death deep into itself.

'Bottoms,' said Felicity, 'up! Have some more champers, darling.

Matron's eating people somewhere else. Besides, she's signed your release. Here's to the future!'

'I'm sticking to the present,' said Myers, 'in future.'

'Perhaps one day we'll see eye to eye over something,' said Felicity.

Myers winced.

'. . . If you'll pardon the expression.'

'Never!' Myers scanned the hospital drive. 'Cab's coming,' he said. 'Good old Lucy. Rescue at last. I hope she's done what I asked; I'm not setting one disabled foot in that taxi until I know it's been recently and comprehensively exorcised by the Archbishop of Canterbury himself.'

Felicity took his glass, giggling.

'Poor old Mortimer,' said Myers. '*He* can't just drive away from all this. Promoted to the ghosthood. Locked away in the past with the rest.'

Felicity held out a supporting arm. 'What did you mean when you said it was all decided? That the accident, the events, were just there waiting for us to set them going? Did the poor man *have* to die?'

Myers shrugged. 'Ouch,' he said.

'But Lucy's warning? Your last-minute realization? Didn't we change anything, then?'

'What happened, happened,' said Myers. 'Who knows?'

HOUSEWARMING

STEVE RASNIC TEM

Judith glanced around the living room once before starting up to bed. Boxes of books and glassware still crowded much of the floor and filled the seats of many of the overstuffed chairs, but at least she'd got the heavy curtains up over the large front windows. She was suddenly startled as two brilliant spots of light blossomed in the cloth, as if a car had turned off the highway and were headed straight across her front yard and into the house.

She laughed lightly to herself. There was a driveway across the road; her neighbours were merely backing up into their garage. She wondered, briefly, if people would be able to see through her curtains, but no, they were too thick, she was sure.

Something scratched at the door and her laughter died. Her nerves jangled as she struggled for control. What was wrong with her? She seemed to be forgetting where she lived now; she acted as if this were her old place, downtown in the inner city. After all, she'd moved into this quiet neighbourhood in the suburbs for her nerves, so why couldn't she relax and enjoy it? She heard the two cats mewling at the door and went to let them in.

The black cat came through first. 'Edge!' she whispered, 'You scared the wits out of me!' Then the grey cat, Myra, slipped through.

Judith closed the door behind them, turned, then looked back over her shoulder at the door once more. She reached over and slid the dead bolt home, then latched the chain lock. It didn't matter she'd found a new place; old habits die hard. Besides, it made her feel better.

The cats had already found their place atop a basket full of towels. They curled together like two fat commas. Judith smiled and opened the door to the stairwell. She stepped inside, then slipped her hand out to switch off the light.

When the door closed she was in a dim yellow darkness, the only light for the stairwell that of a streetlight somewhere north of the house, some of its illumination caught by a small narrow window just above head-level, on the first and only landing. There was a wall lamp at this landing but it didn't work. Judith planned to have it fixed first thing the next day; she hated the dark.

She allowed her fingers to stray to the walls as she ascended the staircase, reminded once more of how lucky she'd been to find such a place out of the congestion of the city but still within easy commuting distance. It was an old house, well-made. The stairwell walls and steps were a beautiful maple, the same maple she thought must be all through the house, although much of it was coated with what was probably a century's accumulation of paint. She'd begun restoring some of that woodwork to its original splendour this very first day, and she knew she wouldn't be happy until it had all been refinished, and the dull, light-absorbing surfaces replaced with shiny wood.

She knew already that redoing the old house wouldn't be easy. It had taken her hours just to chisel away at the first layer of paint. After several coatings of the strongest paint remover she could find the paint still stubbornly adhered. It was almost as if the house were fighting her, holding on to its covering. But apparently her frustration had given her new strength, however, for just as she was ready to give up the scraper had taken away several layers of paint at once, and the old blue carpet was soon covered with large, multicoloured flakes of paint. One brownish layer remained beneath all that, but that had been comparatively easy to strip.

The wood beneath was a brilliant orange-rose, shiny and like new. Judith was startled. She imagined that was exactly as the wood had looked for the first tenants.

Sleep did not come easily. Judith couldn't help mulling over all the things she needed to do the next few days to get the house into shape. She'd have to call the plumber; all the fixtures appeared to be locked up tight. She hadn't even been able to take a bath. She couldn't understand it; the previous tenants had left only a month before.

The furnace was almost as stubborn. It was also quite old, and although she had been able to start a fire, it seemed to give up its heat grudgingly. All the windows on the bottom floor were stuck solid, but then, that mattered little since it was winter. But several of the cupboards seemed to have similar problems, even though for the life of her Judith could find no excuse for their being stuck. They weren't locked, the plunger moved freely back and forth, there was no paint or anything else between the door and the frame – in fact, there seemed to be more than enough clearance all the way around. There just seemed to be no reason for those doors not to open. So most of her things had to remain in boxes; it made her uncomfortable, the house less than home-like when she couldn't at least get her cupboards straightened away. It was as if someone were holding on for dear life to the doorknobs within the cupboards, fighting her.

Many of the lights wouldn't work, storage jars were so jammed into the narrow basement shelves she couldn't budge any of them, and the gas oven's operation was so sporadic she was afraid to use it – the gas seeming to come and go at will. The list seemed endless, and grew longer and longer even as Judith attempted to fall asleep.

A creaking, as if the living-room floor were slowly splitting lengthwise, began somewhere near the window beneath her, and seemed to travel all the way to the bathroom at the rear of the first floor. Judith shifted nervously; she couldn't remember ever hearing a sound of quite that character.

Quickly she began listing all the things it could be: the cats chasing each other, a mouse beneath the floorboards, or most likely the movements of an old house that is in the process of resettling even after a hundred years. She had learned this exercise of list-making as a little girl. It always seemed to calm her a bit, although never completely.

It embarrassed her, being twenty-eight years old and still frightened of sounds in the darkness like a six-year-old. But at least she didn't give in to the fears as she once had.

As a small child she had gone through a period in which she was convinced someone was trying to get in through her bedroom window. Each night she'd covered herself over completely with sheets, blankets, heavy quilts – even in the warmest weather. For a while she'd tried to ignore the sounds coming from her window: the creakings, slidings, tappings, whisperings. But each time she'd eventually have to face those noises, and then her list-making would begin. It could be just a tree branch, but no, it didn't sound like a tree branch scratching. It could be the wind rattling at the pane.

But no, the wind wasn't that rhythmical. So maybe it was a bird, blown in by the wind. Or a wasp. Or the blind had come loose.

But inevitably those years, she lost. And began screaming and sobbing as loudly as she could.

And every time her father had come and turned on the light, and explained to her that actually it had been a branch, the blind, or a small bird blown in against the pane. But each time he had seemed angrier, more impatient, until that last time he'd slapped her and called her a baby, and she'd never screamed for him again, but bit and bit on her lip until she'd thought she'd bitten it through.

It occurred to her some years later that she had always heard more noises, that the dark had been much more frightening, when her father had been angry with her. Then the house hadn't seemed a safe place. She hadn't felt as if she'd belonged. The house hadn't wanted her there.

Something slid on the floor below her. It sounded like a chair, one of the heavy, overstuffed chairs. It could be just a book sliding from its precarious perch. But no, it didn't sound like a book sliding at all.

When she'd first moved into the city she'd made a big mistake taking that apartment downtown. She knew that now, even if it had been cheaper. There were street crimes nearly every day, burglaries, rapes. Not the sort of thing to make one feel secure, especially someone with all her fears. She'd been foolish not to consider that. The apartment was dingy, ill-kept, the years of progressively worse tenants clearly recorded in the walls and furniture. She hadn't belonged there; it could never have felt like home. And she had heard the noises more than ever; she got little sleep living there.

Something, somewhere, rolled then fell a short distance. It could be just a log, but no, it didn't sound anything like a log dropping in the fireplace.

Obviously, just moving hadn't been enough to solve the problem. Here were the noises, the sounds that had always let Judith know she wasn't at home, that she wasn't wanted here, and it was only her first night in the house.

She felt foolish. It was a problem she was going to have to beat if she were to be happy living anywhere. She breathed deeply, fully, trying to remain calm and rational. Sounds were everywhere; they couldn't be avoided. She thought about how one could hear things even in white noise, static, hear almost anything. Judith had left the television on one night, fallen asleep in front of it, and had been sure her father was there in the room, lecturing her about her silly, irrational fears. But it had been the static from the television, that was all. Nothing else.

A few fast creaks in succession. Someone stepping quickly across the living room, reaching for the stairwell door? It could be the cat, one of the cats. But no, it didn't sound anything like a cat.

She'd been a bit apprehensive when she'd first looked at the house, but mainly because she'd just simply never visualized herself as a homeowner. It didn't fit her picture of the future. It had always been difficult for her to imagine living in a house she was totally responsible for, or one that other people had lived in, slept in, before her. Perhaps that was the greatest discomfort about owning an old house for Judith. Who knew how many people had lived and died here before? Countless numbers? In the face of all that, how could she ever feel that she *owned* such a place? How was she to feel at home here, with all those other presences at the back of her mind, evident in every nook and cranny of the house?

Something seemed to snap downstairs, wood from the door-frame, or a window being pried loose? It could have been the works of the cuckoo clock on the dining-room wall, but no, it didn't sound like clockworks.

She had checked the neighbourhood out quite carefully. Most of the residents were elderly, had been here a long time, and claimed they'd never had any trouble, even though a poorer and more violent section of the city was only a few blocks away. Some younger couples had recently moved into houses at both corners, and were spending so much time revitalizing their properties Judith sensed the beginnings of a change in the neighbourhood. Judith was lucky, the real estate agent had told her. She was getting the place before the property values skyrocketed. And although that section of the city but a short distance away made her nervous sometimes, Judith was convinced she'd chosen one of the safest places in the city to make her home.

The door was apparently rattling on its hinges.

A window suddenly banged.

But no, it didn't sound like a tree branch. No, it didn't sound like the wind.

Something heavy slid on the floor below. Something banged the wall as one of her cats screeched.

Without thinking Judith was screaming with her cat, racing down the stairs, her arms tensed and raised. She slammed open the stairwell door and hit the light-switch sobbing.

The sudden glare shocked her system. She looked around the living room wide-eyed, as if she'd suddenly awakened from a bad nightmare and had difficulty adjusting to her bland surroundings.

A few books lay on the floor. One edge of the rug had been curled up. The arm covers of her chairs were all scattered about the floor like empty skins. Typical tricks her cats pulled all the time.

'Edge? Myra?' she called.

The black cat, Edge, came around the side of one of the chairs, crying. Judith picked him up and began stroking his sleek, dark coat. 'Where's your sister, Edge? Where's Myra?'

Judith called for Myra several times. No answer. She finally gave up, hugged Edge to her. 'Guess I'm not the only scaredy cat, huh, Edge?' She chuckled, turned out the light, and carried Edge up to bed with her.

In the darkness a picture suddenly tilted on the wall. A lamp crept to the edge of a table. Several books fell out of their box.

A heavy overstuffed chair slid back from the wall to its original position. The muted yellow glare from a passing car illuminated the green-papered wall behind it, and the matted grey fur speckled with red.

KINDRED SPIRITS

RICK KENNETT

The grass was quite damp as I crawled out of my tent. Droplets hung from its edges and tiny pools filled its hollows. They'd had it 'raining' during the 'night'.

I stood and stretched the cramp out of my joints and muscles, turning as I did to take in the greenery of the surrounding forest. It was a beautiful 'day'. The birds were chirping, there wasn't a cloud in the steel sky, and all the lights above were blazing away to glory. Everything seemed so natural if the 'sky' was ignored. It actually felt like morning in the bush. Only the throb of the engines, whenever they were in use, ever distorted the illusion. That, and whenever the aliens put in one of their rare appearances.

So it was that, as I was about to cross the road to the water-hole with billy in hand, I was a little surprised to see a green-skinned, cone-headed giant flash past in a silver hover-jeep. I watched the being and his humming vehicle disappear down the track, scratched my head, and went about my morning routine.

Sinclair Hayes walked into my camp a few minutes later. He didn't look too happy. He sat down on a log opposite where I crouched, waiting for the billy to boil on the Primus. We exchanged greetings and yawned together. It was still too early to do much else. However, the cobwebs were soon washed away once we got some strong, hot coffee into us.

Sinclair put his enamel mug down, and without preamble said, 'They're throwing me out, David.'

With coffee halfway down my throat I nearly choked.

'What!' I stared up at our pressure-dome sky. 'But that's inhuman!'

He smiled at my choice of adjective. 'Sorry, David. I mean they're taking me out of the forest and putting me down *into* the ship.' He cast his eyes momentarily upwards, and I saw him shudder. 'Hell, you'd never get me out there. It's so impossibly big and lonely. You know what I mean?'

I nodded, and drank some more from my mug.

'So, how did you manage it?' I asked. 'In the right place at the right time?'

He grinned at me over his mug. 'If it wasn't for us being in the right place at the right time – or wrong place at the wrong time – we wouldn't be in this crazy situation.'

'True, but now that we've become used to this "crazy situation" wouldn't you rather be a forest ranger in a purloined piece of bushland, flying through space to places unknown than some homeless wanderer drifting aimlessly around the country?'

'Then, at least, I was on my home planet.'

'Not anymore,' I said, then regretted it. Being accidentally snatched up with this forest by the aliens (who needed it as part of a great regeneration project somewhere in the galaxy) had seemed a godsend to me, an escape from what I viewed as an empty and meaningless life of drifting about. To Sinclair, though, it was little short of tragic. He loved the Earth. He was anxious to return.

At about noon, as I judged it, we had Sinclair's camping gear packed into his hiker's knapsack. We stood at the edge of the bush track that roughly bisected our 2500 hectare tract of spaceborne bushland that I called home. Up until now so had Sinclair Hayes, though only under sufferance.

As we waited for the pick-up I noticed that Sinclair looked rather melancholy. 'Cheer up,' I told him. 'We'll be back on Earth in a few months. Maybe we can write a book about it all. Make a million – or get tossed into adjoining padded cells. Look, Sinclair, I'm the one who'll be stuck here to tend the garden. I'm the one who should be despondent.'

'That's not the point,' he said grimly. 'I had a world and they took me from it. Now they're taking me away from what little I have left of it.'

I didn't know what to say to that. So I said nothing and looked down the road. The sun lights, I noticed, were doing a snappy job of drying it out.

In the distance the dust began to rise as something resembling a whirlwind came down the road. Sinclair picked up his knapsack as the silver hover-jeep came to a halt before us. At its controls sat the only member of the starship's crew I really knew. His name was Jix. He was the cargo officer.

'Good day, Sinclair. Good day, David,' he greeted us in a voice that boomed like a bass drum. He turned his green conical head to Sinclair, his liquid, cat-like eyes seeming to stare right through him. 'Are you ready?'

'Yes,' Sinclair replied dully. He swung his pack into the vehicle's storage locker and climbed into the over-sized seat beside the alien.

'Where will you be working?' I asked.

'Cargo hold power plant; environmental control for the forest. Seems they need me to do some simple repetition work for a while.'

We shook hands.

'Keep those suns burning,' I called to him as the jeep moved off.

'Don't forget the weeding,' he called back, disappearing in a driving explosion of dust.

As the cloud settled I walked back to my camp a few kilometres away on the other side of the forest. I had it to myself now. Alone.

When 'morning' broke the next 'day,' I packed my tent and wandered off down the road, heading to wherever it took me. As instructed by Jix, I (and up until the previous day Sinclair, too) had the job of keeping a check on the forest and its inhabitants; to clear out any potential fire hazards, pick up any injured animals and report any sickness in flora and fauna. A redundant job in many ways, I thought, for there were electronic monitors throughout the forest. But what else could the aliens have done with their reluctant stowaways?

As I walked along, the thick, tall pines either side quivered in the breeze stirred up by the ventilation system. A bird's call echoed through the trees. Somewhere the underbrush cracked as something heavy (kangaroo? wombat?) moved through it. As usual the flies buzzed eternally about my head. *They* were something that could well have been left back on Earth, I mused. Yet I knew they could not, for even flies have their own ecological niche.

I stepped off the road and climbed down into a wide, dry gully that ran beside it. At the moment it was just a dusty rut, but one day it would again flow with thawed mountain snow and be alive with aquatic life – once the forest was fitted to the planetary jigsaw awaiting it somewhere in the galaxy.

I walked along the gully for a distance, and was about to ascend the other bank and strike off into the heart of the bush when sudden darkness fell upon me. I looked up. All the lights within my field of vision, which a second ago had been burning with sun-like radiance, were now flickering a dull red, struggling to maintain a fire-fly glow. After what seemed an eternity, but was probably only thirty seconds, the lights returned, just as bright as before.

I probably wouldn't have thought any more about the incident had I not glanced down the gully again and seen Sinclair Hayes, barely ten metres away. He stood, looking at me with what I can only describe as a sad expression. I blinked, and he'd disappeared.

I was sitting on the edge of the track, worrying about my eyesight or an impending mental crack-up when an unexpected whirlwind came dusting up the road. It was Jix. With excited gestures he motioned me to climb into the jeep. As I did so we took off with an acceleration that must've pulled 3g at least.

'What the hell . . .' I managed, once I began to breathe again.

'You have an appointment with the Director of Personnel Affairs,' Jix answered as if that explained all.

To my astonishment we were already inside the great starship itself, plunging down a wide, high tunnel. People, doors, lights passed in multi-coloured blurs. It was like a mad toboggan ride down a surrealistic slide.

'Why do I want to see the Director of . . .?'

'He is a very busy man,' Jix interrupted. 'We were lucky to get this interview so soon.'

'But what the hell is this all about?'

'Sinclair Hayes has just died.'

'It seems there was an accident at the cargo hold power plant,' the Director of Personnel Affairs, a member of Jix's race, told me; yet I barely heard. The shock had yet to subside. 'He fell against some live circuitry he was servicing and . . .'

The Director swung his desk away on its wall pivot, lifted his long, green figure out of his throne-sized chair and began to pace his office. 'David,' he said as if trying to be tactful, 'since you are now the only human aboard, the Administration believes that it is only fitting for you to conduct the proper rites for the funeral of Sinclair Hayes.'

'Funeral,' I muttered in dull echo. I looked up at him. 'I don't know anything about burials at sea, let alone burials in space.'

'It's quite simple.' The Director stopped his pacing and faced me. 'The body, in a sealed capsule, will be in Airlock Nine two work periods from now. Jix will take you there. Representatives of all sections of the ship will be in attendance.' He began pacing again. 'You will say what needs to be said, pressure helmets will be donned, the airlock will be depressurized and opened, and the pall bearers will slide the capsule –'

'Out there!' I shrieked involuntarily.

The Director stared at me in stunned astonishment.

'Excuse . . . excuse me,' I stammered, springing for the door. 'I'll be there. Airlock whatever-it-was in two work periods. Yes, sir.'

I closed the office door on the Director's bewildered look. I was shaking all over. I was cold, so deathly cold. Such a shock of despair and loneliness had run through me in that moment. Those words – 'Out there!' – the anguished tone, the voice, the emotions that had sparked within me for an instant; none were mine. Something had grabbed at my soul with a clammy grip.

So it was in that state of mind and body that I returned to Jix waiting in the jeep, and in silence he took me back to the forest.

That 'night' I slept fitfully for a number of hours before finally succumbing to deep sleep. Dreams drifted past my mind's eye, vague and transitory. A voice . . . some calling voice from a vast distance seemed to be asking me . . . begging me not to let something happen . . . not to let them do something . . . not to let them do something with . . . with . . .

'Don't let them bury me between the stars!'

I woke up screaming, 'No! No! No!' Then the darkness around me fell back into silence, and there I lay, wide awake and wide-eyed until the lights above began to glow with their imitation of dawn.

They all gathered in a semi-circle in front of me, I standing like a lump next to the two-metre-long tubular plastic capsule lying on the cold metal deck of the airlock. I hugged my space helmet against my side with the crook of my left arm, while the fingers of my hands entangled themselves nervously. The assemblage was looking at me, all waiting for me to say something profound and noble about Sinclair Hayes. But my mind was a blank. My insides were reef-knotting themselves.

Jix was there. So was the Director. Among the other crew members present were a couple of goblin-like humanoids, a being evolved from the lizard rather than the ape, and several bipedal and multi-armed creatures of a grey, featureless jelly substance. And there were more. Many more. To the uninitiated it would have looked an eldritch gathering, and no doubt I was as alien to them as they were to me. Yet they were, in a sense, my shipmates.

Sombre.

I began to speak.

'My friends, we are gathered here at this time and place to pay our last respects to . . . well, to a brother crewman, Sinclair Hayes. No doubt most of you didn't know him, other than being one of the two aliens lifted along with the forest from Earth. A good companion and close friend, we now give his soul over to God, and commit his body to the stars.'

I glanced about sharply, for I thought I heard someone whisper, 'No!' But no one had, it seemed; I tried to shrug it off as imagination.

I raised my helmet, signalling that it was time.

Helmets were fitted to spacesuits, and once all was secure the lock was depressurized. I bent down and took hold of one of the capsule's handgrips. Jix took the opposite position. Two goblins shuffled up and took their places at the rear. Gravity was switched off, and we lifted the weightless capsule until it floated a metre above the deck. The outer door slid open, and the depths of the universe were revealed.

Respectfully we began to slide the capsule out – and it wouldn't budge! It was frozen where it floated above the deck, immovable as something held in a determined grip.

'Sinclair!' I shouted.

The din it caused inside my helmet made my ears ring. Yet above their complaining buzz came a sound I should never have heard. A bleak wind was whipping up in the vacuum of the airlock.

It whirled and swirled about me like a tornado of thick mud. The capsule was buffeted, and began slowly rotating. Jix and the other pall bearers moved back towards the lock's inner door. A pang of acute isolation cut through me, and I moved to join them. That's when an invisible hand seized my throat and jerked me against the wall.

'Don't do this to me, David,' a thin, pathetic voice wailed in my brain. 'I don't want to drift a billion years through empty space!'

I grabbed instinctively at the hand that held me fast. But there was nothing there.

'Close the lock!' I screamed into my helmet mike. 'Close the lock!'

The lock door all-too-slowly slid shut. The air poured in. Gravity returned. The capsule settled to the deck. The pressure fell from my throat. The others surged towards me as I collapsed onto the deck.

The Powers-That-Be aboard that massive starship moved not only in mysterious ways, but quite quickly, too. Five minutes later I found myself before the Board of Ship's Executives to explain why the funeral had not taken place.

I told them exactly what happened. The burial capsule that refused to be moved, the wind in the vacuum, the invisible, intangible force I'd struggled with. For a time they remained unconvinced. It wasn't that they didn't give credence to the supernatural (in fact I found many of the beings aboard had a much better insight into psychic matters than most humans), it was just that something like this had never happened before, and it tended to render them incredulous.

But the facts were there. It had happened. I called Jix, the Director and some of the others present at the attempted funeral. They backed me on every detail. I also told them of my seeing Sinclair at the moment of his death, and of the dream I'd had the previous night.

The Board conferred, and reached an alternative in less than three minutes.

We lowered the burial capsule into a deep, oblong hole underneath the pines of the forest. Thinking it rather pointless to repeat the eulogy, I just stood at the foot of the grave and said, 'Rest in peace now, Sinclair, please.'

The crowd lingered for a while, then, little by little, they drifted back into the ship, back to the sanity of routine. Jix took his shovel, I took mine, and together we filled in the grave. We planted the metal cross the machine shop had fashioned, brushed the dirt from our hands, and joined the others in their return to reality.

I suppose I'd only gone a couple of dozen paces when Jix saw me jump and swing around abruptly. He told me later that he'd seen the hackles stand up on the back of my neck.

'What's the matter?' he asked.

I stood stock-still in the silence of the forest for a few moments before relaxing and letting out a long-held breath. 'Nothing.' I turned and began walking again. 'Just the ventilators sighing through the tree tops, Jix. That's all.'

THE ANKARDYNE PEW

W. F. HARVEY

The following narrative of the occurrences that took place at Ankardyne House in February 1890, is made up chiefly of extracts from letters written by my friend, the Rev. Thomas Prendergast, to his wife, immediately before taking up residence at the vicarage, together with transcripts from the diary which I kept at the time. The names throughout are, of course, fictitious.

February 9th. I am sorry that I had no opportunity yesterday of getting over to the vicarage, so your questions – I have not lost the list – must remain unanswered. It is almost a quarter of a mile away from the church, in the village. You see, the church, unfortunately, is in the grounds of the park, and there is a flagged passage, cold and horribly draughty, that leads from Ankardyne House to the great loose box of the Ankardyne pew. The squires in the old days could come in late and go out early, or even stay away altogether, without anyone being the wiser. The whole situation of the church is bad and typically English – the House of God in the squire's pocket. Why should he have right of secret access? I haven't had time to examine the interior – early eighteenth century, I should guess – but as we drove up last evening in the dusk, the tall gloomy façade of Ankardyne House, with the elegant little church – a Wren's nest – adjoining it, made me think of a wicked uncle, setting off for a walk in the woods with one of the babes. The picture is really rather apt, as you will agree, when you see the place. It's partly a question of the height of the two buildings, partly a question of the shape of the windows, those of the one square, deep-set, and grim; of the other round – the raised eyebrows of startled innocence.

We were quite wrong about Miss Ankardyne. She is a charming little lady, not a trace of Lady Catherine de Bourgh, and is really looking forward to having you as her nearest neighbour. I will write more of her tomorrow, but the stable clock has struck eleven and my candle is burning low.

Febuary 10th. I measured the rooms as you asked me to. They are, of course, larger than ours at Garvington, and will swallow all our furniture and carpets. But you will like the vicarage. It, at least, is a cheerful house; faces south, and isn't, like this place, surrounded by woods. I suppose familiarity with the skies and wide horizons of the fens accounts for the shut-in feeling one gets here. But I have never seen such cedars!

And now to describe Miss Ankardyne. She is perhaps seventy-five, *petite* and bird-like, with the graceful, alert poise of a bird. I should say that sight and hearing are abnormally acute and have helped to keep her young. She is a good talker, well read, and interested in affairs, and a still better listener. Parson's pride! you will exclaim; since we are only two, and if she listens, I must talk. But I mean what I say. All that the archdeacon told us is true; you are conscious in her presence of a living spirit of peace. By the way, she is an interesting example of your theory that there are some people for whom animals have an instinctive dislike – indeed, the best example I have met. For Miss Ankardyne tells me that, though since childhood she has had a fondness for all living creatures, especially for birds, it is one which is not at first reciprocated. She can, after assiduous, continuous persevering, win their affection; her spaniel, her parrot, and Karkar, the tortoiseshell cat, are obviously attached to her. But strange dogs snarl, if she attempts to fondle them; and she tells me that, when she goes to the farm to feed the fowls, the birds seem to sense her coming and *run from the scattered corn.* I have heard of cows showing this antipathy to individuals, but never before of birds. There is an excellent library here, that badly needs cataloguing. The old vicar had, I believe, begun the task at the time of his fatal seizure.

I have been inside the church. Anything less like dear old Garvington it would be impossible to find. Architecturally, it has its points, but the unity of design, on which everything here depends, is broken by the Ankardyne pew. Its privacy is an abomination. Even from the pulpit it is impossible to see inside, and I can well believe the stories of the dicing squires and their Sunday play. Miss Ankardyne refuses to use it. The glass is crude and uninteresting; but there is an uncommon chancel screen of Spanish workmanship, which somehow seems in keeping with the place. I wish it didn't.

We shall miss the old familiar monuments. There is no snub-nosed crusader here, no worthy Elizabethan knight, like our Sir John Parkington, kneeling in supplication, with those nicely balanced families on right and left. The tombs are nearly all Ankardyne tombs – urns, weeping charities, disconsolate relicts, and all the cold Christian virtues. You know the sort. The Ten Commandments are painted on oak panels on either side of the altar. From the Ankardyne pew I doubt if you can see them.

February 11th. You ask about my neuritis. It is better, despite the fact that I have been sleeping badly. I wake up in the morning, sometimes during the night, with a burning headache and a curious tingling feeling about the tongue, which I can only attribute to indigestion. I am trying the effect of a glass of hot water before retiring. When we move into the vicarage, we shall at least be spared the attention of the owls, which make the night so dismal here. The place is far too shut in by trees, and I suppose, too, that the disused outbuildings give them shelter. Cats are bad enough, but I prefer the sound of night-walkers to night-fliers. It won't be long now before we meet. They are getting on splendidly with the vicarage. The painters have already started work; the new kitchen range has come, and is only waiting for the plumbers to put it in. Miss Ankardyne is leaving for a visit to friends in a few days' time. It seems that she always goes away about this season of the year – wise woman! – so I shall be alone next week. She said Dr Hulse would be glad to put me up, if I find the solitude oppressive, but I shan't trouble him. You would like the old butler. His name is Mason, and his wife – a Scotchwoman – acts as housekeeper. The three maids are sisters. They have been with Miss Ankardyne for thirty years, and are everything that maids should be. They belong to the Peculiar People. I cannot desire that they should be orthodox. If I could be sure that Dr Hulse was as well served . . .

February 13th. I had an experience last night which moved me strangely. I hardly know what to make of it. I went to bed at half past ten after a quiet evening with Miss Ankardyne. I thought she seemed in rather poor spirits, and tried to cheer her by reading aloud. She chose a chapter from *The Vicar of Wakefield*. I awoke soon after one with an intolerable feeling of oppression, almost of dread. I was conscious, too – and in some way my alarm was associated with this – of a burning, tingling, piercing pain in my tongue. I got up from bed and was about to pour myself out a glass of water, when I heard the sound of someone speaking. The voice was low and continuous, and seemed to come from an adjoining room. I slipped on my dressing-gown and, candle in hand, went out into the corridor. For a moment I stood in silence. Frankly, I was afraid. The voice proceeded from a room two doors away from mine. As I listened, I recognized it as Miss Ankardyne's. She was repeating the Benedicite.

There were such depths of sadness, so much of the weariness of defeat in this song of triumph of the Three Children saved from the furnace of fire, that I felt I could not leave her. I should have spoken before knocking, for I could almost feel that gasp of fear. 'Oh, no!' she said, 'Oh, no! Not now!' and then, as if bracing herself for a great effort: 'Who is it?'

I told her and she bade me enter. The poor little woman had risen from her knees and was trembling from head to foot. I spent about an hour with her and left her sleeping peacefully. I did not wish to rouse the house, but I managed to find the Masons' room and arranged for Mrs Mason to sit by the old lady.

I can't say what happened in that hour we spent together in talk and in prayer. There is something very horrible about this house, that Miss Ankardyne is dimly aware of. Something connected with pain and fire and a bird, and something that was human too. I was shaken to the very depths of my being. I don't think I ever felt the need for prayer and the power of prayer as I did last night. The stable clock has just struck five.

February 14th. I have arranged for Miss Ankardyne to go away tomorrow. She is fit to travel, and is hardly fit to stay. I had a long talk with her this morning. I think she is the most courageous woman I know. All her life she has felt that the house is haunted, and all her life she has felt pity for that which haunts it. She says that she is sure that she is living it down; that the house is better than it was; but that at this season of the year it is almost too much for her. She is anxious that I should stay with Dr Hulse. I feel, however, that I must see this business through. She then suggested that I should invite a friend to stay with me. I thought of Pellow. You remember how we were obliged to postpone his visit last

September. I had a letter from him only last Friday. He is living in this part of the world and could probably run over for a day or two.

The extracts from Mr Prendergast's letters end here. The following are excerpts from my diary:

February 16th. Arrived at Ankardyne House at midday. Prendergast had meant to meet me at the station, but had been suddenly called away to visit a dying parishioner. I had in consequence a couple of hours by myself in which to form an impression of the place. The house dates from the early eighteenth century. It is dignified though sombre, and is closely surrounded on three sides by shrubberies of rhododendrons and laurel, that merge into thick woods. The cedars in the park must be older than any of the buildings. Miss Ankardyne, I gather, has lived here all her life, and the house gives you the impression of having been lived in, a slightly sinister mansion, well aired by a kindly soul. There is a library that should be well worth exploring. The family portraits are in the dining-room. None is of outstanding interest. The most unusual feature of the house is its connection with the church, which has many of the characteristics of a private chapel. It does not actually abut on the building, but is joined to it by a low, curved façade, unpierced by windows. A corridor, lighted from above, runs behind the façade and gives a private entry from the house to the church. The door into this corridor opens into the spacious hall of Ankardyne House; but there is a second mode of access (of which Prendergast seemed unaware) from Miss Ankardyne's bedchamber down a narrow stair. This door is kept locked and has never been opened, as far as Mason, the butler, can recollect. The church, with the curved façade connecting it to the house, is balanced on the other side by the coach-house and stables, which can be approached in a similar manner from the kitchens. The architect has certainly succeeded in conveying the idea that religion and horseflesh can be made elegant adjuncts to the life of a country gentleman. Prendergast came in just before luncheon. He does not look well, and was obviously glad to see me and to unburden himself. In the afternoon I had a long talk with Mason, the butler, a very level-headed man.

From what Prendergast tells me I gather that Miss Ankardyne's experiences have been both auditory and visual. They are certainly vague.

Auditory. The cry of a bird – sometimes she thinks it is an owl, sometimes a cock – sometimes a human cry with something bird-like in it. This she has heard almost as long as she can remember, both outside the house and inside her room, but most frequently in the direction of the corridor that leads to the church. The cry is chiefly heard at night, hardly ever before dusk. (This would point to an owl.) It has become less frequent of recent years, but at this particular season is most persistent. Mason confirms this. He doesn't like the sound, and doesn't know what to make of it. The maids believe that it is an evil spirit; but, as it can have no power over them – they belong to the Peculiar People – they take no notice of it.

Visual and Sensory. From time to time – less frequently, again, of recent years – Miss Ankardyne wakes up 'with her eyes balls of fire'. She can distinguish nothing clearly for several minutes. Then the red spheres slowly contract to pin-pricks; there is a moment of sharp pain; and normal vision is restored. At other times she is aroused from sleep by a sharp, piercing pain in her tongue. She has consulted several oculists, who find that her sight is perfectly normal. I believe she has never known a day's illness. Prendergast seems to have had a similar, though less vivid, experience; he used the term 'burning' headache.

I have elicited from Mason the statement that animals dislike the house, with the exception of Karkar, Miss Ankardyne's cat, who seems entirely unaffected. The spaniel refuses to sleep in Miss Ankardyne's bedroom; and on one occasion, when the parrot's cage was brought up there, the bird 'fell into such a screaming fit, that it nearly brought the house down'. This I believe, for I tried the experiment myself with the reluctant consent of Mrs Mason. The feathers of the bird lay back flat on its head and neck with rage, and then it began to shriek in a really horrible way.

All this, of course, is very vague. We have no real evidence of anything supernatural. What impresses me most is the influence of the house on a woman of Miss Ankardyne's high character and courage.

February 18th. Certainly an interesting night. After a long walk with Prendergast in the afternoon I went to bed early with a volume of Trollope and a long candle. I did what I have never done before – fell asleep with the candle burning. When I awoke, it was within an inch of the socket; the fire had settled into a dull glow. Close to the candlestick on the table by my bedside stood a carafe of water. As I lay in bed, too sleepy to move, I was conscious of the hypnotic effect induced by gazing into a crystal. Slowly the surface of the glass grew dim and then gradually cleared from the centre. I was looking into the interior of a building, which I at once recognized as Ankardyne church. I could make out the screen and the Ankardyne pew. It seemed to be night, though I could see more clearly than if it had been night – the monuments in the aisle, for example. There were not as many as there are now. Presently the door of the Ankardyne pew opened and a man stepped out. He was dressed in black coat and knee-breeches, such as a clergyman might have worn a century or more ago. In one hand he held a lighted candle, the flame of which he sheltered with the other. I judged him to be of middle age. His face wore an expression of extreme apprehension. He crossed the church, casting backward glances as he went, and stopped before one of the mural monuments in the south aisle. Then, placing his candle on the ground, he drew from his pocket a hammer and some tools and, kneeling on the ground, began to work feverishly at the base of the inscription. When he had finished, and the task was not long, he seemed to moisten a finger and, running it along the floor, rubbed the dust into the newly cut stone. He then picked up his tools and began to retrace his steps. But the wind seemed to have risen; he had difficulty in shielding the flame of the candle, and just before he regained the door of the Ankardyne pew, it went out.

That was all that I saw in the crystal. I was now wide awake. I got out of bed, put fresh fuel on the fire, and wrote this account in my diary, while the picture was still vivid.

February 19th. Slept splendidly, despite the fact that I was prepared to spend a wakeful night. After a late breakfast I went with Prendergast into the church and had no difficulty in identifying the monument. It is in the east end of the south aisle, immediately opposite the Ankardyne pew and partly hidden by the American organ. The inscription reads:

IN MEMORY OF
FRANCIS ANKARDYNE, ESQUIRE,
of Ankardyne Hall, in the County of Worcester,
late Captain in His Majesty's 42nd Regiment
of Foot.
He departed this life 27th February 1781.
Rev. xiv. 12, 13.

I brought the Bible from the lectern. 'Here are lives,' said Prendergast, 'which can fitly be commemorated by such verses: "here is the patience of the saints; here are they that keep the commandments of God." Miss Ankardyne's is one. And I suppose,' he added, 'that there may be some of whom the eleventh verse is true.' He read it out to me: '"And the smoke of their torment ascendeth for ever and ever; and they have no rest day nor night, who worship the beast and his image, and whosever receiveth the mark of his name."'

I thought at first that he was right; that the 12 might originally have been engraved as 11. But closer scrutiny showed that, though some of the figures had certainly been tampered with, it was not either the 2 or the 3. Prendergast hit on what I believe is the right solution. 'The R,' he said, 'has been superimposed on an L, and the 1 was originally 5. The reference is to Leviticus xiv. 52, 53.' If he is correct, we have still far to go. I have read and re-read those verses so often during the day, that I can write them down from memory:

'And he shall cleanse the house with the blood of the bird, and with the running water, and with the living bird, and with the cedar wood, and with the hyssop, and with the scarlet:

'But he shall let go the living bird out of the city into the open fields, and make an atonement for the house; and it shall be clean.'

Miss Ankardyne told Prendergast that she was dimly aware of something connected with pain and fire and a bird. It is at least a curious coincidence.

Mason knows nothing about Francis Ankardyne except his name. He tells me that the Ankardyne squires of a hundred years ago had a reputation for evil living; in that, of course, they were not peculiar.

Spent the afternoon in the library in a rather fruitless search for clues. I found two books with the name 'Francis Ankardyne' written on the fly-leaf. It was perhaps just as well that they should be tucked away on one of the upper shelves. One was inscribed as the gift of his cousin, Cotter Crawley. Query: Who is Crawley, and can he be identified with my man in black?

I tried to reproduce the crystal-gazing under conditions similar to those of the other night, but without success. I have twice heard the bird. It might be either an owl or a cock. The sound seemed to come from outside the house, and was not pleasant.

February 19th. Tomorrow Prendergast moves into the vicarage and I return home. Miss Ankardyne prolongs her stay at Malvern for another fortnight, and is then to visit friends on the south coast. I should like to have seen and questioned her, and so have discovered something more of the family history. Both Prendergast and I are disappointed. It seemed as if we were on the point of solving the mystery, and now it is as dark as ever. This new society in which Myers is interested should investigate the place.

So ends my diary, but not the story. Some four months after the events narrated I managed to secure through a secondhand book dealer four bound volumes of the *Gentleman's Magazine*. They had belonged to a Rev. Charles Phipson, once Fellow of Brasenose College and incumbent of Norton-on-the-Wolds. One evening, as I was glancing through them at my leisure, I came upon the following passage, under the date April 1789:

'At Tottenham, John Ardenoif, Esq., a young man of large fortune and in the splendour of his carriages and horses rivalled by few country gentlemen. His table was that of hospitality, where, it may be said, he sacrificed too much to conviviality; but, if he had his foibles, he had his merits also, that far outweighed them. Mr A was very fond of cockfighting and had a favourite cock upon which he won many profitable matches. The last bet he laid upon this cock he lost, which so enraged him that he had the bird tied to a spit and roasted alive before a large fire. The screams of the miserable bird were so affecting, that some gentlemen who were present attempted to interfere, which so enraged Mr A that he seized a poker and with the most furious vehemence declared that he would kill the first man who interposed; but, in the midst of his passionate asseverations, he fell down dead upon the spot. Such, we are assured, were the circumstances which attended the death of this great pillar of humanity.'

Beneath was written: 'See also the narrative of Mr C— at the end of this volume.'

I give the story as I found it, inscribed in minute handwriting on the terminal fly-leaves:

'During his last illness the Rev. Mr C— gave me the following account of a similar instance of Divine Judgment. Mr A— of A— House, in the county of W—, was notorious for his open practise of infidelity. He was an ardent votary of the chase, a reckless gamester, and was an enthusiast in his love of cockfighting. After carousing one evening with a boon companion, he proposed that they should then and there match the birds which they had entered for a contest on the morrow. His friend declaring that his bird should fight only in a cockpit, Mr A— announced that he had one adjoining the very room in which they were. The birds were brought, lights called for, and Mr A—, opening the door, led his guest down a flight of stairs and along a corridor to what he at first supposed were the stables. It was only after the match had begun, that he realized to his horror that they were in the family pew of A— church, to which A— House had private access. His expostulations only enraged his host, who commenced to blaspheme, wagering his very soul on the success of his bird, the victor of fifty fights. On this occasion the cock was defeated. Beside himself with frenzy, Mr A— rushed back to his bed-chamber and, declaring that the Judgment Day had come and that the bird should never crow again, thrust a wire into the embers, burned out its eyes, and bored through its tongue. He then fell down in some form of apoplectic fit. He recovered and continued his frenzied course of living for some years. It was noticed, however, that he had an impediment in his speech, especially remarkable when he was enraged, the effect of which was to make him utter a sound like the crowing of a cock. It became a cant phrase in the neighbourhood: 'When A— crows, honest men must move.' Two years after this awful occurrence, his sight began to fail. He was killed in the hunting field. His horse took fright and, bolting, carried him for over a mile across bad country to break his neck in an attempt to leap a ten-foot wall. At each obstacle they encountered, Mr A— called out, but the noise that came from his throat only seemed to terrify his horse the more. Mr C— vouches for the truth of the story, having had personal acquaintance with both the parties.'

The supposition that the Rev. Mr C— was none other than the boon companion of Francis Ankardyne did not seem to occur to the mind of the worthy Mr Phipson. That such was the case, I have no doubt. I saw him once in a glass darkly; and I saw later at Ankardyne House a silhouette of Cotter Crawley in an old album, and recognized the weak, foolish profile.

Who it was who drew up the wording of the monument in Ankardyne church, I do not know. Probably the trustees of the heir, a distant kinsman and a mere boy. Perhaps the mason mistook the R for an L, the 1 for a 5. Perhaps he was a grim jester; perhaps the dead man guided the chisel. But I can picture the horror of Cotter Crawley in being confronted with those suggestive verses. I see him stealing from the house, which after years of absence he has brought himself to revisit, at night. I see him at work, cold, yet feverish, on the tell-tale stone. I see him stricken by remorse and praying, as the publican prayed, without in the shadow.

Part of this story Prendergast and I told to Miss Ankardyne. The family pew is pulled down, and of the passage that connected the church with the house, only the façade is left. The house itself is quieter than it has been for years. A nephew of Miss Ankardyne from India is coming to live there soon. He has children, but I do not think there is anything of which they need be afraid. As I wrote before, it has been well aired by a kindly soul.

OUTSIDE AGENCY

DAPHNE FROOME

'Really, Grandpa!' Marion Grant protested. 'You shouldn't have given Tommy that large box of chocolates. And on Christmas Eve of all times. If I hadn't spotted it in his bedroom he'd have been ill all through Christmas.' She bent down, shovelling coal on to the sitting-room fire. Her father-in-law refused to budge an inch from his position in the armchair with his legs stretched out so that she was forced to lean awkwardly over them. 'The child's four,' he muttered. 'He ought to be able to eat a few chocolates without coming to harm at that age . . . Whatever possessed you to buy these modern leather chairs I don't know,' he added. 'I think the upholstered ones you had before were much more comfortable.'

'Not everyone's got a nice bright centrally-heated room to sit in, *and* with a coal fire as well lit specially on weekends and holidays,' Marion retaliated. She thrust the shovel angrily back into the coal scuttle and retreated to the kitchen, her face flushed with anger as well as the heat of the fire.

There was the sound of a key in the lock of the front door. The old man heard his son come in and, rising to his feet, went into the hall and reached up to lift his coat from the hall stand.

'You're not going out surely, Dad? It's absolutely bitter cold.'

'I know when I'm not wanted.' Mr Grant pushed his arms into the sleeves of his weather-proof jacket, twisted a muffler about his neck, placed a thick tweed cap on his head and put on a pair of warm gloves. Out on the front step he hesitated, listening to the angry articulation between his son and daughter-in-law.

'You ought to be ashamed of yourself, Marion, turning the poor old man out in weather like this.'

'Nonsense, Bob. I've never known him do anything he didn't want to. It's my belief he was going out anyway . . .'

The voices ceased as Mr Grant, Sr banged the door shut behind him.

Smiling slightly, he made his way to the garage, got out his car, and drove the few hundred yards along the road to the main entrance of the golf club. Driving inside, he parked the car and stood looking about him.

The afternoon certainly was very cold. Snow lay over the length and breadth of the golf course, the shadows in blue patches beside the hedges and walls and in stripes beneath the frosted tracery of the bare trees. The sky was grey, lighted between the clouds with the mauve-blue tints of the winter afternoon. Under a small plantation of south-facing willows the bright midday sun had exposed one solitary area, the sodden grass of the eighteenth green.

Mr Grant began to plough his way towards it along the small path that rimmed the golf course, steadying himself as he negotiated the slippery ground with the putter that he had removed from the boot of his car.

In spite of his sixty-nine years his long game had kept up to standard. He was proud of the fact that he played off a handicap of eight. But lately, for some inexplicable reason, his putting had gone to pieces. In his anxiety to follow the passage of the ball he spoiled many a good stroke by jerking up his head. He ruined short putts by prodding at them with a kind of frantic nervousness; he lunged at longer ones with a force that sent the ball skidding past the hole. Putts that he used to hole in two, or even one stroke, now often took him four. And only last week there had been that disastrous five. From a mere twenty yards at the edge of the green to the hole, he had actually taken five strokes. There had been an awesome silence from his three companions and then one of them, the captain of the club, had laughed. Laughed out loud and then scathingly remarked, 'Grant, you're getting past it, you know. You ought to be at home, man, with your knitting.'

That night the weather had suddenly worsened, but through all the subsequent days of hail and blizzard and deep hard frost Mr Grant had impatiently waited. For he was determined to practise and go on practising until his putting was at least as good as the captain's. Now at last the snow had stopped falling and he had come out.

Not wanting to begin by being too ambitious, he dropped the ball on the fringe of the green nearest the hole, and putted. The resultant stroke was worse than ever. The ball bounced along in erratic hops, skidded on a series of unexpectedly icy patches, struck an isolated pile of frozen snow, and rolled off the high plateau of the green to fall down the treacherously sloping bank.

Mr Grant watched the progress of the ball with his small eyes narrowed and glinting with frustrated fury, his mouth set in a stubborn line, and querulous folds creasing his forehead. He squelched and slithered towards the spot where the wretched little blob had disappeared from view. It was not usually possible to get past the bottom of the bank. As far back as he could remember, even in the driest of summer droughts, a small but lively spring had sent a miniature waterfall splashing into a whirlpool down below. Mr Grant peered over the edge and into the shadow. The stream was frozen and there was the ball, quite easily accessible, sitting on the top.

He made his way down the muddy bank through a gap in the bare thorns and brambles, and tested the stream's surface carefully. He found that it would support his weight and, leaning over, retrieved the ball and pocketed it.

He then stood for a few moments grudgingly admiring the patterns where the water had been stilled into long, white fingers of ice. Almost skeletal, he thought, and for a moment he imagined he could see the joints in them. He turned hastily. A little too hastily, for his feet slithered beneath him. As he fought to keep his balance his hand came into contact with something hard and stick-like embedded in the side of the bank. He grabbed it for support, and the force of his fall wrenched the object from the frosty earth. He ended up seated in an ungainly heap, the stick-like thing beside him. It was a putter.

He got stiffly to his feet, flung the putter up the bank, and climbed after it. Once on top, he wiped away the worst of the mud with his handkerchief to reveal a dirty shaft of hickory wood and a rather rusty blade.

A feeling of magical opportunity suddenly seized him. He took the golf ball from his pocket, dropped it onto the green, and tapped at it. With an ever-worsening feeling of suspense he watched the ball travel across the spongy grass, and then, as with all good putts, seem to be drawn, as if by some extra strong gravitational pull, towards the hole. Mr Grant stood still for many seconds afterwards savouring the slightly hollow plopping sound the ball had made as it fell.

A faint rustle from behind, a cough, and the muffled clapping of gloved hands woke him from his reverie.

For a golfer, one of the greatest pleasures in life is holing a good long putt. It is an even greater pleasure to have someone on hand to witness the act. Mr Grant turned, the corners of his thin mouth stretched into a smile, but he could see no one. The only movement was that of the bare branches of the nearby willows and the tall, distant plane trees set against the gold and pink of the sunset. The lights of the High Street shops glowing in the distance and the faint sounds of the traffic seemed to emphasize his solitude. He edged round the tall hedge that screened his view the other way, and gazed across the bleak, deserted strip of land beyond it. Even the usually brightly-lit windows of the clubhouse were tonight shrouded with thick curtains against the weather outside.

Carrying both putters he trudged in the gathering darkness back to his car.

'Grandpa, did you *have* to bring that filthy old thing in here?' Marion had patiently borne with her father-in-law sponging his newly found putter in the sink. She had even patiently abstained from protesting as he dripped dirty water over the best china and cut glass she had washed, dried, and left stacked on the draining board ready for use during the festivities on the morrow. But having to fight for a corner of the kitchen table while he worked away polishing it up with metal polish and furniture cream was more than her temper could stand.

Bob came and hovered in the doorway. 'You know he dislikes being called "Grandpa",' he said to his wife. 'It makes him feel his age. It's a sure way to pick a quarrel.'

'But I can't get on.' Marion tipped breadcrumbs into a bowl and fiercely shook in suet and herbs.

'Better not have the wretched turkey stuffed at all if you're going to make a row about it on Christmas Eve,' her husband replied. 'Spoiling it all for Tommy.' He turned and went back into the sitting room.

Old Mr Grant collected up the dusters, sending a floating cloud of dried metal polish across towards his daughter-in-law's mixing bowl, and departed to finish his task on the newly polished dining-room table instead.

'Come and look at this, Bob,' he called to his son at last. 'An old hickory putter, and perfect. I'd never have believed it would have cleaned up as well as this. It's as good as new! I never saw the like of it! And exactly the right weight and length for me, too.' He balanced his acquisition carefully in both hands. 'I found it buried in the bank where the waterfall meets the stream when I was looking for my ball at the eighteenth this afternoon.'

'You went out on the golf course, in this weather?'

'You know how my putting's been worrying me.' The old man chuckled. 'Not any more, I reckon. I holed a putt of a good thirty feet with it, even though it was so dirty.' He paused, savouring again the joy of that moment, pushing into the back of his mind the thought of his elusive witness. The person had, of course, hurried away while he was still standing congratulating himself. That was one of the troubles with growing old – you got slow on your feet and thought everyone else was the same. 'I can't wait to see what it'll be like to play with now it's cleaned up,' he went on, enthusiastically.

'Well, it's snowing hard again, so you won't be going out tomorrow, that's for sure,' his son replied.

After Christmas came a rapid thaw and Mr Grant was able to go and practise once more. He would begin on the first green, he decided, and gradually work his way round all eighteen.

Reminding himself that so far he had hit only one good stroke with his new putter, and that that might well have been a fluke, he took up his usual stance, feet a little apart, back slightly bent, and arranged his hands very carefully on the old-style leather grip. The morning had been bright and sunny when he had left the house, but soon after he had arrived the sun had disappeared behind a cloud and now a gentle rain began to drift downwards. The other golfers and the people who exercised their dogs on the path would certainly not stay out in the wet, but Mr Grant was determined to play and paid no heed to the increasing downpour. A flock of ducks went flying low overhead towards the river and, just as he was about to play the stroke, one of them quacked. Mr Grant twitched, and the ball finished up short of the hole and well to one side of it. Waving the putter at the departing ducks, he wished for a moment he could exchange it for a gun.

Then he heard a laugh; not raucous, like the captain's laugh that day when he had taken five strokes to reach the hole, but thin and sneering. Angrily he glanced around. The rain was so heavy it was impossible to see more than five feet in any direction. The laugh had annoyed him so much that he deliberately dropped the ball onto the most difficult spot on the green and banged it furiously down the slope. A series of small hillocks slowed it just enough to make it trickle gently into the hole. He almost danced over to retrieve the ball. As he straightened up he heard a faint rustle, a cough, and a muffled clapping of gloved hands – just as he had heard on the day he had first found the old putter. As before, he could see no one. He stood still, listening, and as he did so he saw the misty grey shape of someone advancing towards him through the drifting rain. It looked a very tall, broad figure to Mr Grant, who, though jaunty, was rather short. As the figure drew closer Mr Grant could see that its eyes were fixed upon him with a stare of such calculating intensity that he was seized with a feeling of panic. He hurled the putter towards it, missed, and stumbled wildly back to the car park. Fumbling in his pocket for the keys, he somehow managed to unlock the door of the car and scramble inside. The rain was torrential now, and he huddled in the driving seat, waiting for the weather to improve, grateful for the presence of the one or two other people sheltering in the cars around him.

After a while the rain began to ease up and rather shakily he turned on the ignition.

'Is this yours?' There was a tapping on the window, and the captain stood, peering inside waving the putter.

Mr Grant wound down the window and nodded.

'I thought it probably would be. I can't think of any other member who is absent-minded enough to leave one of his clubs on the course.' He eyed the putter curiously. 'I see you're trying a different one. I shouldn't imagine it'll bring about any improvement in your game, though. We're seriously considering putting your handicap up to twelve.'

'Twelve!' Mr Grant took the putter and grasped it firmly. His feeling of fury even made him forget for a moment his unsettling brush with the stranger on the course. 'We'll see about that,' he shouted, and accelerated away with a force that sent the car through the puddles in the car park like a speed boat, shooting up a wide arc of spray on each side as it went.

With each of the days and weeks that followed Mr Grant grew more excited and secretive. He would drive along to the club and practise on the greens, very early in the morning when there was no one about or late in the afternoon when it was almost too dark to see. More than once, when he brought off a monster putt, and that was often now, he thought he could just catch the faint rustle, the cough, and the muffled clapping of gloved hands. When he made one of his mistakes, infrequent though they had now become, there was the thin, sneering laugh, irking him so much that his hands trembled as he tried the stroke again. He muttered about it on his journeys to and from the golf course, and even, sometimes, around the house.

But he ignored all of it in the face of the one thing that drove him on – the determination to win the first big competition of the year.

On the day of the big event everyone remarked about the fantastic improvement in his game, and asked about the curious club sitting amid the rest of his up-to-date equipment. Mr Grant displayed the putter proudly, but always at a little distance. He refused to say how he had come by it and would not allow anyone else to so much as touch it.

Just once or twice, after he had played a stroke, he thought he heard what seemed to be an echo, but it was very faint. Neither his son, his daughter-in-law, nor the small group of friends who were following him and his partner round seemed to notice these odd sounds, but they were a noisy group, laughing and talking loudly among themselves.

Mr Grant approached the last green with a round of sixty-four, eight below par, six strokes ahead of his nearest competitor. Mr Grant was the last man to play. Everyone gathered round and briefly, as he lifted the old club for his final putt, he swelled with pride. The ball was actually on its way to the hole when suddenly there was a streak of light and another ball flew across from the direction of the first tee. One or two of Mr Grant's friends, catching a brief glimpse of this swift and unexpected missile, shouted,

'Fore!', but Mr Grant was concentrating on the last, sweet moment of success as the ball dropped gently into the hole, and was oblivious of their call. Indeed, some people maintained afterwards that the ball, flying through the air, had made no sound at all.

It sped, straight and true, towards Mr Grant, and struck him on his head, felling him at the foot of his caddy, who still held the flag he had lifted for Mr Grant's last ever stroke.

Bob and Marion knelt beside him, someone rushed towards the clubhouse shouting for a doctor, other people looked across to the first tee. It was impossible that any player should be teeing off there, not at the end of such an exciting competition. But no one was teeing off. In fact the entire area was deserted.

'Where's the ball, the ball that struck Mr Grant? That'll give us an idea of the fool who played that stroke,' one of the party shouted. Other people gathered, hushed and confused, round the old man, whispering, 'Is he coming round?' 'Is he dead, do you think?' At last a stretcher was brought to carry him away to the waiting ambulance, and as soon as he was gone the others started searching, first close to the eighteenth green and then farther afield. They even eventually cut away the undergrowth and dragged the little stream. But there was no ball to be found.

Many months had passed. Bob Grant had more or less recovered from the death of his father. His wife, now freed from the extra work of looking after old Mr Grant, had taken up her job as a teacher again. She was brighter and altogether less snappish. With the pain of loss eased now Bob Grant decided it was time that Tommy move out of his small bedroom and into the much larger one the old man had occupied. Clearing out his father's cupboard was a sobering task for Bob, made even less agreeable when he came across the bag of golf clubs that he had angrily thrown in there after the accident.

Hastily gathering up the bag, he went down to the garage and straightaway drove to the golf club.

There was only one person in the professional's shop but Bob waited until the customer had finished making his purchases and gone out before approaching the pro.

'Hello, Bob, nice to see you again. Can I help you at all?' The pro looked at his watch. 'I say, I don't want to seem impolite but I'm due to give a lesson in five minutes.'

'I don't need to keep you that long,' Bob Grant replied. 'I'd like you to sell my father's clubs, that's all. You'll probably recall he bought them from you in the first place.'

The professional nodded. 'I remember it well. I had to get them in specially. Very particular he was, cantankerous even. Still, after that last match of his . . .' The pro took the bag and gazed at the clubs in awe. Then he removed the old hickory putter and, turning it about, examined it closely.

Some sudden impulse caused Bob to reach out for it. 'All except this one,' he said firmly. 'I shall keep this as a memento.'

The pro's face fell, then he said, 'You don't know where he got that from, I suppose? I wouldn't ask, only it bears a remarkable similarity to one used by one of our members. Way back in 1939 it was, well before you were born. It was the last golf match he ever played – the next day he got his calling up papers, went off to fight in the Battle of Britain. We both did as a matter of fact, only he didn't come back.' The man's eyes clouded over and he pulled at his huge, white moustache nostalgically. 'The day of the match was wonderfully fine and he was determined to win. Leading all the way he was, too, right as far as the eighteenth hole. Then he three-putted and drew. He left his clubs in the clubhouse. A friend of his bought them soon afterwards. I don't know what became of the putter, though – that evidently disappeared.' Bob remained uninformatively silent, and the pro went on, 'I must shut up shop now. I'll do my best to get a good price for those clubs.'

'Lend me a ball, will you?' Bob said.

'Here you are,' the professional said, handing him one and adding, 'I'll be in touch.'

Bob picked up the old hickory putter and wandered out on to the course. Never a very enthusiastic player, he had given up golf after his father's death. He wondered at the sudden morbid curiosity that compelled him to try out the putter. Lowering clouds overhead made the course oppressive, and the branches of the trees seemed to lean in claustrophobically. Strangely, there was no one about. What else would one expect on a Monday lunch time? he asked himself logically. He walked up to the eighteenth green, placed the ball in the middle of it, and prepared to make a stroke. A faint murmur seemed to pass around him, then it ceased, leaving behind a stillness. Even the clouds, moving lethargically across the sky, propelled by a gentle breeze, hung immobile as he lifted the club to play the stroke.

At the same moment, from the direction of the eighteenth tee, he quite distinctly heard the sound of a driver hitting a ball in his direction. He looked round angrily. He could see along the length of the fairway very clearly. There was no one to be seen, but as he paused he heard the sound again, followed by two voices in sharp articulation, growing more distinct as they approached him. One was young, the other elderly and very familiar.

The eighteenth was three hundred and ninety yards long. That should give him a good few minutes' respite before they reached him.

He turned and raced across the green to peer down at the spot where his father had told him he had found the old putter. Heavy rains had turned the waterfall into a cascade, and the pool below it seethed and bubbled as though at boiling point.

Bob clambered down the bank and precariously balanced himself on the lowest part of the slope, just above the water. He dug frantically with the ancient club but made little progress. Finally he resorted to tearing away at the earth and stones with his bare hands, and when this grave was large enough, he put in the old putter.

Looking up he saw with relief that his father was in the high rough a good hundred yards from the green. Bob could hear him shouting angrily as he thrashed about, and could see the dead bracken wave. But his father's companion had more than likely driven straight along the fairway, and could already be approaching very close. Bob covered the old club and hammered down the earth on top so that it was buried completely.

Then he climbed back up onto level ground. His hands were scratched and bleeding, but the owner of the hickory putter had no power over him now. He would have to be content with only one partner. Knowing his father, Bob decided, that one partner would prove to be more than enough.

THE EMPTY SCHOOLROOM

PAMELA HANSFORD JOHNSON

My mother and father were in India and I had no aunts, uncles or cousins with whom I could spend my holidays; so I stayed behind in the drab and echoing school to amuse myself as best I could, my only companions the housekeeper, the maid, and Mademoiselle Fournier, who also had nowhere else to go.

Our school was just outside the village of Bellançay, which is in the north of France, four or five kilometres from Rouen. It was a tall, narrow house set upon the top of a hill, bare save for the great sweep of beech trees sheltering the long carriage drive. As I look back some twenty-seven years to my life there, it seems to me that the sun never shone, that the grass was always dun-coloured beneath a dun-coloured sky, and that the vast spaces of the lawns were broken perpetually by the scurry of dry brown leaves licked along by a small, bitter wind. This inaccurate impression remains with me because, I suppose, I was never happy at Bellançay. There were twenty or thirty other girls there – French, German or Swiss; I was the only English girl among them. Madame de Vallon, the headmistress, did not love my nation. She could not forget that she had been born in 1815, the year of defeat. With Mademoiselle Maury, the young assistant teacher, I was a little more at ease, for she, even if she did not care for me, had too volatile a nature not to smile and laugh sometimes, even for the benefit of those who were not her favourites.

Mademoiselle Fournier was a dependent cousin of our headmistress. She was in her late fifties, a little woman dry as a winter twig, her face very tight, small and wary under a wig of coarse yellow hair. To pay for her board and lodging she taught deportment; in her youth she had been at the Court of the Tsar, and it was said that at sixteen years of age she was betrothed to a Russian nobleman. There was some sort of mystery here, about which all the girls were curious. Louise de Chausson said her mother had told her the story – how the nobleman, on the eve of his wedding, had shot himself through the head, having received word that certain speculations in which he had for many years been involved had come to light, and that his arrest was imminent... 'And from that day,' Louise whispered, her prominent eyes gleaming in the candlelight, 'she began to wither and wither and wither away, till all her beauty was gone...' Yes, I can see Louise now, kneeling upon her bed at the end of the vast dormitory, her thick plait hanging down over her nightgown, the little cross with the turquoise glittering at her beautiful and grainy throat. The others believed the story implicitly, except the piece about Mademoiselle Fournier's lost beauty. That they could not stomach. No, she was ugly as a monkey and had always been so.

For myself, I disbelieved in the nobleman; believed in the beauty. I have always had a curious faculty for stripping age from a face, recognizing the structure of the bone and the original texture of the skin beneath the disguisings of blotch, red vein and loosened flesh. When I looked at Mademoiselle Fournier I saw that the pinched and veinous nose had once been delicate and fine; that the sunken eyes had once been almond-shaped and blue; that the small, loose mouth had once pouted charmingly and opened upon romantic words. Why did I not believe in the nobleman? For no better reason than a distrust of Louise's information on any conceivable point. She was a terrible teller of falsehoods.

I was seventeen years old when I spent my last vacation at Bellançay, and knowing that my parents were to return to Europe in the following spring I watched the departure of the other girls with a heart not quite as heavy as was usual upon these occasions. In six months' time I, too, would be welcomed and loved, have adventures to relate and hopes upon which to feed.

I waved to them from a dormer window as they rattled away in fiacre and barouche down the drive between the beech trees, sired and damed, uncled and aunted, their boxes stacked high and their voices high as the treetops. They had never before seemed to me a particularly attractive group of girls – that is, not in the mass. There was, of course, Hélène de Courcey, with her great olive eyes; Madeleine Millet, whose pale red hair hung to her knees; but in the cluster they had no particular charm. That day, however, as, in new bonnets flowered and feathered and gauzed, they passed from sight down the narrowing file of beeches, I thought them all beautiful as princesses, and as princesses fortunate. Perhaps the nip in the air of a grey June made their cheeks rose-red, their eyes bright as the eyes of desirable young ladies in ballrooms.

The last carriage disappeared, the last sound died away. I turned from the window and went down the echoing stairs, flight after flight, to the *salle à manger*, where my luncheon awaited me.

I ate alone. Mademoiselle Fournier took her meals in her own room upon the second floor, reading as she ate, crumbs falling from her lip on to the page. Tonight she and I, in the pattern of all holiday nights, would sit together for a while in the drawing room before retiring.

'You don't make much of a meal, I must say,' Marie, the maid, rebuked me, as she cleared the plates. 'You can't afford to grow thinner, Mademoiselle, or you'll snap in two.' She brought me some cherries, which I would not eat then but preferred to take out with me in the garden. 'I'll wrap them up for you. No! you can't put them in your handkerchief like that; you'll stain it.'

She chattered to me for a while, in her good nature trying to ease my loneliness. Marie, at least, had relations in the village with whom she sometimes spent her evenings. 'What are you going to do with yourself, eh? Read your eyes out as usual?'

'I shall walk this afternoon, unless I find it too chilly.'

'You'll find it raining,' said Marie, cocking a calculating eye towards the high windows, 'in an hour. No, less; in half an hour.'

She busied herself wrapping up my cherries, which she handed to me in a neat parcel with a firm finger-loop of string. 'If it's wet you can play the piano.'

'You've forgotten,' I said, 'we have none now, or shan't have till they send the new one.'

Madame de Vallon had recently sold the old instrument, ugly and tinny, and with the money from the sale plus some money raised by parents' subscription had bought a grand pianoforte from Monsieur Oury, the mayor, whose eldest daughter, the musical one, had lately died.

'You can play on Mademoiselle Fournier's,' said Marie, 'she won't mind. You go and ask her.'

'What, is there another piano in the school?' I was amazed. I had been at Bellançay for seven years and had fancied no corner of the building unknown to me.

'Ah-ha,' said Marie triumphantly, 'there are still things you don't know, eh? You don't have to do the housework, or you'd be wiser.'

'But where is it?'

'In the empty schoolroom.'

I laughed at her. 'But they're all empty now! Whatever do you mean?'

'The one at the top,' she said impatiently, 'the one up the little flight of four stairs.'

'But that's the lumber room!'

'There's lumber in it. But it was a schoolroom once. It was when my aunt worked here. The piano's up there still, though *she* never plays it now.' Marie jerked her head skywards to indicate Mademoiselle Fournier upstairs.

I was fascinated by this information. We girls had never entered the lumber room because no attraction had been attached to it: to us it was simply a small, grimy door in the attic, locked we imagined, as we had never seen anyone go in or out. All we knew was that old books, valises, crates of unwanted china, were sometimes stacked up there out of the way.

There! I have failed to make my point quite clear. I must try again. *There was no mystery whatsoever attaching to this room*, which is the reason why no girl had ever tried the handle. Schoolgirls are curious and roaming creatures; how better can they be kept from a certain path than by the positive assurance that it is a *cul-de-sac?*

Dismissing Marie, I determined to go and seek permission from Mademoiselle Fournier to play upon her pianoforte. Since the departure of the old one, I had missed my music lessons and above all my practising; most of the girls were delighted to be saved a labour which to me, though I was an indifferent performer, had never been anything but a pleasure.

Mademoiselle had finished her meal and was just coming out upon the landing as I ran up the stairs to find her. I made my request.

She looked at me. 'Who told you about the instrument?'

'Marie.'

She was silent. Her brows moved up and down, moving the wig as they did so. It was a familiar trick with her when she was puzzled or annoyed. At last she said, without expression, 'No, you may not go up there,' and pushing me, hurried on downstairs.

At the turn of the staircase, however, she stopped and looked up. Her whole face was working with some unrecognizable emotion and her cheeks were burning red. 'Is there *no* place one can keep to oneself?' she cried at me furiously, and ducking her head, ran on.

When we sat that evening in the drawing room, in our chairs turned to the fireless grate, she made no reference to the little scene of that afternoon. I thought she was, perhaps, sorry for having spoken so sharply: for she asked me a few personal questions of a kindly nature and just before bedtime brought out a tin box full of sugared almonds, which she shared with me.

She rose a little before I did, leaving me to retire when I chose. I stayed for perhaps half an hour in that vast, pale room with its moth-coloured draperies and its two tarnished chandeliers hanging a great way below the ceiling. Then I took up my candle and went to bed.

Now I must insist that I was a docile girl, a little sullen, perhaps, out of an unrealized resentment against my parents for (as I thought) deserting me; but obedient. I never had a bad conduct report from any of our teachers. It is important that this fact should be realized, so the reader shall know that what I did was not of my own free will.

I could not sleep. I lay open-eyed until my candle burned halfway down and the moon shifted round into the windowpane, weaving the golden light with its own blue-silver. I had no thought of any importance. Small pictures from the day's humdrum events flashed across my brain. I saw the neatly-looped parcel of cherries, the currant stain at the hem of Marie's apron, the starch-blue bird on the bonnet of Louise de Chausson, who had left Bellançay to marry an elderly and not very rich nobleman of Provence. I saw the leaves scurrying over the grey lawns, saw a woodpecker rapping at the trunk of the tree behind the house. What I did not see was the face of Mademoiselle Fournier upturned from the stairway. She never entered my thoughts at all.

And so it is very strange that just before dawn I rose up, put on my dressing gown and sought about the room until I found a pair of gloves my father had had made for me in India, fawn-coloured, curiously stitched in gold and dark green thread. These I took up, left the room and made my way silently up through the quiet house till I came to the door of the lumber room – or, as Marie had called it, the empty schoolroom. I paused with my hand upon the latch and listened. There was no sound except the impalpable breathing of the night, compound perhaps of the breathings of all who sleep, or perhaps of the movement of the moon through the gathered clouds.

I raised the latch gently and stepped within the room, closing the door softly behind me.

The chamber ran halfway across the length of the house at the rear of it, and was lighted by a ceiling window through which the moonrays poured lavishly down. It was still a schoolroom, despite the lumber stacked at the far end, the upright piano standing just behind the door. Facing me was a dais, on which stood a table and a chair. Before the dais were row upon row of desks, with benches behind. Everything was very dusty. With my finger I wrote DUST upon the teacher's table, then scuffed the word out again.

I went to the pianoforte. Behind the lattice-work was a ruching of torn red silk; the candle stumps in the sconces were red also. On the rack stood a piece of music, a Chopin nocturne simplified for beginners.

Gingerly I raised the lid and a mottled spider ran across the keys, dropped on hasty thread to the floor and ran away. The underside of the lid was completely netted by his silk; broken strands waved in the disturbed air and over the discoloured keys. As a rule I am afraid of spiders. That night I was not afraid. I laid my gloves on the keyboard, then closed the piano lid upon them.

I was ready to go downstairs. I took one glance about the room and for a moment thought I saw a shadowy form sitting upon one of the back benches, a form that seemed to weep. Then the impression passed away, and there was only the moonlight painting the room with its majesty. I went out, latched the door and crept back to my bed where, in the first colouring of dawn, I fell asleep.

Next day it was fine. I walked to the river in the morning, and in the afternoon worked at my *petit-point* upon the terrace. At teatime an invitation came for me. The mayor, Monsieur Oury, wrote to Mademoiselle Fournier saying he believed there was a young lady left behind at school for the holidays, and that if she would care to dine at his house upon the following evening it would be a great pleasure to him and to his two young daughters. 'We are not a gay house these days,' he wrote, 'but if the young lady cares for books and flowers there are a great number of both in my library and conservatory.'

'Shall I go?' I asked her.

'But of course! It is really a great honour for you. Do you know who the mayor's mother was before her marriage? She was an Uzès. Yes. And when she married Monsieur Oury's father, a very handsome man, her family cut her off with nothing at all and never spoke to her again. But they were very happy. You must wear your best gown and your white hat. Take the gown to Marie and she will iron it for you.'

The day upon which I was to visit Monsieur Oury was sunless and chilly. Plainly the blue dress that Marie had so beautifully spotted and pressed would not do at all. I had, however, a gown of fawn-coloured merino, plain but stylish, with which my brown straw hat would look very well.

Mademoiselle Fournier left the house at four o'clock to take tea with the village priest. She looked me over before she went, pinched my dress, tweaked it, pulled out the folds, and told me to sit quite still until the mayor's carriage came for me at half past six. 'Sit like a mouse, mind, or you will spoil the effect. Remember, Monsieur Oury is not nobody.' She said suddenly, 'Where are your gloves?'

I had forgotten them.

'Forgetting the very things that make a lady look a lady! Go and fetch them at once. Marie!'

The maid came in.

'Marie, see Mademoiselle's gloves are nice, and brush her down once more just as you see the carriage enter the drive. I mustn't wait now. Well, Maud, I wish you a pleasant evening. Don't forget you must be a credit to us.'

When she had gone Marie asked for my gloves. 'You'd better wear your brown ones with that hat, Mademoiselle.'

'Oh!' I exclaimed, 'I can't! I lost one of them on the expedition last week.'

'Your black, then?'

'They won't do. They'd look dreadful with this gown and hat.

I know! I have a beautiful Indian pair that will match my dress exactly! I'll go and look for them.'

I searched. The reader must believe that I hunted all over my room for them anxiously, one eye upon the clock, though it was not yet twenty minutes past four. Chagrined, really upset at the thought of having my toilette ruined, I sat down upon the edge of the bed and began to cry a little. Tears came very easily to me in those lost and desolate days.

From high up in the house I heard a few notes of the piano, the melody of a Chopin nocturne played fumblingly in the treble, and I thought at once, 'Of course! The gloves are up there, where I hid them.'

The body warns us of evil before the senses are half awakened. I knew no fear as I ran lightly up towards the empty schoolroom, yet as I reached the door I felt a wave of heat engulf me, and knew a sick, nauseous stirring within my body. The notes, audible only to my ear (not to Marie's, for even at that moment I could hear her calling out some inquiry or gossip to the housekeeper), ceased. I lifted the latch and looked in.

The room appeared to be deserted, yet I could see the presence within it and know its distress. I peeped behind the door.

At the piano sat a terribly ugly, thin young girl in a dunce's cap. She was half turned towards me, and I saw her pig-like profile, the protruding teeth, the spurt of sandy eyelash. She wore a holland dress in the fashion of twenty years ago, and lean yellow streamers of hair fell down over her back from beneath the paper cone. Her hands, still resting on the fouled keyboard, were meshed about with the spider's web; beneath them lay my Indian gloves.

I made a movement towards the girl. She swivelled sharply and looked me full in the face. Her eyes were all white, red-rimmed, but tearless.

To get my gloves I must risk touching her. We looked at each other, she and I, and her head shrank low between her hunching shoulders. Somehow I must speak to her friendlily, disarm her while I gained my objective.

'Was it you playing?' I asked.

No answer. I closed my eyes. Stretching out my hands as in a game of blind man's buff, I sought for the keyboard.

'I have never heard you before,' I said.

I touched something: I did not know whether it was a glove or her dead hand.

'Have you been learning long?' I said. I opened my eyes. She was gone. I took my gloves, dusted off the webs and ran, ran so fast down the well of the house that on the last flight I stumbled and fell breathless into Marie's arms.

'Oh, I have had a fright! I have had a fright!'

She led me into the drawing room, made me lie down, brought me a glass of wine.

'What is it, Mademoiselle? Shall I fetch the housekeeper? What has happened?'

But the first sip of wine had made me wary. 'I thought I saw someone hiding in my bedroom, a man. Perhaps a thief.'

At this the house was roused. Marie, the housekeeper and the gardener, who had not yet finished his work, searched every room (the lumber room, too, I think) but found nothing. I was scolded, petted, dosed, and Marie insisted, when the housekeeper was out of the way, on a *soupçon* of rouge on my cheeks because, she said, I could not upset Monsieur le Maire by looking like a dead body – he, poor man, having so recently had death in his house!

I recovered myself sufficiently to climb into the carriage, when it came, to comport myself decently on the drive, and to greet the mayor and his two daughters with dignity. Dinner, however, was a nightmare. My mind was so full of the horror I had seen that I could not eat – indeed I could barely force my trembling hand to carry the fork to my lips.

The mayor's daughters were only children, eleven and thirteen years old. At eight o'clock he bade them say good night to me and prepare for bed. When they had left us I told him I thought I had stayed long enough: but with a very grave look he placed his hand upon my arm and pressed me gently back into my chair.

'My dear young lady,' he said, 'I know your history, I know you are lonely and unhappy in France without your parents. Also I know that you have suffered some violent shock. Will you tell me about it and let me help you?'

The relief of his words, of his wise and kindly gaze, was too much for me. For the first time in seven years I felt fathered and in haven. I broke down and cried tempestuously, and he did not touch me or speak to me till I was a little more calm. Then he rang for the servant and told her to bring some lime-flower tea. When I had drunk and eaten some of the sweet cake that he urged upon me I told him about the empty schoolroom and of the horror which sat there at the webbed piano.

When I had done he was silent for a little while. Then he took both my hands in his.

'Mademoiselle,' he said, 'I am not going to blame you for the sin of curiosity; I think there was some strange compulsion upon you to act as you did. Therefore I mean to shed a little light upon this sad schoolroom by telling you the story of Mademoiselle Fournier.'

I started.

'No,' he continued restrainingly, 'you must listen quietly; and what I tell you you must never repeat to a soul save your own mother until both Mademoiselle Fournier and Madame de Vallon, her cousin, have passed away.'

I have kept this promise. They have been dead some fourteen years.

Monsieur Oury settled back in his chair. A tiny but comforting fire was lit in the grate, and the light of it was like a ring of guardian angels about us.

'Mademoiselle Fournier,' he began, 'was a very beautiful and proud young woman. Although she had no dowry, she was yet considered something of a *partie*, and in her nineteenth year she became affianced to a young Russian nobleman who at that time was living with his family upon an estate near Arles. His mother was not too pleased with the match, but she was a good woman, and she treated Charlotte – that is, Mademoiselle Fournier – with kindness. Just before the marriage Charlotte's father, who had been created a marquis by Bonaparte and now, by tolerance, held a minor government post under Louis Philippe, was found to have embezzled many thousands of francs.'

'Her father!' I could not help but exclaim.

Monsieur Oury smiled wryly. 'Legend has the lover for villain, eh? No; it was Aristide Fournier, a weak man, unable to stomach any recession in his fortunes. Monsieur Fournier shot himself as the gendarmes were on their way to take him. Charlotte, her marriage prospects destroyed, came near to lunacy. When she recovered from her long illness her beauty had gone. The mother of her ex-fiancé, in pity, suggested that a friend of hers, a lady at the Court of the Tsar, should employ Charlotte as governess to her children, and in Russia Charlotte spent nine years. She returned to France to assist her cousin with the school at Bellançay that Madame de Vallon had recently established.'

'Why did she return?' I said, less because I wished to know the answer than because I wished to break out of the veil of the past he was drawing about us both, and to feel myself a reality once more, Maud Arlett, aged seventeen years and nine months, brown hair and grey eyes, five foot seven and a half inches tall.

I did not succeed. The veil tightened, grew more opaque. 'Nobody knows. There were rumours. It seems not improbable that she was dismissed by her employer . . . why, I don't know. It is an obscure period in Charlotte's history.'

He paused, to pour more tea for me.

'It was thought at first that Charlotte would be of great assistance to Madame de Vallon, teach all subjects and act as Madame's secretary. It transpired, however, that Charlotte was nervous to the point of sickness, and that she would grow less and less capable of teaching young girls. Soon she had no duties in the school except to give lessons in music and deportment.

'The music room was in the attic, which was then used as a schoolroom also. The pianoforte was Charlotte's own, one of the few things saved from the wreck of her home.'

Monsieur Oury rose and walked out of the ring of firelight. He stood gazing out of the window, now beaded by a thin rain, and his voice grew out of the dusk as the music of waves grows out of the sea. 'I shall tell you the rest briefly, Mademoiselle. It distresses me to tell it to you at all, but I think I can help you in no other way.

'A young girl came to the school, a child; perhaps twelve or thirteen years of age. Her mother and father were in the East, and she was left alone, even during the vacations—'

'Like myself!' I cried.

'Yes, like yourself; and I have an idea that that is why she chose you for her . . . *confidante*.'

I shuddered.

He seemed to guess at my movement for, turning from the window, he returned to the firelight and to me.

'In one way, however, she was unlike you as can possibly be

imagined, Mademoiselle.' He smiled with a faint, sad gallantry. 'She was exceedingly ugly.

'From the first, Charlotte took a dislike to her, and it grew to mania. The child, Thérèse Dasquier, was never very intelligent; in Charlotte's grip she became almost imbecile. Charlotte was always devising new punishments, new humiliations. Thérèse became the mock and the pity of the school.'

'But Madame de Vallon, couldn't she have stopped it?' I interrupted indignantly.

'My dear,' Monsieur Oury replied sadly, 'like many women of intellect – she is, as you know, a fine teacher – she is blind to most human distress. She is, herself, a kind woman: she believes others are equally kind, cannot believe there could be ... suffering ... torment ... going on beneath her very nose. Has she ever realized *your* loneliness, Mademoiselle, given you any motherly word, or ...? I thought not. But I am digressing, and that I must not do. We have talked too much already.

'One night Thérèse Dasquier arose quietly, crept from the dormitory and walked barefooted a mile and a half in the rain across the fields to the river, where she drowned herself.'

'Oh, God,' I murmured, my heart cold and heavy as a stone.

'God, I think,' said Monsieur Oury, 'cannot have been attentive at that time ...' His face changed. He added hastily, 'And God forgive me for judging Him. We cannot know – we cannot guess ...' he continued rapidly, in a dry, rather high voice oddly unlike his own. 'There was scandal, great scandal. Thérèse's parents returned to France and everyone expected them to force the truth to light. They turned out to be frivolous and selfish people, who could scarcely make even a parade of grief for a child they had never desired and whose death they could not regret. Thérèse was buried and forgotten. Slowly, very slowly, the story also was forgotten. After all, nobody *knew* the truth, they could only make conjecture.'

'Then how did you know?' I cried out.

'Because Madame de Vallon came to me in bitter distress with the tale of the rumours and besought me to clear Charlotte's name. You see, she simply could not believe a word against her. And at the same time the aunt of Marie, the maid, came to me swearing she could prove the truth of the accusations . . . Three days afterwards she was killed in the fire which destroyed the old quarter of Bellançay.'

I looked my inquiry into his face.

'I knew which of the women spoke the truth,' he replied, answering me, 'because in Madame de Vallon's face I saw concern for her own blood. In the other woman's I saw concern for a child who to her was nothing.'

'But still, you *guessed*!' I protested.

He turned upon me his long and grave regard. 'You,' he said, '*you* do not know the truth? Even you?'

I do not know how I endured the following weeks in that lonely school. I remember how long I lay shivering in my bed, staring into the flame of the candle because I felt that in the brightest part of it alone was refuge, how the sweat jumped out from my brow at the least sound in the stillness of midnight, and how, towards morning, I would fall into some morose and terrible dream of dark stairways and locked doors.

Yet, as day by day, night by night, went by with no untoward happening, my spirit knew some degree of easing and I began once more to find comfort in prayer – that is, I dared once again to cover my face while I repeated 'Our Father,' and to rise from my knees without fear of what might be standing patiently at my shoulder.

The holidays drew to an end. 'Tomorrow,' said Mademoiselle Fournier, folding her needlework in preparation for bed, 'your companions will be back with you once more. You'll like that, eh?'

Ever since my request and her refusal, she had been perfectly normal in her manner – I mean, she had been normally sour, polite, withdrawn.

'I shall like it,' I sighed, 'only too well.'

She smiled remotely. 'I am not a lively companion for you, Maud, I fear. Still, I am as I am. I am too old to change myself.'

She went on upstairs, myself following, our candles smoking in the draught and our shadows prancing upon the wall.

I said my prayers and read for a little while. I was unusually calm, feeling safety so nearly within my reach that I need be in no hurry to stretch out my hand and grasp it tight. The bed seemed softer than usual, the sheets sweet-smelling, delicately warm and light. I fell into a dreamless sleep.

I awoke suddenly to find the moon full on my face. I sat up, dazzled by her light, a strange feeling of energy tingling in my body. 'What is it,' I whispered, 'that I must do?'

The moon shone broadly on the great surfaces of gleaming wood, on the bureau, the tallboy, the wardrobe, flashed upon the mirror, sparkled on the spiralling bedposts. I slipped out of bed and in my nightgown went out into the passage.

It was very bright and still. Below me, the stairs fell steeply to the tessellated entrance hall. To my right the passage narrowed to the door behind which Mademoiselle Fournier slept, her wig upon a candlestick, her book and her spectacles lying on the rug at her side – so Marie had described her to me. Before me the stairs rose to the turn of the landing, from which a further flight led to the second floor, the third floor and the attics. The wall above the stair rail was white with the moon.

I felt the terror creeping up beneath my calm, though only as one might feel the shadow of pain while in the grip of a drug. I was waiting now as I had been instructed to wait, and I knew for what. I stared upwards, my gaze fastened upon the turn of the stairs.

Then, upon the moonlit wall, there appeared the shadow of a cone.

She stood just out of sight, her fool's-capped head nodding forward, listening even as I was listening.

I held my breath. My forehead was ice-cold.

She came into view then, stepping carefully, one hand upholding a corner of her skirt, the other feeling its way along the wall. As she reached me I closed my eyes. I felt her pass by, knew she had gone along the passage to the room of Mademoiselle Fournier. I heard a door quietly opened and shut.

In those last moments of waiting my fear left me, though I could move neither hand nor foot. My ears were sharp for the least sound.

It came: a low and awful cry, tearing through the quiet of the house and blackening the moonlight itself. The door opened again.

She came hastening out, and in the shadow of the cap she smiled. She ran on tiptoe past me, up the stairs.

The last sound? I thought it had been the death cry of Mademoiselle Fournier; but there was yet another.

As Marie and the housekeeper came racing down, white-faced, from their rooms (they must have passed her as she stood in the shade) I heard very distinctly the piping voice of a young girl:

'Tiens, Mademoiselle, je vous remercie beaucoup!'

We went together, Marie, the housekeeper and I, into the room of Charlotte Fournier, and only I did not cry out when we looked upon the face.

'You see,' said Monsieur Oury, on the day I left Bellançay for ever to join my parents in Paris, 'she did make you her *confidante*. She gave to you the privilege of telling her story and publishing her revenge. Are you afraid of her now, knowing that there was no harm in her for *you*, knowing that she has gone for ever, to trouble no house again?'

'I am not afraid,' I said, and I believed it was true; but even now I cannot endure to awaken suddenly on moonlit nights, and I fling my arms about my husband and beg him to rouse up and speak with me until the dawn.

OFF THE DEEP END

PHILLIP C. HEATH

The young boy named Jeffrey squinted up at a bright, cloudless sky, drinking in the wonderful warmth of the afternoon sun. It mirrored the rippling surface of the lake with dazzling flashes of light and rainbow colour. He brought back the tip of his rod to proper position and swung it smoothly forward, pressing the release with his thumb at precisely the right instant in the down-stroke, and sent the line shooting far out in a quick, gentle arc. The lure plunked neatly into the water, began its return.

He crammed three pieces of Juicy-Fruit into his mouth at once and surveyed the surrounding countryside. Bittercrest Lake was a 380-acre body of water nestled in a wide hollow of tree-clad hills. The nearest community, Myrtle Springs, was about seven miles to the south down Shady Mill Road. A dozen or so scattered dwellings rimmed the vast shoreline, half-hidden amid the pines; cozy hideaways that created an air of scenic seclusion. Handy to each, a small dock or boathouse jutted out slightly over the water.

He could barely distinguish one of the cabins on the farthest side of the point – a large two-storey frame house with steeply pitched eaves and a big bay window facing the lake. It was beautifully landscaped, too, and after a while he could make out his Aunt Freda flitting about the place, probably setting out bedding plants purchased in town. Yes, he thought, that's what she must be doing, digging now along the retaining wall he had helped Uncle Harvey build last autumn out of logs cut from the forest. He didn't see anyone else. Uncle Harvey was most likely visiting a neighbour, and his mother was probably inside cleaning or dusting, as always, against Aunt Freda's tolerant wishes.

Jeffrey pulled the dripping lure from the water, adroitly flicking off a bit of brown moss. It was a very special lure, not so much in being a gold-and-white Hellbender Whopper-Stopper absolutely guaranteed to catch 'the big one,' but because it was the first he had ever bought with his own money, at Mr Johnson's Bait Shop. Of course, Uncle Harvey had given him some of his old discards, and periodically Jeffrey had found a few that had been lost or snagged by other fishermen, but this one was different. And so he knew instinctively it would, indeed, bag the big one.

He eased several yards down the shore where a huge rock offered relaxation. There he briefly took aim and cast again. As this was the deepest section of the lake, he let it sink five or six seconds before making the retrieve, measuring speed by the soft clicking whirr of the reel. His wrists and fingers moved almost by themselves, a continuous, patient process.

He cast once more.

Abruptly the line grew taut. At first he worried that he'd encountered a log or a ledge. Then his senses pricked alert: there was a movement, a tentative pull, which gave way to slack, immediately followed with a firm, definite tugging.

Jeffrey nimbly checked the drag, set it, and slowly returned the tension by raising the length of his rod as his uncle had shown him.

A violent yank on the line nearly threw Jeffrey off balance. He had not been prepared for the formidable opposition on the other end of the line. His rod was forced to the left, then something tried to take the line and run.

Jeffrey braced himself for the fury of the fight and felt a delicious exhilaration coursing through him. It was easy to envision some mighty leviathan diving, circling, struggling for its very life down in the untold depths, madly striving to dislodge the long, sharp, barbed hooks of its unwitting captor. His uncle had told him tales of great fish seldom but occasionally seen or even landed. Lunkers, he called them. And Jeffrey remembered photographs in the newspapers – fatigued anglers beaming beside their dangling trophies.

Uncle Harvey would be so proud of him! Maybe this was that 'grandaddy of 'em all,' the one with 'hair on its belly'.

Such frantic anticipations as these danced in Jeffrey's head as he played the creature for a good twenty minutes, his pole bent almost double. It must be big as he was! But now as he drew it nearer the shore he became worried. With dismay he realized the bank was too rugged here to lift his catch out of the water; the twelve-pound test line would probably hold well – as it had thus far – yet he had no net, and was too exhausted anyway. He attempted calling for help, but evidently no one heard.

Swiftly but carefully he started working the fish into some shallows farther down the shore. There he could more safely drag his catch up onto the bank.

The closer he brought it in, the less it seemed to resist him. It was no doubt tired as he was. And towards the end it became merely a dead weight. The battle was won.

He pulled the thing into some straggling sawgrass, where it lay, unmoving. He anxiously approached his prize, then froze; and gagged. The stench was overpowering. It was puffy and pale, a bloated bulk covered with hairlike strands of weed and green scum. The lure was wrapped tightly about the thick neck; one of the man's hands was hopelessly entangled in the line.

The scream died in Jeffrey's throat, as the blackness squeezed his brain.

For two days Jeffrey lay drugged in a hospital bed recovering from the initial shock, his stomach a grinding twist of sickness, the sinister and climactic chain of events flickering repeatedly, unbidden, across his mind.

Ever since his father had been killed in the automobile accident, he and his mother had come to Aunt Freda and Uncle Harvey's for two or three weeks after school let out for the summer. Last year they had driven up later than usual, during Thanksgiving recess. Because the fish weren't biting much, he decided he would have to entertain himself otherwise – such as with Mrs Prescott, an elderly widow who lived just off the point, not far from his aunt and uncle. Mrs Prescott had always been real nice to him, said he reminded her of her own son who was all grown up and married. Jeffrey thought she must be awful lonely living there alone, and he always made a point of visiting her whenever he came. She would usually bake him a fresh blackberry cobbler or something.

The day after they arrived he went over to greet her, but Jeffrey never got to the door. Instead, he was confronted by an unshaven man with stony eyes and worn, threadbare clothes, who stepped around from the side of the house.

'Who are you? Whatcha want?' His voice was a hard hiss.

Jeffrey answered rather hoarsely, explained himself briefly.

The beefy man grinned slackly from beneath dishevelled hair. 'Yeah? Well, Missus Prescott ain't here. She's gone away fer a few days. I'm – a friend. I'll tell her you was by.'

They both stood there a moment.

'What ya waitin' for? G'wan – get.'

So Jeffrey turned and hurried away, confused and somewhat disturbed. Something was wrong. He sensed it. Where could she have gone for so long, and where had her unseemly 'friend' come from? He mulled it over the rest of that day and part of the next, eventually deciding he ought to speak to his uncle.

Uncle Harvey admitted it was rather peculiar and put in a call to the sheriff. Luckily. For the sheriff told them that a couple of dangerous inmates had very recently escaped from the Craven County Mental Institution and were reportedly headed in their direction. Even now an intensive manhunt was in progress.

By dusk state and local authorities had surrounded Mrs Prescott's. Shortly thereafter the two fugitives were confronted by way of a loudspeaker. But apparently the pair had already spied the lawmen's presence, for they had tied up Mrs Prescott and somehow managed to slip out. Then, dramatically, when night had fallen they reared off across the lake in a stolen boat – until a waiting police cruiser appeared out of the gloom and tried to cut them off. The smaller craft swerved recklessly and was ripped open by a partially submerged stump. The launch flipped, flung both men out, and burst into flames.

Neither body was recovered. Officers searched with spotlights all through that night and dragged the lake for almost a week, but all they brought up were fragments of the ruined boat. Someone surmised that the deeper waters, which were getting colder with the approach of winter, were holding the bodies down. That was obviously true, for there the bodies stayed – at least one of them did – until the next summer, until a young boy, fishing . . .

Even long after his mother had taken him back home Jeffrey's nervousness lingered. He could never account for the eerie and unexplained resistance on the line, but dared not reveal his vague disquiet regarding that mystery, dared not confess the nightmares that plagued him, the haunting, restless nights that robbed him of sleep. When he saw himself sinking, head lolling, mouth agape, his soft limbs turning in the murky depths.

The following year Jeffrey and his mother didn't return to Bittercrest Lake. Part of the reason was his mother's change of job, which consequently limited any prolonged absence from work. But also, he concluded, it was because of his dreadful ordeal. Whatever the case, he found himself a little relieved.

The succeeding summer, though, Uncle Harvey and Aunt Freda welcomed them back with hugs and handshakes, his aunt playfully scolding that she was going to have to tie a brick on 'that young rascal's head' to keep him from growing so fast. They talked, unpacked, and lounged about the cabin until Jeffrey could be cooped no longer and wandered outside.

The place was pretty much the same, he discovered, and presently even decided to do a little fishing off the dock a short walk from the house. He had to borrow one of Uncle Harvey's rods, his own having been missing ever since that day, probably picked up by one of the policemen and accidentally taken along. It was practically brand new, too, a gift from his mother. But he put that out of his mind, and concentrated on surprising Uncle Harvey with a panful of fine bluegill. He'd lately managed to forget about the other body as well, although perhaps not entirely – there were some things he doubted he could ever forget – but at least he locked them away.

Ah, it was good to be back again, in spite of it all, for this place always held a certain fascination. He inhaled deeply, idly savouring the crisp, cherished scents of sassafras, cool mint and forest mould.

An hour later as he was about to go inside for supper, he got an exceptional strike. But then he perceived that it was distinctly different – more of a heavy, reluctant, yet steady drag all the way in.

He tried to swallow but there was no moisture in his throat.

Memories, scenes, images, ghosted through his mind.

All at once a hand flopped out of the water and he shrieked, flung the pole aside and raced wildly to the house. Trembling anew with terror, he babbled his story to the astounded adults.

In ten minutes Uncle Harvey returned to the den, a somewhat

strained look on his face. Jeffrey ventured to the door of his room and, peeking downstairs, listened apprehensively.

He saw his uncle bite his lip, as if wondering what to say.

'I found it,' he confided, his voice solemn. 'He snagged something all right . . . a sunken bush.'

Jeffrey's mother gave a muffled sob and his aunt patted her shoulder in condolence.

His uncle sat down. 'Well, after all, you have to consider what he's been through. Poor fellow. Don't worry though, I'm sure he'll get over it as he grows older.'

'But two years now, and he—' Jeffrey's mother said.

'Be patient, my dear. It's just that some wounds heal slower than others. He needs to forget, and so he will. Believe me. Time will erase his unpleasant memories . . .'

His uncle's words trailed away, and Jeffrey climbed back into bed. He closed his eyes then opened them, wanting to flee to sleep, but fearful of what might be waiting there.

Two more years quickly came and went, and the awful event did not fade from his mind. It simply burrowed deeper into his brain like a dormant, virulent seed.

This subtle realization began to prey upon Jeffrey when he and his mother again returned to the house on the lake. But fortunately it was forced aside by an unexpected distraction. Jeffrey's cousin Tim joined them there, was to stay for a couple of months while Tim's parents were abroad on business. Jeffrey and Tim hadn't seen each other for a number of years, but it was like the old days, and they passed most of the time together, even until the last night of Jeffrey's stay.

Sitting out on the porch after sunset, Tim made a suggestion as if to somehow postpone their inevitable parting.

'Hey, let's go frog-gigging. We never did get around to it. Why not t'night?'

'You still want to?'

'Sure, c'mon.'

So they went, equipped with waders, gigs, torch and tow-sack, clogging about in the tussocks of swamp sedge along Mud Creek, the run-off from the lake. Toting a batch of frogs destined for the freezer, they loitered awhile on the way back to watch the weird luminescence of glowworms, and listen to the clamour of crickets and cicadas before eventually heading to the house.

By that time it was growing late, and everyone was getting ready for bed. Tim said goodnight and trudged upstairs. But Jeffrey wasn't very tired yet, and went outside for one more breath of clean evening air before leaving tomorrow for the city. As always, there was the tormenting uncertainty.

He clenched his fists at his sides, brooding.

He couldn't endure this thing the rest of his life. It had to stop. The unspeakable nightmares, the sweaty, sleepless nights – all of it. It had been such a long time ago; five years, in fact. Why, there wouldn't even be anything left of the other – body. But enough of that. He would be enrolling in university this autumn. And he'd turn eighteen come next October. A young man, as his mother had begun to call him, not some runny-nosed kid who happened to be in the wrong place at the wrong time. Soon he would have things to do, places to go. And this had to stay behind. Dead, forgotten. Yes, tonight he must, *would* bury it forever.

Jeffrey strolled towards the lake and struck out along the familiar trail skirting its spacious shoreline. Several times he hesitated, contemplating returning to the cabin, but his earlier conviction goaded him on.

It was shortly before midnight when he finally spotted the old lichen-stained boulder up ahead, just off the deep end, where it all had happened. He sat down on the great rock and collected his thoughts. A full moon gilded the lake, and scraps of shadows lurked under the taller trees. All the world slumbered, save for the ceaseless, rhythmic lapping of foam-flecked water along the bank.

Suddenly he glimpsed something gleaming there, silvery in the moonlight. Jeffrey reached down and picked it up.

It was his old lure, the one he had bought with his own money, lost that same fateful day. He had to hold it closer to believe it was true. Could it have really been lying here all this time, unseen, untouched? Was it possible? Something about it just didn't seem . . . right.

Something else, with wet, chilled hands was knocking on the door of his mind, and a feeling of unreasoning horror slowly seized him as he noticed for the first time the line attached to the lure, leading back into the water.

Then there was a vicious jerk, a piercing pain, and a fierce tension on the line.

The three wicked, treble hooks had dug deep into his hand, bloody and quivering. With the other he clawed vainly at the bank of silty sand, his mind folding up within him, as Jeffrey was slowly but mercilessly dragged out . . .

. . . and under.

THE SUMMER HOUSE

HEATHER VINEHAM

Maureen stared in disbelief through the kitchen window, the coffee cup, half-dried, poised above the draining board. It had happened again! Sylvie was nowhere to be seen.

Maureen didn't like letting her small daughter out of her sight, and up to a minute ago Sylvie had been in full view on the lawn, playing with her big red and white ball. There was the ball, abandoned in the middle of the lawn, but Sylvie had vanished without trace. It was incomprehensible. The garden was too small to allow any hiding place: a pocket handkerchief lawn, bordered by flower beds where a few straggling rose bushes fought for existence in the hard soil. No outhouses, just a coal-cellar the size of a sentry box.

She looked apprehensively towards the wall at the end of the garden – the wall that divided Mr Phillips's garden from her own. It was low enough for a child to scramble over, with plenty of foot-holds in the worn stonework. She had warned Sylvie never to go over there. To Sylvie's provocative query of 'Why not?' she had never been quite sure how to answer. Just that it was naughty to go into other people's gardens; but she knew it was more than that. Maureen was afraid of that garden, and of the queer old man who owned it. She was particularly afraid of the corner just beyond the dividing wall, for a reason she could never explain. The long unkempt grass that covered the rest of the garden stopped abruptly a few yards from the wall in that corner, as though a rectangle of dry rubble had been cut out of the surrounding greenery. And over this barren spot a giant shadow seemed always to be crouching. A shadow of what? She could never discover. There was no tree that might account for it; only a few lifeless, leafless shrubs that seemed to share the blight of this desolate patch.

She ran quickly out into the garden and across the lawn. A glance over the space beyond showed her that her neighbour's garden was as empty as her own. Where could Sylvie be? She had disappeared like this before and had always reappeared inexplicably a few minutes later. But until she did appear, those minutes seemed like hours.

Maureen forced herself to look into that bleak corner just beyond the wall. It was bare, as she knew it would be, except for the shadow, which seemed darker, more menacing than ever. 'Oh Sylvie,' she called in helpless despair, 'why do you do this to me? You are a naughty girl!' Only silence answered her appeal. She must look somewhere else. The coal-cellar? She'd tried looking there before, without success, but she must inspect every possible place of concealment.

She started towards it without much hope, then sensed a movement close beside her. She swung round. Sylvie stood behind her, smiling unconcernedly, her yellow dress a little crumpled, tawny-brown curls hanging round her face.

'Sylvie!' Maureen exclaimed, her voice shaking in a mixture of anger and relief. 'Where *do* you get to, where have you been?' But she knew what the answer would be.

The child looked up at her innocently – a little too innocently, she thought. 'Only in the summer house.'

But there was no summer house.

Maureen automatically looked across the adjacent garden, but she knew it would tell her nothing. And Sylvie had been out of her sight for only a matter of minutes. It was uncanny.

As she led her little daughter back to the house, Maureen resolved to get to the bottom of this mystery. Her nerves could not stand the suspense any more. But how does one go about eliciting secrets from a six-year-old who does not want to share them?

Maureen decided that casualness was the best attitude to adopt. Once back in the kitchen, she continued drying up the dishes as though nothing out of the ordinary had happened. Then, as unconcernedly as possible, she phrased the question: 'Where is your summer house, darling?' Although she would have preferred, at that moment, to say 'you little devil'.

For a moment silence answered her, then Sylvie replied, speaking over her shoulder, her attention temporarily diverted from a teddy bear that was propped against the wall: 'It isn't my summer house, it's Tim's.' Then once again the teddy bear occupied her attention.

Tim – that name again! Frank had laughed away her fears when Maureen told him about Sylvie's obsession with this unseen companion. Just one of the quirks of an only child, he had assured her: she should soon grow out of it, mixing with other kids at school. Sylvie had been babbling about Tim ever since they had moved to Ripley Avenue nearly a year now. It was no one at her school; they had made sure of that. And now these fleeting, but terribly worrying disappearances.

Maureen realized with surprise that Sylvie was speaking again, enlarging on what she had always seemed determined not to discuss.

'Tim was naughty today,' she said. 'He scribbled all over his Indian book.'

Maureen risked showing a little more interest.

'Who is Tim?' she asked, but Sylvie's answering tone made it clear that she had no intention of continuing her confidence.

'Oh, just a boy,' she replied. 'He's always there.'

But where? thought Maureen, and knew that once again a curtain of restraint had fallen between them.

Maureen made sure next morning that Sylvie was well in view as she tidied up the kitchen. She kept an eagle eye on the small yellow-clad figure pulling up daisies on the lawn. Helping to keep the garden shipshape, Maureen hoped, would deflect Sylvie's attention from these inexplicable excursions.

A thundering on the side door sent Maureen running. The milkman always made sure of being heard when it was settling-up day. After the usual scrabbling for change, she returned to the kitchen, the ice-cold milk bottle in her hand. But halfway to the fridge she stopped, dumping the bottle on the table as she stared askance through the window. Not again! But the garden was as bare as it had been yesterday – and she had been so careful, so certain that this time it would be all right. Then something caught her eye for a fleeting second – a nodding yellow blossom just visible through the clump of bushes at the end of the garden. Sylvie's primrose dress, disappearing over the wall into Mr Phillips's garden.

'Sylvie!' she yelled, rushing frantically out once again to the dividing wall. Panting, she craned over, but only the emptiness of her neighbour's long-neglected garden met her eye. Then her heart thumped painfully as the telephone rang inside the house. She blundered back, a rush of hope mingling with fearful apprehension, and snatched up the receiver.

A masculine voice sounded at the other end of the line. It seemed very near.

'Mrs Marsden?' The voice was cold, abrupt.

'Yes.' Maureen drummed her foot impatiently.

'I wish to protest,' said the voice, and in that moment before he continued she knew who the speaker was. 'This is your neighbour, John Phillips. I should be obliged if you would kindly stop your child from entering my garden. I just saw her climbing over the wall . . .'

Indignation momentarily banished the fear that was gripping her, and Maureen answered forcefully: 'I can't find her, Mr Phillips. She's not in your garden – I've just looked!' She could not control the note of near-panic in her voice and added, hardly realizing what she said, 'Is she in your house?'

There was an immediate pause, then the voice continued, a little less aggressively, 'No, Mrs Marsden, she is not in my house.'

The receiver was shaking violently in Maureen's hand, and she realized that she must quieten her nerves. Flaring tempers would not help matters now. She spoke in a quieter tone. 'I'm so worried, Mr Phillips. She keeps disappearing like this, and I don't know where she gets to – '

'Just a moment,' he said, 'while I have another look.'

There was a pause while she waited impatiently; then he took up the receiver again, and his tone was more conciliatory.

'There's no sign of her here,' he said. 'I've just looked across the garden. Would you care to come round and we'll see what's happened.'

'Yes, right away.'

Maureen snatched her latchkey from her purse and ran swiftly round the corner to the more elegant surroundings of Merton Close. The fourth house along, she reckoned, must be Mr Phillips's.

The houses here were larger, less welcoming, she always had felt, than the newer ones in Ripley Avenue. They had steps flanked by spiked iron railings leading down to basements, which gave them a forbidding look. Flights of stone steps led up to the main entrances – tall Victorian front doors topped by ugly green stained-glass. The windows with their heavy looped curtains seemed to look disdainfully at this intruder from the newly built estate, where there had recently been open country.

She wondered what he would be like, this crabbed old man whom no one seemed to know much about. Her garrulous neighbour, Mrs Richards, said he was a recluse. Something had happened to him years ago that had turned him sour. Maureen hoped that sourness was the worst of his characteristics. She pulled the old-fashioned bell knob and heard the sound jangle in the back regions of the house. Her breath was coming quickly, and she tried to control it.

Through the haze of the dull green glass, she saw the outline of a form approaching the door, which opened to reveal a rather bent figure with greying hair, and wearing a sober black suit. Her first impression was that he was not as tall as she had expected; rather less than middle height, she judged. She had been prepared for anger, resentment, perhaps words of abuse, but was surprised to see that the eyes that looked at her from behind thick-lensed spectacles held a scared look. His face was thin, the mouth drawn down with lines of what might be bad temper, but could equally well have been pain. In that moment, part of her fear was dispelled. She sensed that John Phillips was a very frightened man.

'Mrs Marsden,' he said in a softer voice than he had used over the telephone. 'Won't you come in, please.'

There was something in the tone that made her uneasy. As though he were about to tell her something he hardly dared say – something about Sylvie?

In a daze she followed him through the rather dingy hall, and into a large room overlooking the garden. Maureen's eyes flew immediately to the French windows. This garden was longer, wider than their own, extending a considerable way each side of it. The scene was one of long neglect: a few odd bushes here and there, and a broken statue lying among drooping fern leaves, marking the remains of an ornamental pond. It was a dismal place, and the first glance told her it was empty. There was nowhere anyone could possibly be hidden from view.

She sat down on the chair he offered her, and looked up at him pleadingly. This strange, unpredictable old man seemed her only possible link with Sylvie.

He was looking down at her gravely, one elbow resting on the ornate marble mantelpiece.

'Mrs Marsden,' he began, 'I must apologize if I seemed a little abrupt over the phone, but I have had trouble with Mrs Richards's boys climbing over the wall and making a disturbance. I am sure your little girl meant no harm, but—'

'Where is she?' Maureen interrupted. 'That's what I'm concerned with! Please help me if you can!'

His next remark surprised her. Watching her with that apprehensive look still evident behind the thick lenses, he said in a more subdued tone, 'It's not just the boys, or your little girl. They don't do any real harm. It's just that I cannot bear to see children playing there.'

He went to the window and looked across the grass. He was evidently in a state of tension: he was clenching and unclenching his hands nervously. Then he turned to her again, on his face an expression of puzzled concern. 'Your little girl,' he said, 'I saw her there, I certainly saw her. Then while I was phoning she must have gone again, but where?'

Maureen burst out, more vehemently than she had meant, 'That's what I want to know!'

At that moment self-control snapped, and tears blinded her eyes. She covered her face with her hands and gave up all attempt to check her sobs. She felt his hand placed gently on her shoulder.

'I know how you feel,' he said. 'I lost a child myself.'

She looked up in surprise. He was staring at the end of the garden, and once more she saw the expression of fear in his eyes.

'Thirty-nine years ago,' he said, as though talking more to himself than to her, 'I killed him, just at that spot!'

For a moment Maureen did not trust herself to speak. She clutched the arms of her chair, and was aware that her lips were forming the words. 'Killed him?' Was this some ghastly joke? Was he a maniac?

He nodded. 'What else? I sent him to his death. Timothy would be forty-six by now, if he had lived. Yet I always see him exactly as he was that day.'

She watched him dumbly, registering the name almost unconsciously.

He continued, still staring out of the window: 'It was June 16th

1943,' he said, as though reciting a well-known poem. 'Tim's birthday. He was seven years old. Rather a naughty boy, I'm afraid.' He turned to her with a faint smile. It was the first time she had seen him smile. Somehow it did not suit his face.

'My wife was alive then,' he went on. 'She died about five years ago. Her death was a great shock. It seemed to plunge me back to that other time, officially forgotten; but there are some things one never forgets. Since I have been alone, I have seen him so often.'

Seen him? Had his poor bewildered brain given way under the strain? He answered her unspoken question. 'In my mind, of course.' But a quick glance towards the end of the garden suggested something more.

'When Joan – my wife – was alive, she kept the garden reasonably tidy, but now that I'm on my own here, I can't bear to go down there.'

Then, after a pause: 'If we could only have moved – but it was too difficult. House prices were impossible, so we stayed on, but I always hated that spot.'

She knew what spot he meant. For a moment he seemed lost in thought.

'It was Tim's birthday,' she prompted. Perhaps if she kept him talking . . .

'Ah, yes.' He moved away from the window, and sat on the chair facing her. His hands still continued their nervous movements.

'Tim came down that morning full of *joie de vivre*. He had just opened his birthday presents,' he continued, 'and started opening a large box of chocolates. That was a rare thing in those days; I can't think where they came from. His mother told him not to start them before breakfast, but he deliberately took one and popped it into his mouth.

'I don't like disobedience in children,' he added sternly, with a return to the imperious tone he had used on the phone, 'so I told him to put the box away.

'"It's my birthday," Tim insisted, and started stripping the foil from another chocolate.

'This was too much. I went round the table and took him by the collar.

'"Out you go my lad," I told him, "until you've learned to obey your mother," and I started to propel him towards the door.

'He grabbed the book I had given him, one he had particularly requested for his birthday; all about the different Red Indian tribes, I remember. After all, it *was* his birthday. I thought he could read it in the summer house and come back when he was ready to apologize.'

The summer house?

'As I pulled him through the door, still struggling defiantly, his mother called out: "Aren't you going to thank Daddy for the lovely book?"

'He yelled back, "No!" He was in one of his stubborn moods.

'Well, I yanked him across the garden to the summer house. It used to stand in that corner by your wall.'

He nodded in that direction, and Maureen noticed that this time he averted his eyes quickly.

'It was quite a roomy place,' he explained, 'and Tim used it as a playroom. He'd play there for hours when it rained.

'Well, I came back to my half-finished breakfast, rather sorry I had started off his birthday so badly, and Joan suggested she should go and fetch him back, but I didn't see why we should pander to his disobedience.

'It was then that we heard it; that steady *different* sort of droning. Joan looked frightened. "It's one of theirs," she said. "I'll go and get Tim in", and she started for the door.

'I said, "No, better not. He's as safe there as here if anything happens. It's probably one that slipped through the net." We hadn't heard any warning.

'Then it happened. A deafening roar, a violent vibration that sent us crashing to the floor. Furniture was flung about all around us. It's a miracle we weren't crushed. When we scrambled to our feet, bruised and shaken, we realized that the house was still standing – they built them solid in those days; but the windows were blown in and the room was a haze of dust and rubble. Outside, everything seemed to be shrouded in a yellow fog.

'With one accord, we both blundered through the choking atmosphere, across the garden to the summer house; but of course it wasn't there. There was just a gaping crater that had torn up half our garden and large chunks of those on either side.'

'Oh my God, how dreadful!' Maureen's voice broke, her own anxiety momentarily forgotten in the shock of this terrible story.

He paused, staring in front of him as though re-living the scene.

'They said afterwards it was only a small bomb – there were some like that in 1943 – otherwise we wouldn't have survived to tell the tale. The pilot was "discarding his load" they said, when our Spitfires were on his tail.'

Then Mr Phillips seemed to remember his guest, and met Maureen's eyes rather shame-facedly. 'But you came about your little girl,' he said, and for a moment his face relaxed into an expression of kindly concern.

'If you – ' He hesitated, then continued: 'If you would like to search the house – if you would feel happier . . .'

Should I? Maureen wondered. It seemed insulting to harbour suspicions, but she dared not leave anything to chance. She imagined the shadowy coldness of the large empty rooms above their heads. He has a guilt complex, she told herself, and living alone in this sombre place has turned it into an obsession. Could it be possible that Sylvie is somewhere up there, frightened, alone; perhaps – She should not let her thoughts run on like this.

She started to rise from her chair, darting one last look through the French windows, then sprang to her feet with an excited cry.

'Look!' she shouted, hardly believing what she saw. A splash of yellow was visible for a moment on the wall at the far end of the garden, and then disappeared. A second later she was watching it move across the lawn to their own kitchen door.

'She's back!' Maureen cried joyfully as she started for the door, and before he realized what had happened, she had planted a quick kiss on Mr Phillips's astonished face. He was still watching her unbelievingly as she dashed through the front door and down the steps to the street.

She reached the kitchen panting, in time to open the garden door to a rather aggrieved Sylvie.

'I couldn't reach the handle,' she began. Then her expression changed. 'Oh, Mummy, where have you been? You're all out of breath!'

That evening, as Maureen and Frank watched TV, and Sylvie sat busily sketching unlikely animals on a drawing block, an idea suddenly struck Maureen.

'Why don't you draw the summer house?' she suggested. She saw Frank's eyebrows raised in amused exasperation.

For a moment Sylvie was quiet, then: 'All right,' she agreed, 'but I haven't got the right coloured crayons.'

'Never mind,' said Maureen, 'just draw the shape of it.'

Sylvie started scrawling carefully across the paper, to produce a box-like object with two squares for windows, under a three-cornered porch. A rectangle scribbled over fiercely with black represented an open door, and on top of the porch, rather incongruously, was perched a small flag. Next to this geometrical building Sylvie added two tiny 'pin men' with black blobs for heads and four straight lines each for arms and legs. 'That's Tim and me,' she explained.

Maureen felt a chill pass through her at the name, but she forced herself to smile, and said only: 'Oh, that's very good; may I keep it?'

'If you like,' Sylvie said, and tore off the page to start her next cryptic masterpiece, saying casually, 'Mr Phillips is a silly old man. Why doesn't he come down to the summer house? Tim only wants to thank him for the book.'

'Is that all?' Maureen asked.

'Of course,' Sylvie said.

Mr Phillips seemed a little surprised at Maureen's request the next day.

'Why yes, we have a photo – several in fact,' he told her, and went to a small desk by the window. 'I'm so glad,' he added, 'that you found your little girl. I knew she couldn't be very far away.'

He drew out an album with a faded grey cover, and flicked through the pages till he came to one showing a group of people standing in front of a small structure whose shape was immediately familiar.

She recognized a younger, more upright Mr Phillips in the centre, beside him a plump, dark-haired woman holding a small boy by the hand. The boy had a truculent expression, as though having his photo taken was a boring business.

'I can imagine him being naughty,' thought Maureen, and felt no surprise when Mr Phillips pointed him out as 'our son Timothy.'

'Why the flag on the top?' Maureen asked.

He smiled, and this time it suited him better. 'Oh, just one of Tim's larks,' he explained. 'He picked it up at some bazaar, and climbed up to put it there himself, "to show the King was in residence." He looked upon the summer house as his own little castle.'

Maureen fumbled in her pocket for the crayon sketch.

He stared at it in surprise. 'Where did you get this?' he asked, and Maureen told him.

'She said something when she gave it to me,' Maureen added, and repeated Sylvie's words about the book.

He looked at her strangely for a moment.

'He only wanted to thank me?' he asked. 'Is that what she said?'

Maureen nodded.

Then Mr Phillips turned towards the French windows and flung them open. For a brief moment he hesitated, then started to walk slowly down the garden.

Maureen returned home to find Sylvie in her small bedroom upstairs, engrossed in making up 'Crazy Clay Characters' from a box bought at the local toyshop.

Maureen held out the sketch. 'Do you want to keep this with your other drawings?' she asked.

Sylvie glanced at it disinterestedly. 'No,' she decided. 'I shan't want it any more. There isn't any summer house now, is there? I told you Mr Phillips was a silly old man. He should have gone down there years ago.'

Maureen dropped the sketch into the wastepaper basket, and glanced across the vista of the two gardens. From this height she could see a large portion of the corner that had always disturbed her so. Perhaps it was the effect of the sunlight, but it seemed that a faint covering of green was sprouting mushroom-like over that once barren spot.

The shadow no longer crouched there. It had melted into a pattern of shifting leaves.

THE FERRIES

RAMSEY CAMPBELL

When Berry reached Parkgate promenade he heard the waves. He couldn't recall having heard them during his stroll down the winding road from Neston village, between banks whispering with grass, past the guarded lights of infrequently curtained windows. Beneath clouds diluted by moonlight, the movement of the waves looked indefinably strange. They sounded faint, not quite like water.

The promenade was scarcely two cars wide. Thin lanterns stood on concrete stalks above the sea wall, which was overlooked by an assortment of early Victorian buildings: antique shops, cafés that in the afternoons must be full of ladies taking tea and cakes, a nursing home, a private school that looked as though it had been built as something else. In the faltering moonlight all of them looked black and white. Some were Tudor-striped.

As he strolled – the June night was mild, he might as well enjoy himself as best he could now he was here – he passed the Marie Celeste Hotel. That must have appealed to his uncle. He was still grinning wryly when he reached his uncle's address.

Just then the moon emerged from the clouds, and he saw what was wrong with the waves. There was no water beyond the sea wall, only an expanse of swaying grass that stretched as far as he could see. The sight of the grass, overlooked by the promenade buildings as though it was still the River Dee, made him feel vaguely but intensely expectant, as though about to glimpse something on the pale parched waves.

Perhaps his uncle felt this too, for he was sitting at the black bow window on the first floor of the white house, gazing out beyond the sea wall. His eyes looked colourless as moonlight. It took three rings of the bell to move him.

Berry shouldn't feel resentful. After all, he was probably his uncle's only living relative. Nevertheless there were decisions to be made in London, at the publishers: books to be bought or rejected

– several were likely to be auctioned. He'd come a long way hurriedly, by several trains; his uncle's call had sounded urgent enough for that, as urgent as the pips that had cut him off. Berry only wished he knew why he was here.

When at last his uncle opened the door, he looked unexpectedly old. Perhaps living ashore had aged him. He had always been small, but now he looked dwindled, though still tanned and leathery. In his spotless black blazer with its shining silvery buttons, and his tiny gleaming shoes, he resembled a doll of himself.

'Here we are again.' Though he sounded gruff, his handshake was firm, and felt grateful for company. When he'd toiled upstairs, using the banisters as a series of walking-sticks, he growled, 'Sit you down.'

There was no sense of the sea in the flat, not even maritime prints to enliven the timidly patterned wallpaper. Apart from a couple of large old trunks, the flat seemed to have nothing to do with his uncle. It felt like a waiting-room.

'Get that down you, James.' His uncle's heartiness seemed faded; even the rum was a brand you could buy in supermarkets, not one of the prizes he'd used to bring back from voyages. He sat gazing beyond the promenade, sipping the rum as though it was as good as any other.

'How are you, uncle? It's good to see you.' They hadn't seen each other for ten years, and Berry felt inhibited; besides, his uncle detested effusiveness. When he'd finished his rum he said, 'You sounded urgent on the phone.'

'Aye.' The years had made him even more taciturn. He seemed to resent being reminded of his call.

'I wouldn't have expected you to live so far from everything,' Berry said, trying a different approach.

'It went away.' Apparently he was talking about the sea, for he continued: 'There used to be thirteen hotels and a pier. All the best people came here to bathe. They said the streets were as elegant as Bath. The private school you passed, that was the old Assembly Rooms.'

Though he was gazing across the sea wall, he didn't sound nostalgic. He sat absolutely still, as though relishing the stability of the room. He'd used to pace restlessly when talking, impatient to return to the sea.

'Then the Dee silted up,' he was saying. 'It doesn't reach here now, except at spring tides and in storms. That's when the rats and voles flee onto the promenade – hordes of them, they say. I haven't seen it, and I don't mean to.'

'You're thinking of moving?'

'Aye.' Frowning at his clenched fists, he muttered, 'Will you take me back with you tomorrow and let me stay until I find somewhere? I'll have my boxes sent on.'

He mustn't want to make the journey alone in case he was taken ill. Still, Berry couldn't help sounding a little impatient. 'I don't live near the sea, you know.'

'I know that.' Reluctantly he added, 'I wish I lived farther away.'

Perhaps now that he'd had to leave the sea, his first love, he wanted to forget about it quickly. Berry could tell he'd been embarrassed to ask for help – a captain needing help from a nephew who was seasick on hovercraft! But he was a little old man now, and his tan was only a patina; all at once Berry saw how frail he was. 'All right, uncle,' he said gently. 'It won't be any trouble.'

His uncle was nodding, not looking at him, but Berry could see he was moved. Perhaps now was the time to broach the idea Berry had had on the train. 'On my way here,' he said carefully, 'I was remembering some of the tales you used to tell.'

'You remember them, do you?' The old man didn't sound as though he wanted to. He drained a mouthful of rum in order to refill his glass. Had the salt smell that was wafting across the grass reminded him too vividly?

Berry had meant to suggest the idea of a book of his uncle's yarns, for quite a few had haunted him: the pigmies who could carry ten times their own weight, the flocks of birds that buried in guano any ships that ventured into their territory, the light whose source was neither sun nor moon but that outlined an island on the horizon, which receded if ships made for it. Would it be a children's book, or a book that tried to trace the sources? Perhaps this wasn't the time to discuss it, for the smell that was drifting through the window was stagnant, very old.

'There was one story I never told you.'

Berry's head jerked up; he had been nodding off. Even his uncle had never begun stories as abruptly – as reluctantly – as this.

'Some of the men used to say it didn't matter if you saw it so long as you protected yourself.' Was the old man talking to himself, to take his mind off the desiccated river, the stagnant smell? 'One night we all saw it. One minute the sea was empty, the next that thing was there, close enough to swim to. Some of the men would almost have done that, to get it over with.' He gulped a mouthful of rum and stared sharply out across the pale dry waves. 'Only they could see the faces watching. None of us forgot that, ever. As soon as we got ashore all of us bought ourselves protection. Even I did,' he said bitterly, 'when I'd used to say civilized men kept pictures on walls.'

Having struggled out of his blazer, which he'd unbuttoned carefully and tediously, he displayed his left forearm. Blinking sleepily, Berry made out a tattoo, a graceful sailing ship surrounded by a burst of light. Its masts resembled almost recognizable symbols.

'The younger fellows thought that was all we needed. We all wanted to believe that would keep us safe. I wonder how they feel now they're older.' The old man turned quickly toward the window; he seemed angry that he'd been distracted. Something had changed his attitudes drastically, for he had hated tattooes. It occurred to Berry, too late to prevent him from dozing, that his uncle had called him because he was afraid to be alone.

Berry's sleep was dark and profound. Half-submerged images floated by, so changed as to be unrecognizable. Sounds reached him rather as noise from the surface might try to reach the depths of the sea. It was impossible to tell how many times his uncle had cried out before the calls woke him.

'James...' The voice was receding, but at first Berry failed to notice this; he was too aware of the smell that filled the room. Something that smelled drowned in stagnant water was near him, so near that he could hear its creaking. At once he was awake, and so afraid that he thought he was about to be sick.

'James...' Both the creaking and the voice were fading. Eventually he managed to persuade himself that despite the stench, he was alone in the room. Forcing his eyes open, he stumbled to the window. Though it was hard to focus his eyes and see what was out there, his heart was already jolting.

The promenade was deserted; the buildings gleamed like bone.

Above the sea wall the lanterns glowed thinly. The wide dry river was flooded with grass, which swayed in the moonlight, rustling and glinting. Over the silted river, leaving a wake of grass that looked whiter than the rest, a ship was receding.

It seemed to be the colour and the texture of the moon. Its sails looked stained patchily by mould. It was full of holes, all of which were misshapen by glistening vegetation. Were its decks crowded with figures? If so, he was grateful that he couldn't see their faces, for their movements made him think of drowned things lolling underwater, dragged back and forth by currents.

Sweat streamed into his eyes. When he'd blinked them clear, the moon was darkening. Now the ship looked more like a mound from which a few trees sprouted, and perhaps the crowd was only swaying bushes. Clouds closed over the moon, but he thought he could see a pale mass sailing away, overtopped by lurid sketches that might be masts. Was that his uncle's voice, its desperation overwhelmed by despair? When moonlight flooded the landscape a few moments later, there was nothing but the waves of grass, from which a whiter swathe was fading.

He came to himself when he began shivering. An unseasonably chill wind was clearing away the stench of stagnant water. He gazed in dismay at his uncle's blazer, draped neatly over the empty chair.

There wasn't much that he could tell the police. He had been visiting his uncle, whom he hadn't seen for years. They had both had a good deal to drink, and his uncle, who had seemed prematurely aged, had begun talking incoherently and incomprehensibly. He'd woken to find that his uncle had wandered away, leaving his blazer, though it had been a cold night.

Did they believe him? They were slow and thorough, these policemen; their thoughts were as invisible as he meant his to be. Surely his guilt must be apparent, the shame of hiding the truth about his uncle, of virtually blackening his character. In one sense, though, that seemed hardly to matter: he was sure they wouldn't find his uncle alive. Eventually, since Berry could prove that he was needed in London, they let him go.

He trudged along the sweltering promenade. Children were scrambling up and down the sea wall, old people on sticks were being promenaded by relatives. In the hazy sunshine, most of the buildings were still black and white. Everywhere signs said FRESH SHRIMPS. In a shop that offered 'Gifts and Bygones', ships were stiff in bottles. Waves of yellowing grass advanced, but never very far.

He ought to leave, and be grateful that he lived inland. If what he'd seen last night had been real, the threat was far larger than he was. There was nothing he could do.

But suppose he had only heard his uncle's voice on the silted river, and had hallucinated the rest? He'd been overtired, and confused by his uncle's ramblings; how soon had he wakened fully? He wanted to believe that the old man had wandered out beyond the promenade and had collapsed, or even that he was alive out there, still wandering.

There was only one way to find out. He would be in sight of the crowded promenade. Holding his briefcase above his head as though he was submerging, he clambered down the sea wall.

The grass was tougher than it looked. Large patches had to be struggled through. After five hundred yards he was sweating, yet he seemed to be no closer to the far bank, nor to anything else. Ahead through the haze he could just distinguish the colours of fields in their frames of trees and hedges. Factory chimneys resembled grey pencils. All this appeared to be receding.

He struggled onward. Grass snagged him, birds flew up on shrill wings, complaining. He could see no evidence of the wake he'd seen last night: nothing but the interminable grass, the screeching birds, the haze. Behind him the thick heat had blurred the promenade, the crowds were pale shadows. Their sounds had been swallowed by the hissing of grass.

He'd been tempted several times to turn back, and was on the point of doing so, when he saw a gleam in the dense grass ahead. It was near the place where he'd last glimpsed the ship, if he had done so. The gleaming object looked like a small shoe.

He had to persuade himself to go forward. He remembered the swaying figures on the decks, whose faces he'd dreaded to see. Nevertheless he advanced furiously, tearing a path through the grass with his briefcase. He was almost there before he saw that the object wasn't a shoe. It was a bottle.

When inertia carried him forward, he realized that the bottle wasn't empty. For an unpleasant moment he thought it contained the skeleton of a small animal. Peering through the grime that coated the glass, he made out a whitish model ship with tattered sails. Tiny overgrown holes gaped in it. Though its decks were empty, he had seen it before.

He stood up too quickly, and almost fell. The heat seemed to flood his skull. The ground underfoot felt unstable; a buzzing of insects attacked him; there was a hint of a stagnant smell. He was ready to run, dizzy as he was, to prevent himself from thinking.

Then he remembered his uncle's despairing cry: 'James, James . . .' Even then, if he had been able to run, he might have done nothing – but his dizziness both hindered him and gave him time to feel ashamed. If there was a chance of helping his uncle, however impossible it seemed— He snatched up the bottle and threw it into his briefcase. Then, trying to forget about it, he stumbled back toward the crowds.

His uncle was calling him. He woke to the sound of a shriek. Faces were sailing past him, close enough to touch if he could have reached through the glass. It was only a train on the opposite line, rushing away from London. Nevertheless he couldn't sleep after that. He finished reading the typescript he'd brought with him, though he knew by now he didn't want to buy the book.

The state of his desk was worse than he'd feared. His secretary had answered most of his letters, but several books had piled up, demanding to be read. He was stuffing two of them into his briefcase, to be read on the bus and, if he wasn't too tired, at home, when he found he was holding the grimy bottle. At once he locked it in a drawer. Though he wasn't prepared to throw it away until he understood its purpose, he was equally reluctant to take it home.

That night he could neither sleep nor read. He tried strolling in Holland Park, but while that tired him further, it failed to calm him. The moonlit clouds that were streaming headlong across the sky made everything beneath them look unstable. Though he knew that the lit houses beyond the swaying trees were absolutely still, he kept feeling that the houses were rocking slyly, at anchor.

He lay trying to relax. Beyond the windows of his flat, Kensington High Street seemed louder than ever. Nervous speculations kept him awake. He felt he'd been meant to find the bottle, but for what purpose? Surely it couldn't harm him; after all, he had only once been to sea. How could he help his uncle? His idea of a book of stories was nagging him; perhaps he could write it himself, as a kind of monument to his uncle – except that the stories seemed to be drifting away into the dark, beyond his reach, just like the old man. When eventually he dozed, he thought he heard the old man calling.

In the morning his desk looked even worse; the pile of books had almost doubled. He managed to sort out a few that could be trusted to readers for reports. Of course, a drain must have overflowed outside the publishers; that was why only a patch of pavement had been wet this morning – he knew it hadn't rained. He consulted his diary for distractions.

Sales conference 11 a.m.: he succeeded in being coherent, and even in suggesting ideas, but his thoughts were elsewhere. The sky resembled sluggish smoke, as though the oppressive day was smouldering. His mind felt packed in grey stuffing. The sound of cars outside seemed unnaturally rhythmic, almost like waves.

Back at his desk he sat trying to think. Lack of sleep had isolated him in a no-man's-land of consciousness, close to hallucination. He felt cut off from whatever he was supposed to be doing. Though his hand kept reaching out impulsively, he left the drawer locked. There was no point in brooding over the model ship until he'd decided what to do.

Beyond the window his uncle cried out. No, someone was shouting to guide a lorry; the word wasn't 'James' at all. But he still didn't know how to help his uncle, assuming that he could, assuming that it wasn't too late. Would removing the ship from the bottle achieve something? In any case, could one remove the ship at all? Perhaps he could consult an expert in such matters. 'I know exactly whom you want,' his secretary said, and arranged for them to meet tomorrow.

Dave Peeples lunch 12.30: ordinarily he would have enjoyed the game, especially since Peeples liked to discuss books in pubs, where he tended to drink himself into an agreeable state. Today's prize was attractive: a best-selling series that Peeples wanted to take to a new publisher. But today he found Peeples irritating – not only his satyr's expressions and postures, which were belied by his paunch, but also the faint smirk with which he constantly approved of himself. Still, if Berry managed to acquire the books, the strain would have been worthwhile.

They ate in the pub just round the corner from the publishers. Before long Berry grew frustrated; he was too enervated by lack of sleep to risk drinking much. Nor could he eat much, for the food tasted unpleasantly salty. Peeples seemed to notice nothing, and ate most of Berry's helping before he leaned back, patting his paunch.

'Well now,' he said when Berry raised the subject of the books. 'What about another drink?' Berry was glad to stand up, to feel the floor stable underfoot, for the drinkers at the edge of his vision had seemed to be swaying extravagantly.

'I'm not happy with the way my mob are promoting the books,' Peeples admitted. 'They seem to be letting them just lie there.' Berry's response might have been more forceful if he hadn't been distracted by the chair that someone was rocking back and forth with a steady rhythmic creaking.

When Berry had finished making offers Peeples said, 'That doesn't sound bad. Still, I ought to tell you that several other people are interested.' Berry wondered angrily whether he was simply touring publishers in search of free meals. The pub felt damp, the dimness appeared to be glistening. No doubt it was very humid.

Though the street was crowded, he was glad to emerge. 'I'll be in touch,' Peeples promised grudgingly, but at that moment Berry didn't care, for on the opposite pavement the old man's voice was crying, 'James!' It was only a newspaper-seller naming his wares, which didn't sound much like James. Surely a drain must have overflowed where the wet patch had been, for there was a stagnant smell.

Editors meeting 3 p.m.: he scarcely had time to gulp a mug of coffee beforehand, almost scalding his throat. Why did they have to schedule two meetings in one day? When there were silences in which people expected him to speak, he managed to say things that sounded positive and convincing. Nevertheless he heard little except for the waves of traffic, advancing and withdrawing, and the desperate cries in the street. What was that crossing the intersection, a long pale shape bearing objects like poles? It had gone before he could jerk his head round, and his colleagues were staring only at him.

It didn't matter. If any of these glimpses weren't hallucinations, surely they couldn't harm him. Otherwise, why hadn't he been harmed that night in Parkgate? It was rather a question of what he could do to the glimpses. 'Yes, that's right,' he said to a silence. 'Of course it is.'

Once he'd slept he would be better able to cope with everything. Tomorrow he would consult the expert. After the meeting he slumped at his desk, trying to find the energy to gather books together and head for home.

His secretary woke him. 'OK,' he mumbled, 'you go on.' He'd follow her in a moment, when he was more awake. It occurred to him that if he hadn't dozed off in Parkgate, his uncle might have been safe. That was another reason to try to do something. He'd get up in a few moments. It wasn't dark yet.

When he woke again, it was.

He had to struggle to raise his head. His elbows had shoved piles of books to the edge of the desk. Outside, the street was quiet except for the whisper of an occasional car. Sodium lamps craned their necks toward his window. Beyond the frosted glass of his office cubicle, the maze of the open-plan office looked even more crowded with darkness than the space around his desk. When he switched on his desk-lamp, it showed him a blurred reflection of himself trapped in a small pool of brightness. Hurriedly he switched on the cubicle's main light.

Though he was by no means awake, he didn't intend to wait. He wanted to be out of the building, away from the locked drawer. Insomnia had left him feeling vulnerable, on edge. He swept a handful of books into the briefcase – God, they were becoming a bad joke – and emerged from his cubicle.

He felt uncomfortably isolated. The long angular room was lifeless; none of the desks seemed to retain any sense of the person who sat there. The desertion must be swallowing his sounds, which seemed not only dwarfed but robbed of resonance, as though surrounded by an emptiness that was very large.

His perceptions must be playing tricks. Underfoot the floor felt less stable than it ought to. At the edge of his vision the shadows of desks and cabinets appeared to be swaying, and he couldn't convince himself that the lights were still. He mustn't let any of this distract him. Time enough to think when he was home.

It took him far too long to cross the office, for he kept teetering against desks. Perhaps he should have taken time to waken fully, after all. When eventually he reached the lifts, he couldn't bring himself to use one; at least the stairs were open, though they were very dark. He groped, swaying, for the light-switch. Before he'd found it, he recoiled. The wall he had touched felt as though it were streaming with water.

A stagnant stench welled up out of the dark. When he grabbed the banister for support, that felt wet too. He mustn't panic: a door or window was open somewhere in the building, that was all he could hear creaking; its draught was making things feel cold – not wet – and was swinging the lights back and forth. Yes, he could feel the draught blustering at him, and smell what must be a drain.

He forced himself to step onto the stairs. Even the darkness was preferable to groping for the light-switch, when he no longer knew what he might touch. Nevertheless, by the time he reached the half-landing he was wishing for light. His vertigo seemed to have worsened, for he was reeling from side to side of the staircase. Was the creaking closer? He mustn't pause, plenty of time to feel ill once he was outside in a taxi; he ought to be able to hold off panic so long as he didn't glimpse the ship again—

He halted so abruptly that he almost fell. Without warning he'd remembered his uncle's monologue. Berry had been as dopey then as he was now, but one point was all at once terribly clear. Your first glimpse of the ship meant only that you would see it again. The second time, it came for you.

He hadn't yet seen it again. Surely he still had a chance. There were two exits from the building; the creaking and the growing stench would tell him which exit to avoid. He was stumbling downstairs because that was the alternative to falling. His mind was a grey void that hardly even registered the wetness of the banisters. The foyer was in sight now at the foot of the stairs, its linoleum gleaming; less than a flight of stairs now, less than a minute's stumbling—

But it was not linoleum. The floorboards were bare, when there ought not even to be boards, only concrete. Shadows swayed on them, cast by objects that, though out of sight for the moment, seemed to have bloated limbs. Water sloshed from side to side of the boards, which were the planks of a deck.

He almost let himself fall, in despair. Then he began to drag himself frantically up the stairs, which perhaps were swaying, after all. Through the windows he thought he saw the cityscape rising and falling. There seemed to be no refuge upstairs, for the stagnant stench was everywhere – but refuge wasn't what he was seeking.

He reeled across the office, which he'd darkened when leaving, into his cubicle. Perhaps papers were falling from desks only because he had staggered against them. His key felt ready to snap in half before the drawer opened.

He snatched out the bottle, in which something rattled insect-like, and stumbled to the window. Yes, he had been meant to find the bottle – but by whom, or by what? Wrenching open the lock of the window, he flung the bottle into the night.

He heard it smash a moment later. Whatever was inside it must certainly have smashed too. At once everything felt stable, so abruptly that he grew dizzier. He felt as though he'd just stepped onto land after a stormy voyage.

There was silence except for the murmur of the city, which sounded quite normal – or perhaps there was another sound, faint and receding fast. It might have been a gust of wind, but he thought it resembled a chorus of cries of relief so profound it was appalling. Was one of them his uncle's voice?

Berry slumped against the window, which felt like ice against his forehead. There was no reason to flee now, nor did he think he would be capable of moving for some time. Perhaps they would find him here in the morning. It hardly mattered, if he could get some sleep—

All at once he tried to hold himself absolutely still, in order to listen. Surely he needn't be nervous any longer, just because the ship in the bottle had been deserted, surely that didn't mean— But his legs were trembling, and infected the rest of his body until he couldn't even strain his ears. By then, however, he could hear far better than he would have liked.

Perhaps he had destroyed the ship, and set free its captives; but if it had had a captain, what else might Berry have set loose? The smell had grown worse than stagnant – and up the stairs, and now across the dark office, irregular but purposeful footsteps were sloshing.

*

Early next morning several people reported glimpses of a light, supposedly moving out from the Thames into the open sea. Some claimed the light had been accompanied by sounds like singing. One old man tried to insist that the light had contained the outline of a ship. The reports seemed little different from tales of objects in the skies, and were quickly dismissed, for London had a more spectacular mystery to solve: how a publisher's editor could be found in a first-floor office, not merely dead but drowned.

THE NEW OLD HOUSE

ROBERT SOLOMON

'Well old chap,' James Crighton said, putting his hand on his son David's head. 'Here we are, this is our new house.'

They stood in the street by the garden gate; a paved path ran up to the house, between the bracken and weeds and dripping bushes. It ended at a dark green front door, which was surmounted by a wooden canopy. The wall to the left of the door was faced with stucco and had two small windows on the ground floor, though the dirty net curtains shrouding them prevented one from seeing inside. The house was mid-Victorian, at a guess, quite unlike the semi-detached house in a modern housing estate that they had just come from.

'But – it's new? I thought you said it was old, Daddy?' David replied, in the high, clear, controlled voice that children use when they are making sensible conversation with adults.

'I know I did, but it's new for us. We've only just come here, even if it is an older house than 17 Brook Lane.'

'Why have we come here then?' David's small face was knotted with concentration beneath his thick black hair.

'Because it's nearer my work. And because – I don't think we should stay in the house—' Mr Crighton stopped and looked straight ahead.

'Where Mummy died? I don't mind. I feel like she's still there almost.'

His father did not comment. David fell silent also, afraid that he had said the wrong thing. His father was strange now, had been ever since his mother had died suddenly, of a heart attack. His father talked to him either in a forcedly jolly tone, or else in a very solemn fashion. He never got angry with him now; sometimes David wished that he would. He almost thought of doing something so very naughty that his father would have to punish him.

It was better when someone else was present. Even then, though, the atmosphere was strained and the visitor would look at him with an expression of sympathy that he found unbearable. He was still confused by his mother's death – mostly he did not think about it, but then sometimes the fact of his loss would come to him and he would burst into tears. On these occasions whoever was present would comfort him awkwardly, though he preferred to be left alone. They told him that his mother was in heaven, and that he would see her again some day, but at his age he could not imagine a time when he would also die. Besides, if they really believed that she was alive somewhere, why were they so sad?

Mr Crighton opened the gate and they walked up to the house, David trying not to be brushed by the vegetation that encroached on the path. His father finally opened the door, having had difficulty with the unfamiliar key. The hall was dark and they went into the front room. This was bare, and looked large; the floor was of boards, unpainted in the middle where a carpet had been. The walls were papered with a pattern of large dingy roses, also with bare patches where pictures had hung. The room had not been swept for months, and David sneezed from the dust they disturbed.

David's father walked around, opened a low cupboard, pulled aside the net curtain to look out on the front.

'We'll soon have that paper down, old chap, put up something more cheerful, eh?' He did not sound very hopeful.

A door led into the room at the rear. David went over and looked through the window onto the back garden. This was even more overgrown than in front, and the wall at the end was obscured by a huge dead hydrangea and two dwarf cypresses. They went upstairs, and David was shown the attic room that would be his. The bathroom was rather sordid; the bath was flaked and stained, and its claw feet were rusted.

'We'll soon have it spick and span, won't we? An old house has so much more character than a new one, don't you think?'

'Yes, Daddy.'

They went downstairs again. On the right of the hall, just before the kitchen, was another door. David's father opened it and a damp smell arose. There was a flight of stone stairs leading down.

'What's in there?'

'Just the basement. It's completely underground. Come on, let's explore!'

Suddenly David was afraid. He did not like the dark.

'No, I don't want to, no – ' David was almost shouting in his panic.

'Don't be—' his father cut short the reprimand. David could tell that he had been about to tell him off for showing funk. 'Never mind, we'll explore it later, when we're settled in.'

They moved three weeks later. David was allowed to travel in the removal van. A lot had already been done to make the house more habitable – it had been cleaned, and carpets had been put down – and as the big cheerful workmen carried their familiar furniture into the house it gradually became like a home. When the removal was completed they started to unpack and sort things out. David found the case that contained his own precious belongings and arranged them in his bedroom until it was almost the same as his room in their previous house.

In the weeks that followed he slowly became accustomed to the house. His own room was an important refuge, in which he always felt safe, and from that base he explored the rest of the house, becoming familiar with each room in turn until it was no longer strange and menacing.

He was still disturbed by the fact that the house was *old*; he had a fear of ghosts, even though his father had told him that they did not exist, and he thought that they were much more likely to haunt an old house than a new one. He protected himself by little rituals to ward off the spirit world – always taking the first step upstairs with his right foot, taking his socks off as the last item when undressing – and he assured himself that these rituals would keep him safe. He told himself that no ghost would be in action before midnight, by which time he would be asleep in his room, which was anyway a no-go area for ghosts. Sometimes, though, his precautions would not be enough as he went to bed at night, and he would have to keep a tight control on his panic as he went up the stairs. He would rush into the bedroom and slam the door and burrow underneath the sheets, so that whatever there was outside he would not *see* it.

In an intense bout of work Mr Crighton finished the major jobs around the house and then the holidays ended. They both went back to school: David as a pupil in the Junior School, and his father as a teacher in the adjacent Secondary School. It was a move for both of them – his father had thought that a complete change would be best. This turned out to be the right decision, for after a period of nervousness and shyness David settled in at his new school and started to make new friends.

He liked his teachers, and in particular he got on very well with Miss Macpherson, his form-mistress. She was a bright woman in her late twenties, who had a natural aptitude for communicating with children. She dressed boyishly, with close-cropped brown hair and with overalls that she spread wide when she put her hands in the trouser pockets. Her face was squarish, the nose rather small, and she smiled often, showing her white teeth and pink gums.

She knew Mr Crighton as a colleague, and one afternoon she came round to their house after school. David's father put the kettle on, and started preparing the cups and saucers.

She said to David, 'Come on, you must show me your house!'

He took her upstairs to his own room. He showed her his paintings, of cowboys riding over hills and aeroplanes firing guns in every direction. She pointed to a photograph in a frame and asked: 'Who is that?'

'That is Mummy. I mean, that was—'

'I know, David, I'm sorry.' Miss Macpherson spoke in a low sympathetic voice.

He wriggled; she should not have asked. He said, in a very loud voice, almost shouting, 'Come on, let's go downstairs again.'

Outside the kitchen Miss Macpherson halted by the door leading to the basement.

'What's in here, David?' she asked.

'That's stairs, going down,' he said, suddenly inarticulate.

'To a cellar? A spooky dungeon?'

David's father came out of the kitchen, wiping his hands on a tea-cloth.

'Oh, the basement,' he said. 'David's rather scared of going down there.'

'You mean you've never been downstairs?' Miss Macpherson said in a tone of mock astonishment. David shook his head, still staring at the ground. 'Come on, let's explore it!'

She took his hand and opened the door. No amount of teasing by his father had succeeded in persuading him to go downstairs before, but now the fear of seeming a coward in his teacher's eyes overcame his fear of the basement. His stomach was weightless as they descended the narrow, steep stairs. At the bottom of the flight was another door, which stuck as Miss Macpherson pushed it, as it was loose on its hinges. Finally she pushed it free, and it scraped the floor with a dirty gritty sound. The light from above did not penetrate into the room, and with the hand that David was not clasping firmly she had to fumble around on the wall for a while before she found the switch. She flicked it and turned on a bare light-bulb in the middle of the room.

'Well, what have we here?' she said.

David stood very close to her as they surveyed the room. It was low and square, and obviously had not been used for any purpose other than storage for many years. The ceiling was cracked and flaking, and shiny dark yellow paper was peeling from the walls. There was a carpet of sorts on the floor, of an indeterminate brown colour, with bare patches and spotted with mould and obscure stains. Various objects stood around the sides of the room – an old black chest of drawers, a short tin bath, a domed trunk with powdery leather straps, and other things whose purpose, if ever they had had one, was now unidentifiable.

'Gosh!' said Miss Macpherson, expelling her breath vigorously. 'What a collection of junk, eh, David? Pooh!'

'Yes, Miss,' David said quietly. His fear had now subsided, but his heart was still thumping.

'I'm surprised you're so wary of here,' she said brightly. 'You could have great fun exploring and playing down here.'

'Not a very healthy place, though,' came a voice behind them. They both jumped. It was only Mr Crighton, who had followed them silently.

'Oh, you did startle me!' she exclaimed, putting her hand to her heart. 'The spookiness of the place must be getting to me too!'

'It's just sordid, not spooky.' Mr Crighton was slightly annoyed that she was encouraging David's fears.

'No, of course not. I'm just surprised that the basement is so sordid, when you've got the rest of the house looking so nice.'

'Lack of time, I'm afraid. We spent the summer hols sorting out the top of the house, didn't we, David? Maybe we'll tidy up the basement room over Christmas.'

Miss Macpherson paced around the room with long energetic strides.

'This is much smaller than the ground floor, surely? What's under the rest?'

'Foundations, I suppose. Maybe there were other rooms, which have since been blocked in. This would have been where the servant worked, before the kitchen extension was built.'

'Imagine working down here,' Miss Macpherson said. 'No one would stand for it now, that's for sure. Then, I suppose, some poor girl of fifteen would have been glad to take the job, at a pound a month and half a day off a week. It makes me sick to think of the exploitation that went on!'

As she said this she walked up and down the room, making jerky gestures with her hands. Her youth and liveliness seemed to bring a breath of fresh modern air to the musty Victorian cellar. Mr Crighton's eyes followed her about, and his face seemed to be brightened by her enthusiasm. David watched them both, feeling left out of things. Finally his father spoke, sounding as though he had just remembered something vitally important.

'Yes. Anyway, no point in hanging around here. The tea's all ready, if you'd like to come back upstairs.'

Now that he had been into the most dreaded part of the house, David's fear of the night and the dark disappeared. He even went below ground again, accompanied by his father, it is true, but without showing any reluctance.

Half the term had gone, and David felt that he had been at the new school all his life. A play was to be put on towards the end of term, *A Midsummer Night's Dream*, inappropriate though it was for the season. It was a production of the senior school, but juniors were to play the fairies. David was chosen for one of these parts (Moth) in order to involve him more with the school.

Miss Macpherson took David home after he had been told of this, and a few minutes later his father returned, with the two other teachers who were to direct the play.

'So this is our Moth,' said one of them, a balding sports-jacketed man with hair coming out of his nostrils. 'Are you ready to tread the boards, young David?'

'Yes, sir,' he piped up, and they all laughed, David joining in, though he did not see what was funny.

'It's not a very demanding part, is it?' said David's father. 'I mean, only a couple of short lines?'

'Yes, but we'll give him the "Over hill, over dale" speech as well. Are you up to that, David?'

'Oh yes,' Miss Macpherson answered for him. 'David has a very good, clear reading voice.'

David wriggled and blushed scarlet under his cap of black hair at being praised in public. But he liked it.

After his tea and a couple of TV programmes he was packed off to bed. It was before his usual time, and he felt rather peeved at being sent upstairs while the adults were still chatting over drinks downstairs, but he did not want to misbehave in front of his form-mistress.

He awoke in the small hours. He had no idea what time it was, but the house was quiet and so the guests must have gone home and his father to bed. The curtains flapped in the wind, and he pulled them aside to let the moonlight stream into the room. He stood at the window, gazing out at the silvered garden. He felt impelled by some strange force, and, not pausing for thought, went downstairs until he came to the door beside the kitchen. Still without reflection he opened it and started down the stairs to the basement. The stone steps felt cold beneath his bare feet and he shivered. He reached the bottom of the flight and turned the handle of the second door. It opened easily; perhaps he had found the knack. He switched on the light and walked into the room.

Of course the room was the same, but somehow it seemed transformed by the night. It was as though the moonlight was shining in that room, even thought there was no window to the outside. It was still incredibly dirty, but the very dirt sparkled like powdered diamonds. The objects round the wall looked powerful and friendly, despite their decayed condition. David walked around the room, feeling the greasy dank carpet between his toes, and as he passed each object he touched it. The knobs of the black chest of drawers smiled at him as he stroked them; he drew his fingers along the rough inside of the stained tin bath; the domed trunk seemed to glow warmly and breathe. The other things, whose purpose he did not know, he picked up and fondled, wondering what they had ever meant. It did not matter – all the objects seemed to have an interior life more important than the use human beings made of them, and the value or cleanliness of an object were trivial matters compared to this interior life.

After a while he left, knowing that he would return some night in the future. He turned at the door, giving a last look at the room and its contents before turning out the light.

He went back upstairs. As he passed his father's room he heard people talking – was the radio on? Then he identified his father's voice, and then a higher voice. The sound of a woman speaking in his father's room suddenly took him back those few months to before his mother had died, and he was filled with panic again at the thought of what could be behind the door. He ran up to his room, no longer being careful to walk silently on tiptoe. He leapt into his bed, and after a while he heard a tap on the door.

'You all right in there, David?' He heard his father say.

'Yes, Dad. Just went to get a glass of water,' he answered sullenly. Now the house was a place of unease again, but this time it was the basement room that was the refuge, and his father's room the place to be frightened of.

The weeks went by, and the night of the dress-rehearsal of *A Midsummer Night's Dream* came upon them suddenly. It was an exhausting evening, and the rehearsal went on much longer than expected. David had initially been very enthusiastic about the play, but now he was diffident. He no longer felt at ease in Miss Macpherson's company, and she snapped at him several times for gabbling or mumbling his lines. She had never been angry with him before, and now the sight of her gummy mouth opening and shutting with irritation frightened him. She took him home when his part in the rehearsal was finally over.

It was about a couple of hundred yards from the school to his house, and he lagged behind, unwilling to walk with his teacher, jumping from one paving stone to the next because he knew that this was annoying her.

When they got to the house his father sensed their moods and provided a stiff whisky for Miss Macpherson and a Coke for David. He lifted his eyebrows enquiringly at her and she said, 'Impossible!' David knew they were talking about him.

David's supper was prepared quickly, but he was so tired that he kept on falling asleep over the table. He insisted that he was awake, and made a scene when he was told to go to bed. He did not want to leave his father and Miss Macpherson alone together downstairs. Eventually he was taken up to bed, his father allowing him to dispense with the usual routine of face-washing and tooth-brushing.

The call came again in the small hours of that night. He awoke with the firm conviction that there was someone down in the basement waiting for him. He got out of bed and tiptoed downstairs, without lingering in his room to look out over the garden. Again he opened the door beside the kitchen, walked down the stairs to the basement, and turned the handle of the second door.

The cellar was as before. As though it was now an established ritual, he went from one object to the next, stroking the knobs on the black chest of drawers, feeling round the stain marks on the bath.

Though everything was as enchanted as before, he had the feeling that there was something else to be discovered in the room. The cellar and its contents seemed to be urging him on to look further. After walking round the room a few times he suddenly saw the outline of a door in the wall, behind the trunk with the domed lid. He pulled the trunk aside, wondering why neither he nor his father had noticed the door before.

The door was low, about three feet high and two feet across. It was surfaced with the same shiny yellow paper as the wall, and the crack between it and the wall was brown. Halfway down was an enamelled metal ring, and he pulled on this to open the door.

He crouched down to peer in. His body prevented the light from the main room from entering, and so he shuffled forward and stood up. Gradually his eyes became accustomed to the gloom.

The room was low but long; in fact the far end of it seemed to become blurred and indistinct as though it was enshrouded in mist. The floor was of old lino, dark grey as far as could be seen. Along one wall was a huge black kitchen range, with thick black pipes leading up to the ceiling.

He stood there, expectant. As he waited the room became suffused with a reddish, greyish light, emanating from the kitchen range, which now seemed to be glowing. He could see to the far end of the room, and there was the figure of a woman there, facing away from him, dressed in a long white shift and with her long black hair hanging loose down her back. After a while she said, 'Shut the door, David, and come closer.'

He obeyed her. She turned around, and he saw that it was his mother.

Neither spoke. David was surprisingly calm – the emotion he felt was one of relief rather than joy; everything was all right, his mother was still around after all. He took a step towards her, but she stopped him with an uplifted hand. He knew then that he should not touch her, as though she were electrically charged.

'So you, you found our new house then, Mummy?' he said, quavering. 'Our new old house?' She nodded.

'And will you be living with us still? Will you be coming back upstairs?' She shook her head.

'No, David. I live down here now.' Her voice sounded rather distant.

'But – but won't you be coming to see Daddy?' Again she shook her head.

'No, not anymore. He can't come into this room. Only you can come in here, David. You're the only person I'll be seeing from now on.'

David was secretly very glad that he had his mother all to himself now.

'And are you being a good boy, David?' she continued. She moved to and fro in the little inner room; as she walked the outline of her body could not be seen beneath the loose folds of her shift.

'Oh yes, Mummy.'

'Do you brush your teeth morning and night?'

'Oh yes – well – '

'What?' She bent down to face him. Her expression was unsmiling, but he did not feel afraid.

'Not tonight, I was so tired, I fell asleep before bed. Daddy said it was all right.'

'But I've always told you to brush them, David. You must do what *I* say. Do you see that?'

'Yes Mummy. But —'

'But what?' She had straightened up now, and she pushed back the long black hair that had fallen forward. Her hands were thin and grey, though David could not tell if this was dirt or an effect of the light.

'What if Daddy tells me to do something, and you're not there?'

'You must do what I say. You know what is right, I shall tell you that. And when the time comes, you must do it.'

In the little inner room David could hear someone moving outside. He heard whoever it was stumble and a woman's voice softly muttering 'Drat!' It was Miss Macpherson.

'Who is it, David?' his mother asked. He did not reply, but looked awkwardly downwards.

'You must tell me, David. Who is it?'

'Miss Macpherson. My teacher. She comes to see Daddy.'

'Then you must go out to her.'

He did not want to. He was frightened of going out. He was afraid of seeing Miss Macpherson, as though she were a ghost. Nevertheless he found himself leaving the little room and emerging into the basement. Miss Macpherson was wearing a short white nightie, and when she turned round and saw him she gave a scream.

'David, how you startled me! Where have you been hiding, you naughty boy?'

He pointed at the door.

'What, in that horrid old trunk?' The trunk was still in front of the secret door. 'Hiding in there?'

'No, in the room behind.' He did not know how to lie.

'Room behind? There isn't one. You're fibbing, David.'

He shook his head. He did not trust himself to speak, tears were so close behind his eyes. Miss Macpherson bent down to the trunk and tried to shift it.

'Good Heavens, what a weight, I can't move it an inch. What can be in it?'

What *was* in it? David remembered that he had been able to move it easily when he had gone through to the inner room to meet his mother. Was there something horrible inside it? All of a sudden he was overwhelmed by a total dread of the trunk and whatever was inside it. He looked around the room to be comforted by the other objects, but instead of being warm and friendly as they had been before, they seemed to be mocking and wicked, composed of squat putrescent evil. He felt as though they were growing and closing in on him. What was in the black chest of drawers? What had happened in the stained tin bath?

Then his mother was there in front of him, standing looking at him determinedly. He tried to call her, but an inarticulate cry rather than a word came out. Miss Macpherson looked up.

'What are you staring at, David? There's nothing there.' Her voice trembled, she was obviously rattled. She added to herself, 'The child must be half asleep, sleep-walking,' then in a bright tone, 'Well, I'm jolly well going to find out what's in this trunk!' She bent down again and started to unbuckle the straps that held down the lid.

David's mother came towards him. Her black hair was streaming and rippling behind her, even though there was no wind in the room. In her hands she carried one of the mysterious objects, a metal pole about three feet long, bent into a slight curve. She handed it to David, and immediately he realized its purpose.

He looked at the pole, and then at his mother, as if to confirm what he had to do with it. Her face was contorted with rage and glee, and he was suddenly afraid of her. He stepped back and she advanced. He was taken by the awful fear that it was not really his mother, but some evil creature pretending to be her; maybe some woman had lived and died in that cellar long ago, and her ghost had taken the shape of his mother. She laughed, and David screamed.

Miss Macpherson was still bent over the trunk, tugging at the leather straps. Between her short hair and the top of her nightie David could see an expanse of pink shiny skin. She looked up, and David shouted, 'No, no!' as he brought the iron bar down. He did not know which of the white-dressed women he was swinging at.

BAD COMPANY

WALTER DE LA MARE

It is very seldom that one encounters what would appear to be sheer unadulterated evil in a human face; an evil, I mean, active, deliberate, deadly, dangerous. Folly, heedlessness, vanity, pride, craft, meanness, stupidity – yes. But even Iagos in this world are few, and devilry is as rare as witchcraft.

One winter's evening some little time ago, bound on a visit to a friend in London, I found myself on the platform of one of its many subterranean railway stations. It is an ordeal that one may undergo as seldom as one can. The glare and glitter, the noise, the very air one breathes affect nerves and spirits. One expects vaguely strange meetings in such surroundings. On this occasion, the expectation was justified. The mind is at times more attentive than the eye. Already tired, and troubled with personal cares and problems, which a little wisdom and enterprise should have refused to entertain, I had seated myself on one of the low, wooden benches to the left of the entrance to the platform, when, for no conscious reason, I was prompted to turn my head in the direction of a fellow traveller, seated across the gangway on the fellow to my bench some few yards away.

What was wrong with him? He was enveloped in a loose cape or cloak, sombre and motionless. He appeared to be wholly unaware of my abrupt scrutiny. And yet I doubt it; for the next moment, although the door of the nearest coach gaped immediately opposite him, he had shuffled into the compartment I had entered myself, and now in its corner, confronted me, all but knee to knee. I could have touched him with my hand. We had, too, come at once into an even more intimate contact than that of touch. Our eyes – his own fixed in a dwelling and lethargic stare – had instantly met, and no less rapidly mine had uncharitably recoiled, not only in misgiving, but in something little short of disgust. The effect resembled that of an acid on milk, and for the time being cast my thoughts into confusion. Yet that one glance had taken him in.

He was old – over seventy. A wide-brimmed rusty and dusty black hat concealed his head – a head fringed with wisps of hair, lank and paper-grey. His loose, jaded cheeks were of the colour of putty; the thin lips above the wide unshaven and dimpled chin showing scarcely a trace of red. The cloak suspended from his shoulders mantled him to his shins. One knuckled, cadaverous, mittened hand clasped a thick ash stick, its handle black and polished with long usage. The only sign of life in his countenance was secreted in his eyes – fixed on mine – hazed and dully glistening, as a snail in winter is fixed to a wall. There was a dull deliberate challenge in them, and, as I fancied, something more than that. They suggested that he had been in wait for me; that for him, it was almost 'well met!'

For minutes together I endeavoured to accept their challenge, to make sure. Yet I realized, fascinated the while, that he was well aware of the futility of this attempt, as a snake is of the restless, fated bird in the branches above its head.

Such a statement, I am aware, must appear wildly exaggerated, but I can only record my impression. It was already lateish – much later than I had intended. The passengers came and went, and, whether intentionally or not, none consented to occupy the seat vacant beside him. I fixed my eyes on an advertisement – that of a Friendly Society I remember! – immediately above his head, with the intention of watching him in the field of an eye that I could not persuade to meet his own in full focus again.

He had instantly detected this ingenuous device. By a fraction of an inch he had shifted his grasp upon his stick. So intolerable, at length, became the physical – and psychical – effect of his presence on me that I determined to leave the train at the next station, and there to await the next. And at this precise moment, I was conscious that he had not only withdrawn his eyes but closed them.

I was not so easily to free myself of his company. A glance over my shoulder as, after leaving the train, I turned towards the lift, showed him hastily groping his way out of the carriage. The metal gate clanged. The lift slid upwards and, such is the contrariness of human nature, a faint disappointment followed. One may, for example, be appalled and yet engrossed in reading an account of some act of infamous cruelty.

Concealing myself as best I could at the bookstall, I awaited the next lift-load. Its few passengers having dispersed, he himself followed. In spite of age and infirmity, he *had*, then, ascended alone the spiral staircase. Glancing, it appeared, neither to right nor left, he passed rapidly through the barrier. And yet – *had* he not seen me?

The Collector raised his head, opened his mouth, watched his retreating figure, but made no attempt to retrieve his ticket. It was dark now – the dark of London. In my absence underground, minute frozen pellets of snow had fallen, whitening the streets and lulling the sound of the traffic. On emerging into the street, he turned in the direction of the next station – my own. Yet again – had he, or had he not, been aware that he was being watched? However that might be, my journey lay his way, and that way my feet directed me; although I was already later than I intended. I followed him, led on no doubt in part merely by the effect he had had on me. Some twenty or thirty yards ahead, his dark shapelessness showed – distinct against the whitening pavement.

The waters of the Thames, I was aware, lay on my left. A muffled blast from the siren of a tug announced its presence. Keeping my distance, I followed him on. One lamp-post – two – three. At that, he seemed to pause for a moment, as if to listen, momentarily glanced back (as I fancied) and vanished.

When I came up with it, I found that this third lamp-post vaguely illuminated the mouth of a narrow, lightless alley between highish walls. It led me, after a while, into another alley, yet dingier. The wall on the left of this was evidently that of a large garden; on the right came a row of nondescript houses, looming up in their neglect against a starless sky.

The first of these houses *appeared* to be occupied. The next two were vacant. Dingy curtains, soot-grey against their snowy window-sills, hung over the next. A litter of paper and refuse – abandoned by the last long gust of wind that must have come whistling round the nearer angle of the house – lay under the broken flight of steps up to a mid-Victorian porch. The small snow clinging to the bricks and to the worn and weathered cement of the wall only added to its gaunt lifelessness.

In the faint hope of other company coming my way, and vowing that I would follow no farther than to the outlet of yet another pitch-black and uninviting alley or court – which might indeed prove a dead end – I turned into it. It was then that I observed, in the rays of the lamp over my head, that in spite of the fineness of the snow and the brief time that had elapsed, there seemed to be no trace on its surface of recent footsteps.

A faintly thudding echo accompanied me on my way. I have found it very useful – in the country – always to carry a small electric torch in my greatcoat pocket; but for the time being I refrained from using it. This alley proved not to be blind. Beyond a patch of waste ground, a nebulous, leaden-grey vacancy marked a loop here of the Thames – I decided to go no farther; and then perceived a garden gate in the wall to my right. It was ajar, but could not long have been so because no more than an instant's flash of my torch showed marks in the snow of its recent shifting. And yet there was little wind. On the other hand, here was the open river; just a breath of a breeze across its surface might account for this. The cracked and blistered paint was shimmering with a thin coat of rime – of hoarfrost, and as if a finger had but just now scrawled it there, a clumsy arrow showed, its 'V' pointing inward. A tramp, an errand-boy, mere accident might have accounted for this. It may indeed have been a mark made some time before on the paint.

I paused in an absurd debate with myself, chiefly I think because I felt some little alarm at the thought of what might follow; yet led on also by the conviction that I had been intended, decoyed to follow. I pushed the gate a little wider open, peered in, and made my way up a woody path beneath ragged unpruned and leafless fruit trees towards the house. The snow's own light revealed a ramshackle flight of steps up to a poor, frenchified sort of canopy above French windows, one-half of their glazed doors ajar. I ascended, and peered into the intense gloom beyond it. And thus and then prepared to retrace my steps as quickly as possible, I called (in tones as near those of a London policeman as I could manage):

'Hello there! Is anything wrong? Is anyone wanted?' After all, I could at least explain to my fellow passenger if he appeared that I found both his gate and his window open; and the house was hardly pleasantly situated.

No answer was returned to me. In doubt and disquietude, but with a conviction that all was not well, I flashed my torch over the walls and furniture of the room and its heavily framed pictures.

How could anything be well – with unseen company such as this besieging one's senses! Ease and pleasant companionship, the room may once have been capable of giving; in its dirt, cold and neglect it showed nothing of that now. I crossed it, paused again in the passage beyond it, and listened. I then entered the room beyond. Venetian blinds, many of the slats of which had outworn their webbing and heavy, crimson chenille side-curtains concealed its windows. The ashes of a fire showed beyond rusty bars of the grate under a black marble mantelpiece. An oil lamp on the table, with a green shade, exuded a stink of paraffin; beyond was a table littered with books and papers, and an overturned chair. There I could see the bent-up old legs, perceptibly lean beneath the trousers, of the occupant of the room. In no doubt of whose remains these were, I drew near, and with bared teeth and icy, trembling fingers, drew back the fold of the cloak that lay over the face. Death has a strange sorcery. A shuddering revulsion of feeling took possession of me. This cold, once genteel, hideous, malignant room – and this!

The skin of the blue loose cheek was drawn tight over the bone; the mouth lay a little open, showing the dislodged false teeth beneath; the dull unspeculative eyes stared out from beneath lowered lids towards the black mouth of the chimney above the fireplace. Vileness and iniquity had left their marks on the lifeless features, and yet it was rather with compassion than with horror and disgust that I stood regarding them. What desolate solitude, what misery must this old man, abandoned to himself, have experienced during the last years of his life; encountering nothing but enmity and the apprehension of his fellow creatures. I am not intending to excuse or even commiserate what I cannot understand, but the almost complete absence of any goodness in the human spirit cannot but condemn the heart to an appalling isolation. Had he been murdered, or had he come to a violent but natural end? In either case, horror and terror must have supervened. That I had been enticed, deliberately led on, to this discovery I hadn't the least doubt, extravagant though this, too, may seem. Why? What for?

I could not bring myself to attempt to light the lamp. Besides, in that last vigil, it must have burnt itself out. My torch revealed a stub of candle on the mantelpiece. I lit that. He seemed to have been engaged in writing when the enemy of us all had approached him in silence and had struck him down. A long and unsealed envelope lay on the table. I drew out the contents – a letter and a Will, which had been witnessed some few weeks before, apparently by a tradesman's boy and, possibly, by some derelict charwoman, Eliza Hinks. I knew enough about such things to be sure that the Will was valid and complete. This old man had been evidently more than fairly rich in this world's goods, and reluctant to surrender them. The letter was addressed to his two sisters: 'To my two Sisters, Amelia and Maude.' Standing there in the cold and the silence, and utterly alone – for, if any occupant of the other world had decoyed me there, there was not the faintest hint in consciousness that he or his influence was any longer present with me – I read the vilest letter that has ever come my way. Even in print. It stated that he knew the circumstances of these two remaining relatives – that he was well aware of their poverty and physical conditions. One of them, it seemed, was afflicted with Cancer. He then proceeded to explain that, although they should by the intention of their mother have had a due share in her property and in the money she had left, it rejoiced him to think that his withholding of this knowledge must continually have added to their wretchedness. Why he so hated them was only vaguely suggested.

The Will he had enclosed with the letter left all that he died possessed of to – of all human establishments that need it least – the authorities of Scotland Yard. It was to be devoted, it ran, to the detection of such evil-doers as are ignorant or imbecile enough to leave their misdemeanours and crimes detectable.

It is said that confession is good for the soul. Well then, as publicly as possible, I take this opportunity of announcing that, there and then, I made a little heap of envelope, letter and Will on the hearth and put a match to them. When every vestige of the paper had been consumed, I stamped the ashes down. I had touched nothing else. I would leave the vile, jaded, forsaken house to reveal its own secret; and I might ensure that that would not be long delayed.

What continues to perplex me is that so far as I can see no other agency but that of this evil old recluse himself had led me to my discovery. Why? Can it have been with this very intention? I stooped down and peeped and peered narrowly in under the lowered lids in the light of my torch, but not the feeblest flicker, remotest signal – or faintest syllabling echo of any message rewarded me. Dead fish are less unseemly.

And yet. Well – we are all of us, I suppose, at any extreme *capable* of remorse and not utterly shut against repentance. Is it possible that this priceless blessing is not denied us even when all that's earthly else appears to have come to an end?

THE OLD RECTORY WELL

PATRICIA MOYNEHAN

The Old Rectory lay snugly in the angle of two country lanes, with the grey and red stone village church behind it and the little grassy churchyard in between.

The house had belonged to a couple who had lived there for all their married years – fifty three – then the husband had died and his wife had followed him in the next summer. Darrel Cohen, a millionaire American singer, and his sculptress mistress, Nerissa McMahon had bought it from the executors.

There were two very large drawing rooms downstairs, both facing west across the fields and wooded hills surrounding the tiny village of Askham. Darrel took for his study the room with French windows opening onto the croquet lawn, and had his grand piano installed there.

Nerissa took the other room. Its doors led to the garden on the south side, and its large bay window overlooked the lawn to the west. When her kilns and desks and other paraphernalia were installed she turned her attention to an odd little annex on the north side of the house – the church side – which adjoined Darrel's study.

It was a long, narrow, empty room that had been used as a storage 'cellar' because it had only one large window facing west, next to the door that led out into the lawned garden. The annex seemed to have been built a few years later than the house. It was a dark place, its longest wall being of bare, dark red brick, and with black painted shelves along the full length of it. The floor had been concreted over.

It struck Nerissa as odd, and irritating, that the kitchen should be located downstairs where the cellars ought to have been, and that the cellar was on the ground floor, where the kitchen ought to have been.

Her liking for convenience soon prompted her into engaging builders to convert the room into a kitchen. But they had to dig up the solid stone floor in order to lay one of suspended timber and they found an old well sunk deep into the earth beneath.

Nerissa was delighted. 'We can build the floor timbers up to its mouth and then put a little circular brick wall around it. It'll go very well with the pine furniture. But we'd better put a mesh hood on the top to stop people falling into it.'

Darrel laughed. 'People? They'd have to be spaced out or something to fall in. We could leave it open.'

She glared at him. 'Don't be stupid. My sister's children are only four and six. They could fall into it, easily.'

He shrugged. 'OK. It doesn't matter. What're you getting so mad about?'

By the end of the week, the workmen had finished laying the timber flooring and removed the rotted wooden cover from the well. In the same afternoon, the village carpenter came along and fitted a very stout wire mesh hood.

'Good,' she said, surveying the finished work, that evening, 'I feel much happier now that's been secured.'

Darrel looked at her quizzically. 'Why?'

'Because – because – I don't know, it was unsafe.'

A noisy fortnight ensued while the rest of the kitchen was being fitted out but it was completed by mid-June, in time for them to appreciate the coolness of the place.

As Nerissa and Darrel sat together in the garden late one night, suffering the close heat, the idea of the cool kitchen crossed her mind.

'The kitchen's not bad at all, is it?' she said.

'I'm glad you like something around here,' he muttered.

She frowned. 'What do you mean?'

'You've been snapping my head off since we moved in here. I can't say one word before you're on my back.'

'I haven't,' she denied emphatically, then reflected for a moment. 'Have I?'

He nodded.

'Maybe it's the strain,' she pondered. 'Setting up the classes, trying to get the kitchen fixed up, and sorting out all the other downstairs rooms . . .' She stopped as she realized that Darrel's bright blue eyes were not on her but looking past her towards the open kitchen door. She turned round and caught a glimpse of something, some movement, in the centre of the kitchen, as if the light had flickered. 'What's the matter?' she asked.

When she turned back, Darrel was standing up, looking out over the garden.

'It's really beautiful here, so much green,' he said, 'makes you glad you're alive. I'd like to make England my permanent home.'

There was a sudden cry, like a loud sob. She lifted her head to listen, unable to tell from which direction the sound had come.

'What was that?' she said.

'Probably a bird or something,' he replied, turning back to her. 'OK, I'm going to bed. I feel really tired. Sep messes up my lyrics too much and I had my fill of him today.'

He went into the kitchen and she followed. 'Is he coming back tomorrow?'

'No, he is not – thank God. Tomorrow I'm alone with my music – just me and my piano.'

As she crossed the threshold into the kitchen the coldness of the room clung to her and made her gasp. She shook off the feeling and said, 'My sculpture class begins tomorrow afternoon. Still, they won't bother you, I won't let them.'

'No, don't do that,' he said. 'I like them. Long as they're all pretty . . . well, no – long as they're all girls.'

'Honestly! Sometimes I wonder why you live with me,' she teased.

He came over to her and kissed her, softly. 'Because I love you,' he replied, 'more than anything else in the world.'

'How much?' she persisted.

'Lemme see,' he murmured, slipping his arms around her and drawing her up against him, 'as much as I love life?'

She smiled up at him, then sniffed the air curiously, as a faint musty smell swept around her. Looking over his shoulder, she saw the three foot wall around the well's surface, and shuddered. Here and there its white stones glistened greenly with wet moss under the kitchen light.

'How . . ?' She slid out of his embrace and went to it.

'What?' he said.

But when she ran her finger over the surface of the stones, it was dry and clean.

She did not linger long downstairs after Darrel had gone to bed, and when she switched off the lights and headed for the staircase, their little beagle puppy, Simon Kilpatrick, came haring after her. She stared past the pet into the darkness of the hall and fancied she could see something green and glowing beyond the glass panels in the kitchen door.

She was drawn back, fascinated, but on opening the door, she saw only the empty, dark kitchen with the round, shadowed shape of the well waiting silently at the centre of the room. She closed the door quickly and went upstairs.

Darrel seemed to be sleeping when she got into bed. She had not been lying beside him for more than a few minutes when he spoke to her in a sleepy voice.

'You won't leave me?' he asked slowly, 'Will you?'

She raised herself up on one elbow and looked at the back of his head. 'No, of course not. Why?'

'I'd be so lonely without you . . .'

She snuggled up to his back and kissed his warm shoulder. 'You are silly . . .'

As she settled back on her pillows and drifted into sleep she noticed a strange musty smell on his skin.

When she woke up the next morning, she was alone.

On her way down the upstairs hall, she stopped outside the bathroom door as the sound of movement inside caught her attention.

'Darrel?' She closed her fingers around the handle and a shiver ran up her arm.

The sound of footsteps ceased as she pushed the door open. Inside, the hazy sunlight poured across the saffron circular bath and sparkled over the gold fittings. Her spider plants hung in their baskets, still and quiet in the morning light. But there was that faint musty smell mixed in with the scents of soap and perfume that she kept on the glass shelves around the fiery mosaic walls.

The other 'thing' swirled around her coldly. She retreated and slammed the door, but it followed her onto the landing and chased her, swirling around her like some fetid invisible swamp mist, until she reached the kitchen, where it suddenly vanished.

She went into Darrel's study. Darrel was playing his white grand piano with one hand and eating a sandwich from the other.

'*Since then I've been thinking of you*
And things are looking black
In England.'
'What are you doing?' she asked.
'Ssh!' he snapped. And went on,
'*Was it really ages ago?*
Can you hear my sobs where you are
In England?'

'That isn't right—' she began, but he slammed his fist down on the piano top and turned on her.

'Look, get out of here, will you! Quit harassing me when I'm working. Beat it! Beat it!'

His eyes, which normally shimmered with gentleness, were blazing angrily at her.

'Those words aren't the ones you put to that melody,' she said, defiantly. 'And how dare you tell me to beat it? Sod off, yourself!' She turned away from him and went back into the kitchen. The room was too cold, unnaturally cold.

He began to play again, to play the melody that had no place with those words but belonged to a musical parody about San Francisco going on his next album.

'I'm going to have that well filled in,' she said, suddenly. And as she said it, she felt a violent hostility oozing out of its open mouth at her and she backed off, startled, into Darrel's study. Hands gripped her shoulders and she was whirled around to face Darrel's usually dreamy face now glowering horribly.

'Can't you leave the damn' thing alone! It hasn't done *you* any harm, for God's sake!' He turned his back on her and sat down at the piano.

She waited for a moment and then his voice came back to her, apologetically.

'I'm sorry. But I need peace and quiet to work in. The France tour is coming up in a couple of weeks. I feel exhausted.'

'You didn't sleep well?' She heard a low laugh, a wry laugh, a sad laugh. It was not Darrel.

'I don't think so. I must've been dreaming, I guess. But I can't remember about what.'

He had not heard the laugh. She looked back at the well. 'Sleeping well.' She shivered again.

'Please, let me fill that thing in,' she said, quietly.

'Give me one good believable reason,' he said but did not wait for her reply and, instead, resumed his playing and began to sing, softly:

'*Since then I been thinking of you . . .*'

In the afternoon, when the students came in for their first sculpture lesson, he was more like his old self. Inevitably, they sneaked into his study and he willingly entertained them. He also played the melody for San Francisco, as it should have been played.

She began to think seriously about getting the builder in to brick up the well, when Darrel was out of the house.

In the evening, when they were, as had become their habit, sitting out in the garden under the clear night sky, she broached the subject again.

'Don't you feel there's something wrong about it?'

'About what?'

'The well.'

'Oh, for God's sake, forget it, will you! It's getting to be an obsession with you. You're gonna start seeing things next!' He got up and walked off down the garden.

She felt frightened because she was beginning to feel helpless. If the well was not filled in, she dare not stay.

'You won't leave me,' he said. He was at the bottom of the garden but he sounded as if he was behind her. 'You promised.'

She jumped to her feet and took a step in his direction but a loud banging sound coming from the kitchen checked her and she looked behind her towards the open door.

Something was in the kitchen, something hammering at the mesh hood, trying to get it off. She stared at the shadow hunched over the well. Tendrils of grey mist wound around and between the wired dome, like fingers pulling at the lid. She felt herself drawn towards the sight and the air growing colder and clinging to her face, freezing the breath in her body before she could exhale it. As she came nearer to the shape, she saw that it was not trying to get the meshing off. Its mist-like fingers were holding the lid of the well down and some other unseen hand was hammering, hammering, hammering something on.

The grey wisps protruding from the shadowy arms left the hood and wavered in the air as whatever it was turned what must have been its head towards her. She could not see any features but she could feel its burning stare. Then, slowly, it turned its whole grey transparent mass. The hammering grew louder and louder until it was beating inside her skull. The misty grey tendril-like fingers snaked along the freezing air.

She stumbled backwards, in panic, and fell over the kitchen threshold into the warm night.

'Darrel!' she screamed.

But there was no reassuring sound of his footsteps racing up the lawn. Instead, she heard a low brutal laugh, and suddenly the hammering stopped and the shadow was gone.

She spun round, still breathless with fear, and found herself staring up at her lover's furious face.

'What the hell is wrong with you, now!' he demanded, angrily.

She looked at the kitchen and the open door to the garden slammed shut.

He strode over to it and threw it open.

An old man stood in the doorway; he was dripping with dark green slime. She was close behind Darrel and could smell an awful stench. She cried out and pulled the door closed, shutting out the horrible sight.

Darrel looked at her, amazed, and opened the door again. 'What's the matter with you?' he asked, in a more tolerant tone of voice. 'Is there a rat in there?'

'I – not a rat. Didn't you see it!'

His expression darkened again. 'See what?' he snapped, and disappeared into his study.

She lay in bed and the faint musty rotting smell danced around her head as he tossed and turned beside her. Quietly, she slipped from the sheets and went across to the window. She could almost hear voices, low conversation, and that hammer-hammer-hammer again.

Darrel clenched his fists and rolled on to his back. His eyes were closed but he was murmuring restlessly. She looked out at the garden and the moon-silvered lawn. The bushes by the fence cast strange shadows on the grass and the clouds scudding across the moon caused long-legged shades to stalk across the lawn. In the sky there were no clouds when she looked up once more. The moon was bright and round and the stars shone icily clear. Everything was very, very still. There was no longer any sound at all and the air was as heavy and sepulchral as if it had been sealed for centuries in a tomb.

'Can't breathe . . . can't breathe . . . no – no – let me out . . .'

She looked back at Darrel, he was throwing his head from side to side and his red-gold curls were soaking and sticking to his forehead.

Looking back through the window, she saw in the garden below those long-legged shadows still moving over the silvered grass. They melted away into the darkness of the bushes and then something shone and sparkled in the moonlight, something in the grass, polished and gleaming, and attached to a dark boot – a buckle?

'Let me out! Let me out!' Darrel screamed out and sat up in bed. He stared at her as she watched him from the window. 'What the hell are you doing?' he snapped. 'You know how important my sleep is to me.'

He threw the sheets away from him and got out of bed. Most of his slim tanned body was shining with sweat but he did not seem to notice as he pulled on his bathrobe.

'Christ,' he muttered, 'I don't know how long I can stay in a house with a crazy woman.'

He stormed out of the bedroom and slammed the door behind him.

Tears blurred her vision as she looked back down into the garden. But she could see nothing now. Then, very softly there floated up from the bushes that soft cruel laugh she had heard the previous night. She pulled the curtains together defiantly and got back into bed. Darrel's music drifted faintly up to her from the floor below.

When she woke to the morning sunlight streaming reassuringly into the room, Darrel was wrapped around her; he had forgiven her for disturbing his precious sleep.

They had breakfast late that day and just as they had finished, the doorbell rang, and Darrel went to answer it. Heather, Nerissa's sister, en route for her lover's house in London, had called in with the intention of staying overnight. Nerissa had said drop in, after all, she explained, so here she was with three white suitcases and two very boisterous daughters.

Nerissa came out into the hall to see what all the noise was about. Nerissa watched Darrel; he liked Heather and her maverick way of life. 'How long are you staying?' he asked.

Heather's daughters grabbed his legs and he crouched down to hug the little girls.

'Just one night,' Heather said.

'Where's your puppy?' Lisa, the six year old, asked.

'Oh, how'd you know about that?' he smiled.

Heather picked up one of her white suitcases. 'I told them. Nerissa wrote to me about it.'

'Leave the baggage,' he said. 'I'll get it.'

He called the puppy and it came bounding down the stairs. But when he held out his hand to it, it backed off and yelped at him.

'That's strange,' he said, pursuing the little beagle, but the puppy shot past him through the kitchen, and out through the open back door.

'Well, let's see if we can catch him,' Darrel laughed, and took the children's hands, leading the two little girls off through the kitchen with him, and out into the garden.

Heather went through into the kitchen but Nerissa lingered on the threshold. What was the matter with Simon Kilpatrick?

'Coming in?' Heather prompted. 'Anything wrong?'

'What?' Nerissa moved forward, steeling herself against the coldness of the room, as she always did now. 'I was just wondering whether to check the kilns for this afternoon's class or not. But I feel fairly sure I left everything running properly.'

Heather looked at her suspiciously. 'Yes, I'm sure you did. You plan everything so well.' Then she added, in a soft voice, 'You've got him well organized, haven't you!' Nerissa didn't reply, so Heather went on, 'I don't know how you got him interested in you in the first place. It's a pity he's such a good little Jewish boy or I suppose he would have married you by now – unless, of course, you don't want to marry him and you're simply using him.'

'How do you mean?' Nerissa said, shocked. 'You don't use people you love. But I don't suppose you'd know that.'

'No,' she smiled. 'But I like him. He looks like a particularly *good* little boy, to me. Some of them are so gentle – particularly the ones who are close to their mothers. However, you and I are sisters, so I wouldn't dream of taking him away from you. You've been together six years now, haven't you? Does he still pay the running costs of your class?'

'You know he does,' Nerissa conceded and suppressed her anger by changing the subject. 'Will you want breakfast? I know the children will, but what do you have these days?'

She had black coffee, which Nerissa felt was very appropriate.

So, the following morning, while the children tucked into cornflakes and boiled eggs, and Darrel went on sleeping upstairs, Heather drank her black coffee and made polite conversation with Nerissa, whom she hardly ever saw, except when in need of a favour.

'Who was the old man in the hall, Auntie Nessa?' Lisa asked, between bites of soldiers.

Nerissa looked quickly across at the newly opened well but the hood was still firmly bolted in place. She turned back to her niece and smiled. 'Darrel, probably. He looks terrible in the mornings.'

'He was crying, he said he was lonely,' Dina, the little one, added.

'Then he went,' Lisa said.

'Where?' Heather asked.

'Through the wall,' Lisa said, disarmingly honest.

'He did,' the little one backed her elder sister up.

Heather laughed, not noticing that Nerissa was biting her lip. 'What lies, you two! Hurry up and eat your breakfast, we have to meet your Uncle Ronald for lunch in London in an hour and a half.'

They left just before eleven; Darrel came downstairs around quarter past and found Nerissa in the garden.

He wandered out in his bathrobe and walked up behind her. 'Gone, I suppose,' he said.

She stiffened with fright.

He rested his long fingers on her shoulder. 'I didn't startle you, did I? You could've woken me. Did they say when they were coming back?'

'You know what my sister's like. She never says when she'll be anywhere.'

Inwardly she wondered whether or not she should have asked Heather to stay longer. Darrel did not believe her about the well and she was beginning to feel an increasing dread of it.

She watched him wander into the kitchen and help himself to some orange juice. He looked as if he was quite happy in there, as if he belonged in there.

Her class began at half past two and finished at five. Sep called in, in the middle of the afternoon and was still with Darrel arguing and swearing about musical arrangements, when she slipped out at half past five and walked across the little graveyard to the church.

The weathered, wrought-iron ring on the church door yielded to her hand and the door swung inwards on to that strange perfumed atmosphere of shadows and Christianity that wrapped itself around the pillars and the pews. Diffused sunlight slanted in through the high, narrow, arched windows along each side and at the bottom of the church – or perhaps it was the top – three large pointed stained-glass windows mutilated the summer brightness so that the altar beneath was shaded and darkly fluid.

She wandered quietly down the centre aisle and stopped when she reached the little rail that barred the way to the red carpeted altar steps. To her right she saw what she had been told by the locals was always kept available in the church: A great leather-bound register with faded gold leaf tracery on its cover lay upon a dark brown highly polished lectern that was standing against the wall. The stout chain through the spine of the register at one end was set into the marble pillared wall behind.

'Great lengths to go,' she murmured. 'You could easily tear the book away from it, I suppose.'

'Why would you want to do that?'

A man's voice echoed down the aisles to where she was standing. She swung round.

The vicar smiled at her. 'Voices carry very well in here. I take it you were only musing to yourself?' He came down the centre aisle to join her. 'Anyway, now I know your intention, better not carry it out, eh? You're from the Old Rectory, aren't you? I've been meaning to call on you.'

'Hello,' she said.

'Are you Church of England?'

'No, no. Oh ... no, I'm not here out of duty. Out of curiosity, actually.' She turned to the register. 'This is a record of the village, isn't it?'

'Goes back four hundred years.' He smiled. 'And tells you everything you need to know about your next door neighbour. It was kept secretly at first, in Cromwellian times, by one of my ancient predecessors, and then, when the establishment took a more tolerant view of my profession, it was brought out for public display. Now, if you hadn't thought of looking in there first, perhaps I could have done and called on you with the excuse of telling you a bit of the Old Rectory's history – which I don't know anything about, as a matter of fact. I did know the old owners, Mr and Mrs Brendon, but they're gone now ... It's quite unusual that we have a ... what is he – a musician?'

'Yes ... in a way,' she laughed. 'Pop star, I suppose, although he's not very fond of that description. Still, what does it matter?' She looked at the book and touched its ancient binding. 'Beautiful,' she said.

'Yes, I believe it's very valuable, but it's stood out here in the open for three centuries unharmed, so I dare say it'll be here for a good while yet.'

She opened the book slowly, carefully, and looked at the beautiful copper plate lettering inside. 'This is a work of art,' she said.

'You're an artist yourself, I think. Artistic people are often far more sensitive and impressionable to things that the rest of us hardly notice. Well, I'll leave you to appreciate it, alone. I lock the church doors at half past ten, tonight, so you have,' he glanced at his watch, 'just under five hours to enjoy yourself.'

He said goodbye and walked off down the church.

There was a shallow marble ledge running along the wall behind the lectern, about knee level. She lifted the great book from its perch and sat down on the ledge with the register on her knees.

The villagers' births, marriages and deaths had been recorded right up to the present year. She found Brendon and worked backwards. But the Brendons had lived all over the village and there was nothing in the register that told her anything about the Old Rectory. She turned the pages back, carefully, moving gently backwards through the centuries and becoming increasingly fascinated by the stories about the dwellers in Askham.

Much later, she reached the beginning. The register had first been installed in the church secretly in the time of Oliver Cromwell, as the vicar had told her.

The first name in the book was Kemp; he was a landowner who lived in the Old Rectory with his family. His younger son, John was the local priest; the elder boy, Peter, was his heir; he had one daughter, Elizabeth. There was no mention of his wife. Then, later on, Nerissa read that Mistress Kemp had died twelve years earlier. It was all normal biographical stuff until she reached the second side of the first page. There was a great deal of old-fashioned writing on this. Unusually, it was in English, archaic English, but she could understand it nevertheless. It seemed to be a story that started on May 23rd, 1650. It was an odd coincidence – was it not – that she and Darrel had moved into the Old Rectory on May 23rd of the current year. She began to read:

'Be it nowne that upon thys day, ye twentye thirde daye offe Maye in thys yere of Our Lorde Onye thousande sic hundredde and fiftye thyre came to ye dwellinge plays offe onye Joseph Kemp ye Earle of Tonridge who dyde flee custodye off ye battalyons of ye Lorde Protector, and dyde seke hym asylum with ye familye offe Kemp who dyde haffe sympathye for ye late Kyng's cawse and hys followyrs.

They, noweing the Lorde Protector's men to be close bye, dyde secret ye Earle in ye welle on ye northe syde of thyre dwellinge. Ye soldyrs dyde fynd no trays offe ye Earle. Thyre Captyn, onye Edward Shepherd, commandyd ye welle to be selde.

Thys don, he dyde then comman ye familye Kemp entyre into ye churchyard besyde ye lande on which ye sayde welle dyde lye.

Thyre, fathyr, sonnes and dawtyr were putte to dethe and thyre bodyes lefte in ye churchyarde to be exampyls to the pepyls offe Askham. Ye Captyn dyde command ony offe hys men to stay besyde ye welle to be certyn it was notte unselde. He dyde stay in ye village from thatte daye, which be Mundye, to ye following Sabbathe. When he dyde departte, notte onye dyde dayr uncovyr ye welle for they newe it to be of no worth to courtte dethe at ye Lorde Protector's hands for onye who must now hymselfe, haffe dyde.'

There was no more to the story. She looked up from the book and found that it was dark outside and the electric lighting in the church had come on. It was horrible to imagine that man dying alone, trapped in the darkness. If he were given a Christian burial maybe that would rid the well of its ghosts.

The church doors rattled as the vicar came in.

'Good heavens, still here? Did you find what you were looking for, are you coming back tomorrow?'

She put the book back on the lectern. 'Yes, to both questions. I think my – I think Darrel would like to see the book. Very interesting.' She walked back to the church doors. Surely, it was all the proof she needed to convince Darrel that she was not imagining things.

'Must be very interesting, indeed,' the vicar remarked. 'It's locking-up time, you know. Would you like me to walk back to the Old Rectory, with you?'

She thought about it for a moment, then wondered what Darrel would say if she brought the vicar back to supper at such a late hour. He wouldn't like it. 'Men of the cloth' tried his patience – particularly if one of their visits infringed on his precious sleep.

'No thank you. But call in tomorrow afternoon, if you like – after my class finishes, at five. I'd like to discuss something with you, if you don't mind. You can have tea with us.'

The little graveyard was well lit by the still-full moon and the sky was cloudless. She slipped into the garden through the little side gate and looked up at their bedroom window over Darrel's study.

The moonlight danced eerily over the glass. He was looking down at her. She lifted her hand to wave and then realized that it wasn't Darrel. The face was too old, the hair grey, the skin shining as if it were wet . . .

As she looked the head became transparent – as if it were shifting and changing with the light – as if it were old one moment, and young the next. Grey-haired – then – red-haired.

She shut her eyes tightly and then looked again. There were two men. There was Darrel and there was – no – there was not. The other image seemed to melt behind him, or in front of him or into him . . .

She ran to the open French windows of his study and turned on every light as she raced through the house.

When she reached the top of the stairs, she found Darrel standing outside the bedroom door.

'Hi.' He smiled, 'What's the matter?'

The smell was terrible. She reached out for the landing light-switch and flicked it on.

Darrel looked at her with a naive, puzzled expression; he seemed totally unaware that his shirt was saturated in green slime.

'Where've you been?' he asked.

She could not answer. She felt as if she were staring at two faces, one old, hovering before one young.

He came towards her. 'I've missed you. You've been away such a long time.' He touched her hand with his own cold and wet fingers and brought his face, its face, close to hers. 'I'm so lonely,' he said. 'You promised never to leave.'

The smell was dreadful, like something terrible and rotting that had been shut away for centuries and had now been freed to – to –

'Darrel — ' she sobbed. Her mind began to reel, she couldn't breathe, the smell was so bad, it was everywhere – everywhere . . . darkness and cold everywhere . . . everywhere . . .

The terrible piercing cold of the kitchen shocked her into consciousness. Darrel was carrying her towards the centre of the kitchen where the well waited with its hungry mouth umuzzled – the mesh cover lying where it had been flung, against the wall beneath a broken window.

He stopped at the edge of the little circular wall. She stared up at the old face – young face. She tried to say his name but her voice had been frozen to a croaking whisper.

'You promised you'd never leave me,' she heard him say, as she fell, fell, fell down into the stinking darkness.

STREETS OF THE CITY

TONY RICHARDS

The first thing Marshall Harris noticed as he rounded the corner of Lexington and 23rd was the bright red wash of light across the entire street. Three squad cars and a black police sedan were parked outside the entrance to the Hotel *Fiorella*, where Harris had lived these past eight years. And, as he watched, an ambulance pulled up, two paramedics disgorged themselves and hustled their furled stretcher through the hotel's revolving doors. A huge crowd was already gathering, the few police outside were trying to hold them back, but all that Harris could see were the lights, the bright red strobing beacons on the cars. They swept across the buildings, lit the pavements with their flame. And it was just as though some small section of hell had been transplanted outside the hotel. Harris came untensed, shifted the bag of groceries from his right arm to his left and, despite his forty-one years, sprinted across the busy street and began to push his way through the crowd.

By the time that he was thirty-five, Marshall Harris had realized that he would never direct a show on Broadway. It had taken him, perhaps, another year to adjust to that fact, to realize that he had not *failed* in any way, but simply that his talent lay in other fields of theatre, less glamorous and less well-paid for sure, but noble nonetheless. Nobility had become his cornerstone in life. He drank little, smoked a pipe, and never doped at all. His physique was good, his appearance immaculately groomed without becoming dandyish. The clothes he wore were calm and unpretentious, young but not *too* young. At that time of life, in that profession, with that lack of pure financial success, most other men would have become embittered and seedy. Marshall Harris was neither, and it earned him respect from everyone from his fiancée Patty to the kids in the little theatre on Mercer where he was currently directing an updated version of Ibsen's *An Enemy of the People*. He had stopped rehearsals at six-thirty that day, showered and changed by seven, and suddenly, instead of going back to the hotel, decided he wanted to eat kosher that evening. If he had gone straight back, he reflected later, then he might actually have been able to do something. But he walked to his favourite deli on Delancey Street, spent forty minutes chatting to the proprietor, and caught the IRT uptown almost an hour late. He jogged up the subway steps at 23rd and Park, and headed east, towards the bright red lights.

By the time he reached the inner circle of the crowd, the word was going round that somebody was dead. A uniformed cop moved forward to stop Harris from progressing farther, but the director snapped that he lived here, sidestepped, and went on through. There were more uniforms in the hotel lobby. A young man, plainclothes, was interviewing the desk porter. Ignoring the lift, Harris took the steps two at a time up to the second floor. And it was there, in corridor 212–236, outside his own room, that the main body of policemen was clustered. It was there that something terrible had taken place.

His first thought was of Patty. She might have dropped by unexpectedly, found him not there, let herself into his room. She might have waited there alone. And in this city . . . Harris ran, bursting through the reinforced-glass fire doors, groceries still tucked under his arm as though he were a quarterback breaking with the ball. He had rammed, actually rammed, past two plainclothes detectives before he realized his mistake. His own door, 224, was shut. It was the room immediately adjacent that was the centre of attention.

The white-emulsioned inside of door 225 was splattered up and down with blood. It was still quite fresh, had not begun to darken yet, and its colour reminded Harris of the whirling lights out on the street. He stepped forward gingerly until he had an unobstructed view of the room.

They had not covered up the body yet. The police photographer was still at work, and the glare of his flashbulb brought the butchered corpse into sudden and obscene relief. The torso had been laid wide open, gutted like a fish. Every limb was hacked at; there were fingers missing from the hands. And the face – one eye missing, hardly any lower jaw at all. Only the long and tangled mass of blood-stained, mousy hair testified that this had been a human being once, a girl.

Mousy hair.

Harris had seen that kind of hair before, stained and tangled in that self same way, attached to a corpse that had been mutilated in an identical manner. A young girl. A very pretty, very sweet young girl who had lived and died a whole lifetime ago. And though Harris had never once forgotten, he had managed to sublimate the memory till now. Standing in front of that open, dripping door, he could hold it down no longer, and it came rushing out of his subconscious, crashed down on him like a wave. Mousy hair. Mousy, mousy, mousy hair.

His knees buckled and he slumped against the far wall of the corridor. The bag of groceries slipped from his grasp. Pastrami, bagels, haimishe pickles and cheese blintzes spilled across the rug. They went unnoticed, because at that moment Marshall Harris's mind went far away from him, and all of human sanity was lost.

She was waiting for him, in that place beyond the world and thought and time. She had not aged at all in twenty one long years. Her long, mousy hair was bright and freshly-washed, and cut into a style that had been all the fashion two decades ago. Darkness and void surrounded her, but in the far, far distance Harris could make out the glow of myriad lights, sodium lamps, as though the dark streets of the city somehow threaded through this limbo land. She smiled at him, but there was no love in her smile any more. And her expression seemed to say: This is only the beginning. There is more and worse to come . . .

When he returned, he was sitting bolt upright against the wall, like an old derelict gone rigid from booze. The oldest of the plainclothes men was squatting down in front of him, popping the groceries back into the paper bag. His badge, clipped to the front of his coat, identified him as Lieutenant James Carrera, Homicide Division, and he looked vaguely annoyed. He was, Harris realized, one of the men he had rammed into in his headlong dash.

Carrera looked up sharply as Harris opened his eyes.

'You OK? You gonna be sick?'

'No, I . . . I think I'm all right now.'

'It's OK by me, either way. You know, the intern was sick when he saw that mess. I always thought those guys had stomachs made of lead.' Carrera laughed; the corners of his eyes did funny crinkly things, humourless things. 'I'm gonna have'ta ask you a few questions.'

It all went down in the Lieutenant's small black book, all the details that Harris could muster from his blood-fogged mind.

Firstly about himself, his name, age, occupation, what he had been doing for the past hour and who could verify those facts. And then about the girl. Her name was Shirley DeVane. She had moved in six months ago from Cleveland, Ohio. She was a 'gipsy,' a chorus girl, and she had settled here, so long a walk from Broadway, because the hotel offered reduced rates to theatricals, and because she couldn't stand the YWCA or the all-women's hotels, and because somebody had told her, when she first arrived, that the East Side was safer than the West. It was a generalization for which she had paid dearly.

'Did she have many friends?'

'A few, I think. I didn't know her that well.'

'Any enemies?'

'I doubt it. She was a nice kid.'

'When was the last time you saw her, Mr Harris?'

'Just . . .' It seemed hard to believe. '. . . this morning. I bumped into her on the stairs.'

'Did she seem troubled in any way? Upset?'

'No, quite the opposite. She'd just landed a job in the new Sondheim musical. She was pretty well over the moon.'

Carrera snapped his notebook shut. 'OK, that's all for now. Thank you for your co-operation, Mr Harris.' He stood up and helped Harris to his feet, handed him the paper bag. 'It looks like a routine case. She disturbs an intruder in her room. The guy panics, goes berserk.'

'*That* berserk?'

'It happens. But we have to make sure.'

The two paramedics, sick-looking themselves, were carrying the body out. It was thankfully covered up, but a lock of mousy hair had fallen out from under the red blanket, dangled in full view. Harris turned away.

Carrera had lumbered halfway back down the corridor before Harris's shout brought him to a halt.

'Lieutenant? Can I ask you a question?'

The detective turned, nodded cautiously. 'Sure.'

'Was the girl . . . was she . . . assaulted?'

It was as if all the suspicion for all the crimes in New York City fell on Harris right then. The look that the Lieutenant gave him seemed compounded of pure surprise and sheer anger, with lots of native instinct and experience thrown in. A dark-eyed, knowing look from a man who'd just realized Marshall Harris was far more involved than he was letting on. 'Yes, Mr Harris,' Carrera said slowly. 'Yes, she was.' He seemed on the verge of enquiring why Harris had asked that particular question, but his experience and instinct drew him short, and he simply grimaced, turned back round, and lumbered on. He looked back once, from the glass fire doors, and then was gone.

In his own room, with the door locked tight and the bolt and the chain on, Harris dumped the groceries into the wastepaper basket, drew all the blinds and threw himself out full-length on the bed. He lay quite still there, in a semi-darkness that gradually deepened to neon-slivered black. He lay there for hours. Some time around nine, his bedside phone rang persistently a dozen times, then stopped, and rang again. He did not even bother to reach across to answer it, though he knew that it was probably Patty calling him. They were due to get married early next month, and he loved her dearly. But he could not get that girl out of his mind.

And the worst thing was, he was afraid even to sleep. Rigid terror filled him every time he began to doze. For Marshall Harris knew that, in his impending dreams, *she* would be waiting for him. She, with her mousy hair.

It was well past midnight when Harris decided to get some coffee. He got up slowly, stiffly, from the bed, made some vague attempt to straighten out the wrinkles in his clothes, then unlocked his door and peered out. His gaze was returned blearily by a uniformed policeman sitting on a hard chair outside 225. Harris ignored the cop, unsure whether to acknowledge him or not, and wandered down the corridor still dangling the room keys from his hand.

The *Fiorella*, like most of New York's older hotels, had seen more glamorous days. The ghosts of the Gatsby era still wheeled and tinkled through its dimly-lit halls; the whole building was saturated with the memory of the Charleston and bright chatter and cocaine. Perhaps Dorothy Parker had once partied here. Perhaps James Thurber and his wife had sipped martinis in one of the sumptuous suites. Those days were long gone, but it remained a friendly place. No sterile modern decor here, no plastic and no chrome. Like Marshall Harris, the hotel retained its nobility.

And then there was the ground-floor coffee shop.

It was empty of customers when Harris wandered in. That

pleased him. He liked, late at night, to sit at the far corner of the counter so that he could swivel around on his stool and watch Lexington Avenue through the big, velvet-draped window in the wall. From a distance, and through glass, the streets of the city were beautiful after dark. He sat, he swivelled, watched. Down at the far end, behind the counter, Rahsaan began fixing him a cup of sanka, unasked.

'Coffee please, Rass,' Harris said. He would need the caffeine to keep him away from sleep.

The big Black man nodded and complied, then came limping along the back of the counter with the cup in his steadier hand. Harris winced inwardly every time he saw that limp, that tremble. Rahsaan Kirk Ali had once been a top amateur sprinter, hundred yards, one of the best. A row of honours on the top shelf behind the counter testified to that. There were shields and cups and medals and, most prized of all, a two-foot-high silver-plated figurine of an athlete in full pantheresque flight. That had been Rahsaan ten years ago until a speeding car had broken him completely, finished any promise of a full professional career. He set the cup down carefully, then leaned against the counter out of breath.

'Buh-bad business with that girl tuhday.'

'Uh-huh, very bad.'

'She wuz only a kid. Who the hell'ud go'n do a thing like that?'

'The police reckon it was a burglar.'

'Yeah, makes sense in this damn town.' He wiped his mouth uncomfortably. 'Her folks must know buh now. Shee-it! Ah keep thinkin', what if it was one'a mine, man? What if it was one'a mine?'

Harris had no answer to that. He sat, and sipped his coffee.

'Y'know,' the Black man continued, 'ah wish ah'd bin on up theyuh. If ah'd've only heard her scream, ah'd've *nailed* that bastard. May not be so strong as ah use'ta be, may not be so fast, but ah'd've had a damn good *go*.'

And he sincerely meant it; it was not just brag. And something heavy churned around in Harris's gut. Here was a man who was a virtual cripple, who had trouble carrying a cup of coffee ten yards up a bar, and yet who would still face an armed lunatic willingly to save a young girl's life. Harris would have liked to imagine he would do the same, but his own past denied that. Most emphatically.

'Goodnight, Rass,' he said, making no attempt to conceal the sharpness in his tone. He set the half-empty cup down on the counter, walked out of the coffee shop as fast as dignity allowed, still feeling the man's amazed stare on his neck.

Seven minutes after he had left, three scrawny white youths slouched into the shop, held Rahsaan up at knife-point and proceeded to raid the till. Just as they were leaving, almost as an afterthought, they took the two-foot silver trophy down from the shelf and beat the man to death with it. Nobody heard him scream, least of all Marshall Harris. And by one o'clock that morning, the squad cars and the black sedan were back outside the hotel. The streets of the city were once more awash with red.

Room 224 went away from Harris, and the void and the darkness returned. She was there, still smiling, and her hair was blowing in an insubstantial breeze that came from the direction of the sodium streetlights. And on that breeze there came a noise, the sound of tinkling laughter...

He was tired and puffy-eyed when he met Patty the next morning, somewhat less well-groomed than usual, somewhat less noble, somewhat slouched. She seemed surprised at first, until, over ham and eggs in the small diner just off Gramercy Park, he started to recount the story of the two concurrent murders. He was near to tears. An old Italian waitress who had been slathering the opposite, empty table with a dishcloth stopped to listen, stare, and Patty, noticing her, slammed five dollars onto the Formica, grabbed Harris by the arm and hustled him out of there. They wandered for an hour through the quiet streets of the teens, talking softly, staving off the pangs of fear with words layered on words. And Harris told her everything. Except about the past. Except about the mousy hair.

Patty was a stunning brunette, six years his junior. She worked with handicapped children in the slums of the Barrio, and if Harris respected her just as much as he loved her, he felt that was *right*, that was *important*, that respect. He hoped she felt the same for him. And he hoped he would never give her cause to lose it. He was not about to start now. A wind had sprung up from the south, blowing in from the Upper Bay. It caught the old newspapers and the discarded candy wrappers and the dust, set the window frames in the surrounding blocks to rattling, and Harris faced right into it and straightened, stiffened like a lofted sail. He smiled. The old nobility was back.

'How about we find somewhere where we won't be disturbed?' he said.

'How about my place?'

The smile turned to an open grin.

Rehearsals began again that afternoon, and Harris approached them with all the confidence he'd ever known. He had been through a bad time of bloodshed and haunted guilt-ridden dreams, and the mere act of passing through unscathed had left him stronger. Marshall Harris: a pair of glowing, watching eyes in the darkness beyond the footlights, a voice so certain that it could not be ignored. He absorbed himself, completely.

And he stopped rehearsals half an hour early, perplexed and annoyed. Jaqueline Sarn was one of the most talented young actresses he'd ever had the pleasure of working with. He had cast her in the role of Petra, Stockmann's daughter, and she had played that small part with a degree of honesty and grace astonishing to watch. Until today, when she muffed her lines and stuttered and looked so self-conscious it could make you scream.

He took her to one side after the others were gone, and asked her, gently, what was wrong. And heard an old, old story. She had been on the little theatre circuit for six years now. She had tried for bigger productions, been turned down with those flimsy excuses commercial directors apply when a kid is so good that she might upstage the bigger names. And she was sick to death of it. She *knew* she had the wherewithal, she *knew* that she could make it, and if New York wouldn't take her then perhaps Hollywood might. Even if it meant working commercials and TV. Even if it meant hanging out at Schwab's with all the silicone-puffed starlets, waiting for the right producer to come along. She had sunk the last of her savings in a Greyhound ticket to L.A., had sat up all night clutching the damned thing, trying to decide whether to tear it up or not. Harris talked to her quietly, just as Patty had talked to him, weighing up the pros and cons, the chances and the risks. It was an idiotic scheme in his opinion, but he kept that to himself; the girl was old enough to run her own life. The only concrete advice he could offer was that she could get a refund on the ticket if she forewent the symbolic act of ripping it to shreds. She seemed satisfied. He had helped.

While Harris was taking his customary shower, Jaqueline Sarn got her things together and wandered out of the back door of the theatre – straight into the arms of a wild-eyed, unknown man. She was assaulted on the spot, then brutally murdered with what proved to be, when the police found it in a nearby dustbin later, a fifteen-inch meat cleaver. The killer was escaping just as Harris turned the water off. He stepped out, dripping, onto the latex mat, feeling uncomfortable all of a sudden. There was a sharp chill on the air. He felt as though he were being watched. He turned around twice, satisfied himself that he was alone in the cubicle, and then glanced at himself in the mirror. Staring over his right shoulder, reflected in the steamy glass, was a young woman, a girl. Smiling. Mousy hair. Twenty-one years dead.

Lieutenant James Carrera sat on the edge of the bed in Harris's room, gazing at the broken man who occupied the armchair opposite. Harris had been trembling long before the detective arrived; he was not near to stopping yet. His hands were clenched one around the other till the knuckles had gone white. Only the eyes were invisible, lost in pools of shadow. Carrera did not particularly care to see those eyes.

He pulled the notebook out again, toyed with it but did not open it.

'I'd have you under suspicion,' he commented, 'except you've got perfectly good alibis for two of the killings. Forensics can disprove you did the last.'

Harris looked up. 'Fine.' He did not sound convinced.

'But I know one thing,' the Lieutenant continued. 'Somehow, you're the focus for these three deaths. Each one came in close contact with you; each one was murdered shortly after in an abnormally brutal manner. I think you're the key to all this, Mr Harris. And I'm damned if I know why. Like'ta tell me?'

'Perhaps some lunatic is doing this.' He was clutching at straws; he knew it. 'A madman, out to hurt me by getting at people I know.'

'Uh-uh, it's not one man.'

'*What?*'

'We caught Shirley DeVane's killer, *two hours* before Jackie Sarn got hers. Found him blind drunk in an alley, mumbling how sorry he was. A bag-snatcher, Mr Harris. A petty, small-time thief who'd faint at the sight of his own blood. He doesn't know why he did it.

He has no history of violence, no psychiatric record. And yet, dig this, he claims he heard voices telling him to kill the girl. One voice, specifically. A young woman's voice.'

'Oh my God!'

'What was that?'

'I said, oh my *God*! Will you leave me alone?'

Carrera stayed where he was. 'The fingerprints on the trophy and the meat cleaver don't match up. That's three *separate* killers, Mr Harris. All centred around you.'

'Get out of here!'

'Make me.' And the swipe came at Carrera from nowhere; just a blur where Harris had been sitting, and then that clenched fist sweeping in from the left corner of his vision. The Lieutenant caught Harris's wrist before the blow was landed, and the two were locked like that for a second, fury against will, before Harris went limp. Carrera shoved him back into the chair, then began talking quickly and evenly. 'It's not going to end with those three people, Mr Harris. I know that in my bones. You know it too. And there's something you're not telling me. Why won't you let me help?'

'It happened a long time ago. I don't think it's any use to you.'

'Well let me be the judge of that.'

Harris rubbed his hands against his cheeks, as though the motion would erode some of his weariness and fear. 'OK,' he whispered. 'All right, you win.' But he would not look at Carrera.

'Kris and I were going to be married. It was summer, the beginning of the sixties, and it seemed like a good time. We'd both just graduated from the High School of Performing Arts, and we'd got part-time jobs in one of the big restaurants on Fifth. I was a waiter, she was a waitress; we worked the evening shift. That night . . . we knocked off around one and headed for my apartment on 94th. We took a short cut across the Park – it was supposed to be safe in those days. And then *they* showed up.'

His face began to cloud.

'Remember those street gangs we used to have?'

Carrera nodded. He had pounded a beat in the South Bronx from '54 through to '57. He remembered the street gangs only too well.

'There were six of them, way off their turf. God knows what they were doing there! They were all drunk or stoned on something, and they began to chase us. We ran, of course, and I thought Kris was right beside me till I heard them laugh. She'd fallen over. She was wearing those damn stupid little stiletto heels and she'd been too scared to take them off. I stopped and I looked back and . . . they were all around her.' His hands covered his eyes, concealing far more than mere tears. 'I looked at them. They were huge. They were all armed. And I didn't know what to do. A guy's supposed to defend his girl, right? A guy's supposed to risk everything for someone he loves. It *says* so in every book and movie that you've ever read or seen. And yet to go back into that mob was to die. And I . . . didn't . . . want . . . to die.'

His words had become long, husking sobs by now, barely coherent at all. Carrera sat there waiting, eyes like frosted glass, till the man had calmed down.

'I ran,' Harris told him. 'Don't ask me where, just anywhere away from there. I was so ashamed and confused I didn't even try to get help. I must have passed a squad car, God knows how many phone boxes. But I just ran, and kept on running. I huddled in an alley until dawn, and then I pulled together enough courage to go to my folks' home. They'd been looking for me, frantic. The cops had been dredging the lake for me. When I told them where I'd been . . . the looks on their faces . . .

'I went down to the morgue. I wanted to see her one last time. The gang . . . when they'd finished with her, they tore her apart like wild animals. They used knives, bike chains, broken bottles, even their hands. There was hardly any of her left. Her family was there. God, it was *terrible*!'

A long while later, when he had finished rocking back and forth, finished clutching himself, finished crying, Carrera said: 'Mr Harris, nobody would blame you for backing off, for not getting yourself killed too.'

'But I could have got help. I could have saved her if I'd only called the cops. I didn't even *try*, don't you understand?'

'OK, you made a big mistake. We're all entitled to one.'

'Even if it costs another life? Tell me, what kind of man just runs away and lets another human die? What kind of person does that and retains the right to live?'

'A lot of people do it these days, Mr Harris.'

'That makes it *better*? Cowardice by popular consent?'

'Perhaps that's the way we've all become.' Carrera was still toying with his notebook. 'I still don't understand. What's all this got to do with the killings?'

From somewhere in that room, Harris could hear the laughter. From somewhere in the room, Harris could feel that breeze. Sodium lamps twinkled at the periphery of his vision. Limbo land. Streets of the city. The Lieutenant could not hear or feel or see it, and Harris knew that he would never understand.

'I keep seeing her.'

'The girl? Kris?'

Harris nodded. 'She appears to me, in visions, dreams. She's been dead twenty-one years, and yet she's still out there somewhere. I sound crazy, don't I?'

'That's not for me to say,' Carrera replied, standing up. 'Have a drink and get some sleep. I'd be a little crazy too.'

'You aren't going to . . .'

'I'll check out the girl's family. That might give us a lead. But I deal in reality, Mr Harris, not in dreams.'

When he was gone, Harris crossed to his window and gazed down on Lexington. The streetlamps were hard at work down there, weaving their bright glow into the folds of night. But the light that they cast was not nearly enough.

It was in the papers the next morning. Lieutenant James Carrera, who only dealt in reality, had stopped a battered black Chevvy on a routine investigation, walked round to the driver's door and asked the kid inside to show his licence. The kid had reached into the glove compartment, pulled out a Saturday Night Special and with two shots blown the Lieutenant's brains out through the back of his skull.

When questioned later, the kid claimed he had heard a woman's voice telling him to do it, the voice of a young girl.

That had been the morning Harris was due to take Patty up to 47th Street to buy the ring. He had promised to pick her up at nine and when, by nine thirty, he had not moved from his room, she phoned him. He let it ring twelve, fifteen times before picking it up.

'Marsh, where *are* you? I've been sitting here for ages.'

His jaw moved, but he could not answer her.

'Marsh, are you all right?'

'One of the kids got killed yesterday,' he said. 'One of my actors.'

'Oh, no!'

'The cop who questioned me, he got killed too. That's four dead, all because of me.'

'Because of . . . what on earth are you talking about?'

He told her about Kris, about that summer from his long dead youth. Every lousy detail, to the last bright drop of blood, and he hoped that she forgave him. She sounded shocked and slightly stunned, but not less loving for all that. Then he told her about the visions and the dreams.

'Marsh, that can't be.'

'Can't, but is. Call it a ghost, call it a psychic manifestation of my guilt, call it anything, but it's *real*, and it's out to get me.'

'Stop talking like that. That's insane.'

Harris almost grinned. Like a torture victim does, in that rictus of a smile when the whips and the branding irons break through the wall that marks the outer limit of pure human pain. 'You want insane, I'll give you insane. Tell me, Patty. What's the one thing worse than dying?'

There was something wrong with the line, as if it had been crossed. A sound like a breeze blowing, a noise like someone laughing in the void.

'Nothing's worse than dying, Marsh.' She honestly believed that or she would have given up on her job long ago.

'You're wrong, so wrong. There is one thing. It's to live while everybody else dies. It's to be the immune carrier of some fatal disease. To stand back and watch while everyone you love, everyone you care for, everyone you talk to or open to or touch is cut to shreds, and then to have to live on with the memory of that. To know that it's your fault. To know there's nothing you can do, because you had your chance long ago and you blew it. She's worked it out well, Patty. She's had twenty-one long years.'

She seemed to be considering that, seemed to half-believe it. 'But even if it *is* true,' she said, 'why wait till now? Why wait so very long?'

It was the single thing he did not understand. It did not fit. He had been pondering the question since he had read about Carrera, and the answer would not come . . .

Until that moment. When he listened to her voice over the line, and heard the noise of laughter and of wind, and knew. Suddenly *knew*! Twenty-one years he had stumbled through life, setting up a noble pose, trying to forget. And, in all that time he had never found another girl like Kris, a woman he could love. Until he had met Patty. They were due to be married in a few weeks, just as he and Kris . . . The terror in him mounted to a fever point.

'Patty! Get off the phone!'

'I can't hear you! The line—!'

'Don't call me, don't try to see me, ever again! Forget about me, please!'

'I don't understand. Marsh, I'm coming round there, now!'

'I won't be here! I'm going where you'll never find me! Stay away, don't even *try*!'

She was crying, hurt and lost. God, if she only knew how small a pain that was.

'This is ridiculous, Marsh. I—' And she stopped dead. 'Hold on will you, please? There's someone pounding on the door.'

'*No*!'

The wind on the line caught his scream and hurled it back at him. He knew she had not heard it.

'Patty, don't answer it! Stay away from there!'

But there was no reply. She had already gone.

He heard the latch click back, heard it with such terrifying clarity he knew more than the phone had picked it up. As though the sound were being relayed through a void. He heard Patty begin to speak, then heard the first word muffled as something like a leather glove was pressed against her mouth. There was the scuffle of someone pushing somebody else backwards, and then the noise of the door shutting. The thump of her body against the rug. The sudden rip of cloth. A scream that never quite made it beyond her covered mouth.

Get help!

Call the police!

Harris hammered at the phone and nothing happened. *She* had called *him*. He could not clear the line.

There was a phone box in the lobby. It would take him two minutes to run there, many more minutes for the police to arrive. Too late. Twenty-one years too late. He'd had his chance; he would not get another.

And he sat, listening, transfixed. The assault was over. He could hear the knife go in for the first time, of many.

It was a century later when he heard the thud of sneakers, the reopening and the quick closing of the door. He was still as stone and bled completely dry. His eyeballs burned for lack of moisture.

Patty, somehow, was still breathing, making ragged, frothing sounds that had no human origin. He could hear her dragging herself across the rug to the phone, moving in short, seal-like flops as one of her crippled children might move. It took her a very long while.

'Pa–tty.'

'Marsh...' Her voice was no more than a graveyard whisper. 'Marsh. Help ... me...'

The breeze came back, far stronger than before. It blew until it was a howling gale that deafened Harris, echoed through his room. And then, abruptly, it was gone. The line went very dead.

Marshall Harris sprang to his feet, bolted for the door and ran. Through the lobby, ignoring the doorman and the porter and the clerk. Down Lexington, east on 23rd. Running, running, just as he had run on that summer so long ago, not knowing where he was running, just anywhere, away. He dodged and ducked, trying desperately to avoid contact with any other person.

But there were crowds. He collided with a middle-aged executive, and saw a garishly painted Olds draw up beside the man and two young hoods step swaggeringly out. He brushed against an old woman walking into her apartment building, and saw a tall Black junkie draw a straight razor and follow her inside. There was no place to run, no place to ever hide.

The streets of the city were awash with blood.

KECKSIES

MARJORIE BOWEN

Two young esquires were riding from Canterbury, jolly and drunk, they shouted and trolled, and rolled in their saddles as they followed the winding road across the downs.

A dim sky was overhead and shut in the wide expanse of open country that one side stretched to the sea and the other to the Kentish Weald.

The primroses grew in thick posies in the ditches, the hedges were full of fresh hawthorn green, the new grey leaves of eglantine and honeysuckle, the long boughs of ash with the hard black buds, the wand-like shoots of sallow willow hung with catkins and the smaller red tassels of the nut and birch. Little the two young men heeded of any of these things, for they were in their own country that was thrice familiar; but Nick Bateup blinked across to the distant purple hills and cursed the gathering rain.

'Ten miles more of the open,' he muttered, 'and a great storm blackening upon us.'

Young Crediton, who was more full of wine, laughed drowsily. 'We'll lie at a cottage on the way, Nick – think you I've never a tenant who'll let me share board and bed?' He maundered into singing:

'There's a light in the old mill
Where the witch weaves her charms,
But dark is the chamber
Where you sleep in my arms.
Now come you by magic, by trick, or by spell
I have you and hold you,
And love you right well!'

The clouds overtook them like an advancing army; the wayside green looked vivid under the purple threat of the heavens and the birds were all still and silent.

'Split me if I'll be soaked,' muttered young Bateup. 'Knock up one of these boors of thine, Ned – but damn me if I see as much as hut or barn.'

'We come to Banells farm soon – or have we passed it?' answered the other confusedly. 'What's the pother? A bold bird as thou art and scared of a drop of rain?'

'My lungs are not as lusty as thine,' replied Bateup, who was indeed of a delicate build and more carefully dressed in greatcoat and muffler.

'But thy throat is as wide!' laughed Crediton. 'And God help you, you are shawled like an old woman – and as drunk as a Spanish parrot.

'Tra la la, my sweeting,
Tra la la, my May,
If now I miss the meeting
I'll come some other day.'

His companion took no notice of this nonsense, but with as much keenness as his muddled faculties would allow, was looking out for some shelter, for he retained sufficient perception to able him to mark the violence of the approaching storm and the loneliness of the vast stretch of country where the only human habitations appeared to be some few poor cottages far distant in the fields.

Ned lost his good humour and as the first drops of stinging cold rain began to fall, he cursed freely, using the terms common to the pot-houses where he had intoxicated himself on the way from Canterbury.

Urging their tired horses, they came onto the top of the little hill they ascended; immediately before them was the silver ashen skeleton of a blasted oak, polished like worn bone, standing over a small pool of stagnant water (for there had been little rain and much east wind), where a few shivering ewes crouched together from the oncoming storm.

Just beyond this, rising out of the bare field, was a humble cottage of black timber and white plaster and a deep thatched roof. For the rest of the crest of the hill was covered by a hazel copse and then dipped lonely again to the clouded lower levels that now began to slope into the marsh.

'This will shelter us, Ned,' cried Bateup.

''Tis a foul place and the boors have a foul reputation,' objected the lord of the manor. 'There are those who swear to seeing the devil's own fizz leer from Goody Boyle's windows – but anything to please thee and thy weak chest.'

They staggered from their horses, knocked open the rotting gate, and leading the beasts across the hard dry grazing field, knocked with their whips at the tiny door of the cottage.

The grey sheep under the grey tree looked at them and bleated faintly; the rain began to fall like straight yet broken darts out of the sombre clouds.

The door was opened by a woman very neatly dressed, with large scrubbed hands, who looked at them with fear and displeasure; for if her reputation was bad, theirs was no better. The lord of the manor was a known roisterer and wild liver who spent his idleness in rakish expeditions with Sir Nicholas Bateup from Bodiam, who was easily squandering a fine property. Neither was believed to be free of bloodshed, and as for honour they were as stripped of that as the blasted tree by the lonely pool was stripped of leaves.

Besides they were both now, as usual, drunk.

'We want shelter, Goody Boyle,' cried Crediton, pushing his way in as he threw her his reins. 'Get the horses into the barn.'

The woman could not deny the man, who could make her homeless in a second; she shouted hoarsely an inarticulate name and a loutish boy came and took the horses, while the two young men stumbled into the cottage, which they filled and dwarfed with their splendour.

Edward Crediton had been a fine young man, and though he was marred with insolence and excess, he still made a magnificent appearance, with his full, blunt features, his warm colouring, the fair hair rolled and curled, and all his bravery of blue broad-cloth, buckskin breeches, foreign lace, top boots, French sword, and gold rings and watch-chains.

Sir Nicholas Bateup was darker and more effeminate, having a cast of weakness in his constitution that betrayed itself in his face; but his dress was splendid to the point of foppishness and his manners even more arrogant and imposing.

Of the two he had the more evil repute; he was unwed and, therefore, there was no check upon his mischief; whereas Crediton had a young wife, whom he loved after his fashion and who checked some of his doings and softened others, and stayed very faithful to him and adored him still after five years of a wretched marriage, as is the manner of some women.

The rain came down with slashing severity; the little cottage panes were blotted with water.

Goody Boyle put logs on the fire and urged them with the bellows. It was a gaunt white room with nothing in it but a few wooden stools, a table, and an eel-catcher's prong.

On the table were large, fair, wax candles.

'What are these for, Goody?' asked Crediton.

'For the dead, sir.'

'You've dead in the house?' cried Sir Nicholas, who was leaning by the fireplace and warming his hands. 'What do you want with dead men in the house, you trollop?'

'It is no dead of mine, my lord,' answered the woman with evil civility, 'but one who took shelter here and died.'

'A curse, witch!' roared Crediton. 'You hear that, Nick? Came here – died. And now you'll put spells on us, you ugly slut—'

'No spells of mine,' answered the woman quietly, rubbing her large clean hands together. 'He had been long ailing and died here of an ague.'

'And who sent the ague?' asked Crediton with drunken gravity. 'And who sent him here?'

'Perhaps the same hand that sent us,' laughed Sir Nicholas. 'Where is your corpse, Goody?'

'In the next room – I have but two.'

'And two too many – you need but a bundle of faggots and a tuft of tow to light it – an arrant witch, a confest witch,' muttered Crediton; he staggered up from the stool. 'Where is your corpse? I've a mind to see if he looks as if he died a natural death.'

'Will you not ask first who it is?' asked the woman, unlatching the inner door.

'Why should I care?'

'Who is it?' asked Sir Nicholas, who had the clearer wits, drunk or sober.

'Robert Horne,' said Goody Boyle.

Ned Crediton looked at her with the eyes of a sober man.

'Robert Horne,' said Sir Nicholas. 'So he is dead at last – your wife will be glad of that, Ned.'

Crediton gave a sullen laugh. 'I'd broken him – she wasn't afraid any longer of a lost wretch cast out to die of ague on the marsh.'

But Sir Nicholas had heard differently; he had been told, even by Ned himself, how Anne Crediton shivered before the terror of Robert Horne's pursuit, and would wake up in the dark crying out for fear of him like a lost child; for he had wooed her before her marriage and persisted in loving her afterwards with mad boldness and insolent confidence, so that justice had been set on him and he had been banished to the marsh, a ruined man.

'Well, sirs,' said Goody Boyle in her thin voice, that had the pinched accents of other parts, 'my lady can sleep of nights now – Robert Horne will never disturb her again.'

'Do you think he ever troubled us?' asked Crediton with a coarse oath. 'I flung him out like an adder that had writhed across the threshold—'

'A wonder he did not put a murrain on thee, Ned. He had fearful ways and a deep knowledge of unholy things.'

'A warlock – God help us!' added the woman.

'The devil's proved an ill master then,' laughed Crediton. 'He could not help Robert Horne into Anne's favour – nor prevent him lying in a cold bed in the flower of his age.'

'The devil,' smiled Sir Nicholas, 'was over busy, Ned, helping *you* to the lady's favour and a warm bed. You were the dearer disciple.'

'Oh, good lords, will you talk less wildly with a lost man's corpse in the house and his soul riding the storm without?' begged Goody Boyle; and she latched again the inner door.

Murk filled the cottage now; waves of shadow flowed over the landscape; without the rain blotted the window and drowned the valley; in the bitter field the melancholy ewes huddled beneath the blasted oak beside the bare pool, the stagnant surface of which was now broken by the quick rain drops; a low thunder grumbled from the horizon and all the young greenery looked livid in the ghastly light of heaven.

'I'll see him,' said Ned Crediton swaggering. 'I'll look at this gay gallant in his last smock – so that I can swear to Anne he has taken his amorous smile to the earthworms – surely.'

'Look as you like,' answered Sir Nicholas, 'glut your eyes with looking—'

'But you'll remember, sirs, that he was a queer man and died queerly, and there was no parson or priest to take the edge off his going or challenge the fiends who stood at his head and feet.'

'Saw you the fiends?' asked Ned curiously.

'Question not what I saw,' muttered the woman. 'You'll have your own familiars, Esquire Crediton.'

She unlatched the inner door again and Ned passed in, bowing low on the threshold.

'Good day, Robert Horne,' he jeered. 'We parted in anger; but my debts are paid now and I greet you well.'

The dead man lay on a pallet bed with a coarse white sheet over him that showed his shape but roughly; the window was by his head and looked blankly onto the rain-bitten fields and dismal sky; the light was cold and colourless on the white sheet and the miserable room.

Sir Nicholas lounged in the doorway; he feared no death but his own, and that he set so far away it was but a dim dread.

'Look and see if it is Robert Horne,' he urged, 'or if the beldame lies.'

And Crediton turned down the sheet. ''Tis Robert Horne,' he said.

The dead man had his chin uptilted, his features sharp and horrible in the setting of the spilled hair on the coarse pillow. Ned Crediton triumphed over him, making lewd jests of love and death and sneering at this great gallant who had been crazed for love and driven by desire, and who now lay impotent.

And Sir Nicholas in the doorway listened and laughed and had his own wicked jeers to add; for both of them had hated Robert Horne as a man who had defied them.

But Goody Boyle stole away with her fingers in her ears.

When these two were weary of their insults they replaced the flap of the sheet over the dead face and returned to the outer room. And Ned asked for drink, declaring that Goody Boyle was a known smuggler and had cellars of rare stuff.

So the lout brought up glasses of cognac and a bottle of French wine, and these two drank grossly, sitting over the fire; and Goody Boyle made excuse for the drink by saying that Robert Horne had given her two gold pieces before he died (not thin pared coins, but thick and heavy) for his funeral and the entertainment of those who should come to his burying.

'What mourners could he hope for?' laughed Ned Crediton. 'The crow and the spider and the death-watch beetle?'

But Goody Boyle told them that Robert Horne had made friends while he had lived an outcast on the marshes; they were no doubt queer and even monstrous people, but they were coming tonight to sit with Robert Horne before he was put in the ground.

'And who, Goody, have warned this devil's congregation of the death of Robert Horne?' asked Sir Nicholas.

She answered him – that Robert Horne was not ill an hour or a day, but for a long space struggled with fits of marsh fever, and in between these bouts of the ague he went abroad like a well man and his friends would come up and see him, and the messenger who came up to enquire after him was Tora, the Egyptian girl who walked with her bosom full of violets.

The storm was in full fury now, muttering low and sullen round the cottage with great power of beating rain.

'Robert Horne was slow in dying,' said Sir Nicholas. 'Of what did he speak in those days?'

'Of a woman, good sir.'

'Of my wife!' cried Ned.

Goody Boyle shook her head with a look of stupidity. 'I know nothing of that. Though for certain he called her Anne, sweet Anne, and swore he would possess her yet – in so many words and very roundly.'

'But he died baulked,' said Ned, swaying on his stool, 'and he'll rot outside holy ground.'

'They'll lay him in Deadman's Field, which is full of old bones none can plough and no sheep will graze,' answered the woman; 'and I must set out to see lame Jonas, who promised to have the grave ready – but maybe the rain has hindered him.'

She looked at them shrewdly as she added: 'That is, gentles, if you care to remain alone with the body of Robert Horne.'

'I think of him as a dead dog,' replied Ned Crediton.

And when the woman had gone, he, being loosened with the French brandy, suggested a gross jest.

'Why should Robert Horne have all this honour, even from

rogues and Egyptians? Let us fool them – throwing his corpse out into the byre, and I will lie under the sheet and presently sit up and fright them all with the thought it is the devil!'

Sir Nicholas warmly cheered this proposal and they lurched into the inner chamber, which was dark enough now by reason of a great northern cloud that blocked the light from the window.

They pulled the sheet off Robert Horne and found him wrapped in another that was furled up under his chin, and so they carried him to the back door and peered through the storm for some secret place where they might throw him.

And Ned Crediton saw a dark bed of rank hemlock and cried, 'Cast him into the kecksies!' that being the rustic name for the weed.

So they flung the dead man into the hemlocks, which were scarce high enough to cover him, and to hide the whiteness of the sheet, broke off boughs from the hazel copse and put over him, and went back laughing to the cottage, and there kept a watch out from the front window, and when they saw Goody Boyle toiling along through the rain, Ned took off his hat and coat and sword and folded them away under the bed; then Sir Nicholas wrapped him in the under sheet, so that he was shrouded to the chin, and he lay on the pillow and drew the other sheet over him.

'If thou sleepst, do not snore,' said Nicholas, and went back to the fire and lit his long clay full of Virginian tobacco.

When Goody Boyle entered with her wet shawl over her head, she had two ragged creatures behind her who stared malevolently at the fine gentleman with his fine clothes and dark curls lolling by the fire and watching the smoke rings rise from his pipe.

'Esquire Crediton has ridden for home,' he said, 'but I am not minded to risk the ague.'

And he sipped more brandy and laughed at them, and they, muttering, for they knew his fame, went into the death chamber and crouched round the couch where Sir Nicholas had just laid Ned Crediton under the sheet.

And presently others came up, Egyptians, eel-catchers and the like, outcasts and vagrants who crept in to watch by the corpse.

Sir Nicholas presently rolled after them to see the horror and shriekings for grace there would be when the dead man threw aside his shroud and sat up.

But the vigil went on till the night closed in and the two wax candles were lit, and still Ned Crediton gave no sign, nor did he snore or heave beneath the sheet; and Sir Nicholas became impatient, for the rain was over and he was weary of the foul air and the grotesque company.

'The fool,' he thought (for he kept his wits well even in his cups), 'has gone into a drunken sleep and forgot the joke.'

So he pushed his way to the bed and turned down the sheet, whispering, 'This jest will grow stale with keeping.'

But the words withered on his lips, for he looked into the face of a dead man. At the cry he gave they all came babbling about him and he told them of the trick that had been put upon them.

'But there's devil's work here,' he ended. 'For here is the body back again – or else Ned Crediton dead and frozen into the likeness of the other.' And he flung the sheet end quickly over the pinched face and fair hair.

'And what did ye do with Robert Horne, outrageous dare-fiend that ye be?' demanded an old vagrant.

And the young lord passed the ill words and answered with whitened lips: 'We cast him into yon bed of kecksies.'

And they all beat out into the night, the lout with a lantern.

And there was nothing at all in the bed of kecksies . . . and Ned Crediton's horse was gone from the stable.

'He was drunk,' said Sir Nicholas, 'and forgot the part – and fled that moment I was in the outer room.'

'And in that minute did he carry Robert Horne in alone and wrap him up so neatly?' queried Goody Boyle.

'We'll go in,' said another hag, 'and strip the body and see which man it be—'

But Sir Nicholas was in the saddle.

'Let be,' he cried wildly; 'there's been gruesome work enough for tonight – it's Robert Horne you have there – let be. I'll back to Crediton Manor—'

And he rode his horse out of the field, then more quickly down the darkling road, for the fumes of the brandy were out of his brain and he saw clearly and dreaded many things. At the cross-roads when the ghastly moon had suddenly struck free of the retreating clouds he saw Ned Crediton ahead of him riding sharply, and he called out:

'Eh, Ned, what have you made of this jest? This way it is but a mangled folly.'

'What matter now for the jest or earnest?' answered the other. 'I ride home at last.'

Sir Nicholas kept pace with him; he was hatless and wore a shabby cloak that was twisted about him with the wind of his riding.

'Why did not you take your own garments?' asked Sir Nicholas. 'Belike that rag you've snatched up belonged to Robert Horne—'

'If Crediton could steal his shroud, he can steal his cloak,' replied Ned, and his companion said no more, thinking him wrought into a frenzy with the brandy and the evil nature of the joke.

The moon shone clear and cold with a faint stain like old blood in the halo, and the trees, bending in a seaward wind, cast the recent rain that loaded them heavily to the ground as the two rode into the gates of Crediton Manor.

The hour was later than even Sir Nicholas knew (time had been blurred for him since the coming of the storm) and there was no light save a dim lamp in an upper window.

Ned Crediton dropped out of the saddle, not waiting for the mounting-block, and rang the iron bell till it clattered through the house like a madman's fury.

'Why, Ned, why this panic home-coming?' asked Sir Nicholas; but the other answered him not, but rang again.

There were footsteps within and the rattle of chains, and a voice asked from the side window.

'Who goes there?'

And Ned Crediton dragged at the bell and screamed: 'I! The master!'

The door was opened and an old servant stood there, pale in his bedgown.

Ned Crediton passed him and stood by the newel-post, like a man spent yet alert.

'Send someone for the horses,' said Nick Bateup, 'for your master is crazy drunk. I tell you Mathews, he has seen Robert Horne dead tonight—'

Crediton laughed: the long rays of the lamplight showed him pale, haggard, distorted, with tumbled fair hair and a torn shirt under the mantle, and at his wrist a ragged bunch of hemlock thrust into his sash.

'A posy of kecksies for Anne,' he said. The sleepy servants who were already up began to come into the hall, and looked at him with dismay.

'I'll lie here tonight,' said Sir Nicholas; 'bring me lights into the parlour. I've no mind to sleep.'

He took off his hat and fingered his sword and glanced uneasily at the figure by the newel-post with the posy of kecksies.

Another figure appeared at the head of the stairs. Anne Crediton holding her candle, wearing a grey lute-string robe and a lace cap with long ribbons that hung on to her bosom; she peered over the baluster and some of the hot wax from her taper fell onto the oak treads.

'I've a beau pot for you, Anne,' said Crediton, looking up and holding out the hemlocks. 'I've long been dispossessed, Anne, but I've come home at last.'

She drew back without a word and her light flickered away across the landing; Crediton went up after her and they heard a door shut.

In the parlour the embers had been blown to flames and fresh logs put on, and Sir Nicholas warmed his cold hands and told old Mathews, in a sober manner for him, the story of the jest they had striven to put on Goody Boyle and the queer monstrous people from the marsh and the monstrous ending of it, and the strangeness of Ned Crediton; it was not his usual humour to discourse with servants or to discuss his vagrant debaucheries with any, but tonight he seemed to need company and endeavoured to retain the old man, who was not reluctant to stay, though usually he hated to see the dark face and bright clothes of Nick Bateup before the hearth of Crediton Manor.

And as these two talked disconnectedly, as if they would fill the gap of any silence that might fall in the quiet house, there came the wail of a woman, desperate yet sunken.

'It is Mistress Crediton,' said Mathews with a downcast look.

'He ill uses her?'

'God help us, he will use buckles and straps to her, Sir Nicholas.'

A quivering shriek came brokenly down the stairs and seemed to form the word 'mercy'.

Sir Nicholas was an evil man who died unrepentant, but he was not of a temper to relish raw cruelty or crude brutalities to women; he would break their souls but never their bodies. So he went to the door and listened, and old Mathews had never liked him so well as now when he saw the look on the thin, dark face.

For the third time she shrieked and they marvelled that any human being could hold her breath so long; yet it was muffled as if someone held a hand over her mouth.

The sweat stood on the old man's forehead.

'I've never before known her complain, sir,' he whispered. 'She is a very dog to her lord and takes her whip mutely—'

'I know, I know – she adores his hand when it caresses or when it strikes; but tonight, if I know anything of a woman's accents, that is a note of abhorrence—'

He ran up the stairs, the old man panting after him with the snatched-up lantern.

'Which is her chamber?'

'Here, Sir Nicholas.'

The young man struck on the heavy oak panels with the hilt of his sword.

'Madam – Madam Crediton, why are you so ill at ease?'

She moaned from within.

'Open to me. I'll call some of your women – come out—'

Their blood curdled to hear her wails.

'Damn you to hell,' cried Sir Nicholas in a fury. 'Come out, Ned Crediton, or I'll have the door down and run you through.'

The answer was a little break of maniac laughter.

'She has run mad or he,' cried Mathews, backing from the room. 'And surely there is another clamour at the door—'

Again the bell clanged and there were voices and tumult at the door; Mathews went and opened, and Sir Nicholas, looking down the stairs, saw in the moonlight a dirty farm cart, a sweating horse, and some of the patched and rusty crew who had been keeping vigil in Goody Boyle's cottage.

'We've brought Esquire Crediton home,' said one; and the others lifted a body from the cart and carried it through the murky moonlight.

Sir Nicholas came downstairs, for old Mathews could do nothing but cry for mercy.

'It was Edward Crediton,' repeated the eel-catcher, shuffling into the hall, 'clothed all but his coat and hat, and that was under the bed – there be his watches and chains, his seals and the papers in his pockets – and for his visage now, there is no mistaking it.'

They had laid the body on the table where it had so often sat and larked and ate and drunk and cursed; Sir Nicholas gazed, holding up the lantern.

Edward Crediton – never any doubt of that now, though his face was distorted as by the anguish of a sudden and ugly death.

'We never found Robert Horne,' muttered one of the mourners, trailing his foul muddy rags nearer the fire and thrusting his crooked hands to the blaze.

Mathews fell on his knees and tried to pray, but could think of no words.

'Who is upstairs?' demanded Sir Nicholas in a terrible voice. 'Who is with that wretched woman?'

And he stared at the body of her husband.

Mathews, who had loved her as a little child, began gibbering and moaning.

'Did he not say he'd have her? And did not yon fool change places with him? Oh God, oh God, and has he not come to take his place—'

'But Robert Horne was *dead*. I saw him dead,' stammered Sir Nicholas, and set the lantern down, for his hand shook so the flame waved in gusts.

'Eh,' shrieked old Mathews, grovelling on his hands and knees in his bedgown. 'Might not the devil have lent his body back for his own pitchy purposes?'

They looked at him a little, seeing he was suddenly crazed; then Sir Nicholas ran up the stairs with the others at his heels and thundered with his sword, and kicked and shouted outside Anne Crediton's chamber door.

All the foul, muddy, earthy crew cowered on the stairs and chittered together, and in the parlour before the embers old Mathews crouched and huddled and whimpered.

The bedroom door opened and Robert Horne came out and stood

and smiled at them, and the young man in his fury fell back and his sword rattled from his hand to the floor.

Robert Horne was a white death, nude to the waist and from there swathed in grave clothes; under the tattered dark cloak he had ridden in was his shroud knotted round his neck; his naked chest gleamed with ghastly dews, and under the waxen polish of his sunken face the decayed blood showed in discoloured patches; he went down the stairs and they hid their faces while his foul whiteness passed.

Sir Nicholas stumbled into the bedchamber. The moonlight showed Anne Crediton tumbled on the bed, dead and staring, with the posy of kecksies on her bare breast and her mouth hung open and her hands clutching at the curtains.

The mourners rode back and picked up Robert Horne's body whence it had returned to the kecksie patch and buried it in unholy ground with great respect, *as one to whom the devil had given his great desire.*

ABOVE AND BEYOND

CHARLES BRAMELD

You don't normally think of ghosts in connection with modern, high-rise blocks of flats, do you? Mention ghosts and, virtually automatically, you call to mind castles, Tudor manor houses and the like; ancient buildings where someone who was murdered years ago comes back to haunt the place; not tall, modern structures made in concrete, steel and glass. Yet Fullingford Court had its ghost even before its first human occupants took up their tenancies. Well, it did according to Mrs Stellintini, anyway. I remember in detail the occasion when mention of a ghost there first came to public notice, over seven years ago.

The tower block wasn't even finished and builder's workers still seemed to be everywhere: electricians fitting lights, plumbers fitting pipes, carpenters, odd-job men and plenty of others. Nevertheless, Helthingham Council had already begun to allocate the flats, and the first fifty families were being shown round. I imagine the idea was to persuade them there were delights in store that they had never dreamed of. Councillor Fullingford himself, Chairman of the Housing Committee, was acting as chief guide. And proud of it he was too. After all, his name now graced a brand-new bronze plaque alongside the main entrance. FULLINGFORD COURT, it announced to all who cared to look.

'Look at that view,' said Councillor Fullingford. He was in the living room of one of the topmost flats on the fifteenth floor. 'You'd have to pay the earth for a penthouse flat like this in London. And eight local families will have one for a standard council rent.'

'Is it true that your son and his wife are allocated one of these top flats?' Among the thirty or so people who had crowded into the room with him it wasn't clear to me who had yelled out the question. It didn't matter much anyway since Councillor Fullingford, somehow, didn't seem to have heard.

There was no doubt, though, who it was that yelled out next. 'Excuse me, Councillor,' called Mrs Stellintini. There was no way anybody could pretend not to hear Mrs Stellintini when she intended to be heard. 'Excuse me. I'd like one of these top flats. The flat they've given me's on the fourteenth floor. Can you tell me how to go about getting a swap for one on this top level?'

'Oo, no, no! You can't do that. No! I mean, where should we be if everybody wanted to be changing about all the time? We can't plan things that way. And after all, these flats have been allocated fairly. We drew lots, we did. No, it's just not on.'

There was a sudden hush and thirty-odd heads turned to see how Mrs Stellintini reacted. Most of the families who were due to be moved in came from Jubilee Street and Paradise Row, which had long been ready for demolition, and mostly they knew each other. And better than anything, they knew Mrs Stellintini! They watched her closely, eyes already lit up with amused expectancy.

And Mrs Stellintini didn't disappoint them. She pursed her lips angrily, scowled, then suddenly looked round with an expression of perplexity, fear even. She hunched her shoulders and shivered visibly.

'Oh my goodness,' she said. 'Oh dearie me! Did you feel that? I've known there was something wrong up here. I knew it the minute we reached this top floor, but I couldn't quite put my finger on it. But now I've got it! Oh yes, I've got it now . . . There's a presence here! That's what it is! There's a spirit floating in the air. Can you feel it? It's stronger in here than it was out on the landing.'

As you might guess, this caused a wide stir of amusement, grins on many faces, one or two open guffaws. After all, it was so blatant, so manifest that Mrs S was putting it on. Obviously she was hoping to scare somebody, somebody booked for a top flat, to do a swap with her for her own new flat, one storey lower.

Well, there were no takers. Mrs Peasegood, a widow, was in the crush, squeezed in between George Cousins and his wife. I was close by and heard what she said.

'I've been given a key for one of these top flats, Mary,' she whispered to Mrs Cousins, 'but Martha Stellintini's not getting her hands on it. She can whistle for it, she can. I'm sticking to it.'

Looking back on that occasion, you might argue that she'd made a bad decision – indeed a fatal decision. Mrs Peasegood, you see, was the first victim, if victim's the word. But that wasn't until nine months later.

During those first few months, rumours about unnatural happenings kept springing up and being mentioned around, but in most cases they were quickly traced back to Mrs Stellintini and so nobody paid them much attention.

'Have you heard?' one woman would say to another as they waddled slowly up the thirteenth stairway carrying the inevitable plastic shopping bags. 'She's at it again. Telling everybody in the laundrette this morning that in the night she keeps hearing funny noises – creaks, groans, rattling chains. Straight up above her head, she says, on the fifteenth floor. But then, she caps it, the daft ha'porth, by asking if anybody on the top floor wants to swap flats with her. Who does she think she'll fool that way?'

The tale that gave me a little chuckle to myself was one I heard three men discussing over a smoke on one of the open landings.

'Heard the latest?' asked one. 'Mrs Stellintini's saying there's a grey-haired man keeps appearing around the top decks. He's not real, she says, but he's very distinguished-looking.'

'Wishful thinking, happen,' cackled one of the others.

'It seems she first saw him on the top landing,' the first went on. 'But he disappeared right before her eyes. She went up to him to ask who he was – she would, wouldn't she? But he melted into thin air in front of her. It's happened twice more since then, so she says.'

'Eh!' the third chap butted in, sounding more serious. 'I've heard of somebody else that that happened to. That ginger-haired woman on landing six. Perhaps there's something in it.'

'Go on, Ted! Start talking like that, you'll soon be as daft as they are.'

As I say, nobody heeded these tales. Not, that is, until Mrs Peasegood's sudden death. Nine months after Alice Peasegood declared she was sticking to her top flat, the merry widow proved conclusively she wasn't. She came crashing down from the fifteenth floor, over the landing rails and down to the concrete flags below. Death was instantaneous, of course.

Nobody could say for certain how it happened, although plenty were ready to air their guesses. The landing rail was reasonably high. Certainly it was possible to get over it, but to do that needed effort. It would be difficult, if not impossible, to fall over accidentally. And yet, in due course the verdict at the inquest was 'Accidental death.'

In the few days between the death and the funeral, rumour really got going.

'She told me she was a bit bothered,' related one of Mrs Peasegood's cronies. 'She's been hearing things in the night. Not chains and things like Mrs Stellintini. Just gentle sighs and moans, that's how she put it. But they bothered her.'

'Yes, I was there, wasn't I, Lil?' said another. 'And she'd tidied her shelves then gone down to do her shopping. And when she got back, some things on the shelves had been moved and a couple of china pieces were on the floor. Yet she'd left the door locked. And it was still locked when she got back.'

If the tales from Mrs Stellintini hadn't caused much of a ripple, these from Mrs Peasegood stirred up quite a swell. After all, Mrs Peasegood was dead, very, very dead. Within a week, I reckon every one of the hundred and twenty family units in Fullingford Court had heard of them. And seven different individuals claimed they'd seen the grey-haired man, the stranger who either disappeared before their eyes or turned a corner but was nowhere to be seen when they rounded the same corner seconds later.

Once Mrs Peasegood was lowered into the ground, the waves of gossip began to subside again, which is what you might expect, but they didn't disappear entirely. From then on, until Fullingford Court became completely untenanted, there was a wariness, an expression in the eye, to be noticed by anyone observant of the occupants of that tower block. I found that even I couldn't help noticing this whenever I saw any of them going up and down within the massive complex of flats.

The resident who changed most, but who, uncharacteristically, had nothing to say was Mrs Stellintini. After Mrs Peasegood's funeral, she was never again heard to refer to clanking chains, nor to the grey-haired man, not even to swapping flats.

But she didn't talk about much else, either. From being renowned as the biggest gossip in Helthingham, she became withdrawn and rarely spoke. Almost overnight, she looked older. Almost overnight, she changed from being a lively, middle-aged lady with slightly greying hair and a sense of humour to a morose old woman whose hair quickly turned snow-white.

The next really major incident at Fullingford Court was two and a half years after Mrs Peasegood's fatal fall. In between, there were occasional flurries of suppressed excitement when people claimed to have seen the ghost again, the grey-haired man with the ability to disappear at will. But, although the claims were now taken seriously, there was no enthusiasm for any open discussion of them.

It was the same with further instances of articles moving about of their own accord on shelves and ledges, and reports of noises in the night. Tales about such happenings were regularly being passed around, but the passing was never done openly. Incidents were whispered about, and that's all. It seemed to me that people hoped, perhaps, that a show of no interest might keep any manifestations to a minimum. Nevertheless, there was no lack of spreading rumour, spoken of in undertones and passed on in half-completed hints. The result was an even stronger atmosphere of something frightening below the surface.

The tempest came with the dreadful episode of the Briggs family. Again, nobody was sure how it happened. Afterwards, with the clarity of hindsight, everyone could explain that it was wrong from the start to put a woman whose husband had left her, and with young twin boys to look after, into a top-floor flat. But that was when experience all over the country was proving that high-rise flats are entirely the wrong places for young children to live in. In fairness, it should be remembered that when Mrs Briggs was given the tenancy everybody thought she was lucky, and plenty were jealous and would gladly have changed places into her penthouse flat with its magnificent views.

This time it began as a double tragedy. The two boys, Barry and Brian, four years old with Barry the older by fifty minutes, were found lying on the concrete flagstones a few paces from where Mrs Peasegood had died two years and more earlier. As far as anybody could tell, they must have been playing around and climbing on the railing. It was suggested that perhaps one had slipped, grabbed his brother, and that they both had crashed down together. But that was guessing again, and guessing wasn't going to change anything.

'Pity it had to be Mrs Stellintini who found them,' said one old dear on the stairways. 'State she's in, it could send her round the bend completely.' It was an easy forecast to make. It took only a fortnight for it to be proved correct.

The shock of it all was so massive that tongues started operating openly again. Opinion was voiced that the building and particularly its fifteenth floor were accursed. Tongues wagged in another direction too.

'She ought to have known better,' said Mrs Gardiner to four other ladies on the fourteenth landing. 'Fancy letting four-year-olds play out at that height. And only a railing to stop them falling. Asking for trouble!'

The twins' mother, Mrs Briggs, one landing higher, could hear every word, the stairwell acting as a natural ear trumpet.

Mrs Briggs herself put a speedy stop to such talk. Five days after the deaths of her sons, the day after their funeral, she followed the same route that they had taken and finished on the same patch of concrete paving. The double tragedy became a triple one and Fullingford Court had claimed its fourth life.

The deaths of the mother and her sons marked the beginning of the end of the tower block. Helthingham Council found it impossible to re-let the Briggs's top-floor flat, nor would anyone consider the tenancy on the fourteenth floor when Mrs Stellintini was taken away to spend the rest of her days in a hospital for the mentally ill.

From then on, the Council was under increasing pressure as one after another of over a hundred tenants pestered to be rehoused. Slowly, as months grew into years, some began to be moved out, and there was no question, no question whatever, of them being replaced by other families moving in.

At one stage, the Council called in experts who were able to explain that the tall block had actually been designed to sway slightly in the wind, and this oscillation could easily explain both the eerie sighing noises in the night and the slight drift of small, loose objects on smooth surfaces. This may have eased a few worries for some, but personally I doubt it. I reckon few occupants were ready to see things so rationally. The increasingly frantic requests for re-housing seemed to confirm my view. The powers-that-be eventually rationalized it all themselves by saying that high-rise flats were a mistake anyway, they'd all have to come down.

It took over four years after the Briggs's tragedy before Fullingford Court was finally emptied of its tenants, but this has at last been achieved. As a matter of fact, the last family of all moved out yesterday. Once their taxi set off to follow the removal van, they'd all gone, all the one hundred and twenty families who less than eight years earlier had moved with mixed feelings into the brand-new tower.

So now, you see . . . once again it's mine . . . all mine and mine alone. And that, really, you know, is how I like it. This is MY patch. Oh, yes, yes, they're going to pull it down, I know that. But that doesn't bother me. Not a bit. After all, I was here before they put it up . . . And after it's gone, I'll still be around.

THE CHAIR

RONALD CHETWYND-HAYES

The old man in the second-hand furniture shop had a pointed grey beard, a mass of white hair and spoke with a faint foreign accent.

'The chair came from a house with an unfortunate history.'

This tantilizing statement was further enhanced when the old fellow refused to elaborate further, but I dismissed it as nothing more than a rather unique sales gimmick, for who can resist buying an item of furniture with a mysterious past?

'The gentleman will note,' he said patting the winged-back, 'the brocade, which is so marvellously well-preserved; the claw feet; the graceful curve of the arms. It is indeed a bargain at eighty pounds.'

'Early eighteenth-century,' I murmured, determined to appear well-versed in antiquarian lore. 'Fifty pounds.'

He shrugged thin, bowed shoulders. 'The gentleman drives a hard bargain and as a sign of deep respect I will reduce the price to seventy pounds.'

We finally settled for sixty-five.

The chair looked well against the wall that faced the foot of my four-poster bed. I had only to raise my head from the velvet-covered pillow and there it was – a relic from some long-dead yesterday. The brocade – as the old man had said – was in an excellent state of preservation: its pattern of tiny pink roses only slightly faded, the silver background still gleaming with a satisfying sheen.

One more item.

My bedroom was now a haven carved out of the rock of time. Tudor bed, early Georgian wardrobe and dressing-table, Queen Anne cabinet, Jacobean commode – and now the chair. I was not certain of its age. Maybe Queen Anne; most likely the first George. Certainly not later. Now I could sleep and dream of ladies in long, flowing dresses and of gentlemen in black velvet doublets and crimson hose. The realm of what-might-have-been was so much more interesting than a world of roaring machines, rustling income-tax forms and flickering television screens. Yesterday the great walked with earth-shaking steps; today the small scamper across an asphalt desert and leave a trail of corruption in their wake.

I lay in my vast four-poster bed, monarch of a kingdom that was born when the Tudors strutted the corridors of Whitehall. In my hands was a facsimile of a newspaper dated August 28 1828. I experienced a thrill of delicious ecstasy while I read an account of the execution of William Corder – he of Red Barn fame. A mere hundred and fifty years ago, but a sufficiently long journey back along the eternal road to create a buffer of years between me and the age of mechanical confusion.

I turned a page. The paper acquired a crease – I shook it – lowered it – then raised it again. But the threefold action had been fatal to my peace of mind. For, as I had momentarily looked over the lowered newspaper, I had seen a woman seated in the chair. The tiny print became a jumbled mass of black lines, the paper trembled as I tried to dismiss that brief vision of a long white face and large dark eyes that had glittered – or maybe glared – from beneath slim, black brows.

I did not think that perhaps my faculties had become deranged, or toy with words – such as optical illusion, imagination and other like clichés. One does not practise self-deception under these circumstances, for the human eye and brain are loyal servants and rarely attempt to deceive their master.

No – from behind my frail barricade of paper I knew there was a strange woman seated in the chair and she had not entered through the doorway, or crawled from under the bed, or slid silently from the wardrobe – but had suddenly come into being. I lowered the newspaper inch by inch and gradually unveiled the face of truth.

She was so still. A study in black and white. Black hair, brows and dress; white face, hands and shoes. The long face might have been thought beautiful by those who like smooth unlined skin and thin red – so red – lips. I noticed that the hands – which lay one on each knee – were extraordinarily long; and on the left middle finger was a large stone, possibly a ruby, encased in a gold filigree setting.

We stared at each other; and her dark eyes did not blink, only glittered with a faintly mischievous gleam – or so it seemed to me, who sat upright, wrapped in the cold mantle of fear – and maybe there was a pale ghost of a smile twisting the thin red lips.

Then she raised her right hand and beckoned.

It was not an imperious gesture. Rather a coy invitation; a seductive bending of four fingers; a subtle command that it would be well to obey. But prolonged fear curdles and becomes anger. Suddenly I was yelling, mouthing obscenities, aware of a burning hatred for that seated figure, which did nothing more than beckon. My outstretched hand gripped a gilt bedside clock and I hurled it straight at the white face.

She vanished just before the clock crashed against the chair back.

I am a person who can come to terms with any situation.

I remember being interviewed by an Officer's Selection Board during the war, when a stupid old fool of a colonel asked me: 'What would you do if you met a battleship walking across a field?' I gave the only possible, positive answer: 'Find out why.'

It was not of course the answer they wanted. I was supposed to smile and say: 'Take more water with it,' or some such nonsense. But I still maintain that such a phenomenon would have aroused the curiosity of a reasonably intelligent man, once he had mastered his quite natural alarm. I believe there are only two basic laws in the universe – Cause and Effect. Let us take the case of the walking battleship. One must assume the vessel had acquired legs. Were they formed from metal or flesh and blood? The gentlemen on the selection board, for some reason best known to themselves, declined to answer this simple question, and in fact, refused to pursue the matter any further.

But if I had been supplied with this basic information, there is no doubt in my mind that I would have solved the mystery and so demonstrated my gift for dealing with any untoward contingency.

Thus, on the morning after my disconcerting experience, I first admonished myself for having given way to alarm and despondency, then set out to discover why a ghost should haunt a second-hand item of furniture.

I examined the chair most thoroughly. The upholstery was not stained in any way; there was no sign of damage, repair, recent French polishing on legs or visible woodwork – nothing in fact that might supply even an irrational explanation.

The seat, back and arms were well padded – with horsehair I imagined, and which appeared to have lost none of its resilience. A good solid chair with plenty of room to stretch out, curl up, sleep in, read in, do whatever-you-like-in; but certainly not intended to haunt in.

The physical examination of the chair – if I may be permitted the expression – was now complete, and for all the good it had done me, I might as well have gone for a long walk. I then passed on to a line of reasonable conjecture: Sometime during the past two hundred years, a woman with a beautiful, long, white face, had sat in the chair and saturated the upholstery with her personality. On occasion, someone tuned in on the right wave-length had recreated her image. Last night that person had been me and when I threw the clock, the line of contact had been broken. It was as simple as that.

I felt quite pleased with my reasoning powers and did a little dance round the room. Within the space of ten minutes I had solved a mystery that would have had a normal person gibbering in the fireplace, or smashing a valuable chair to pieces with an axe. 'Fear is the child of stupidy,' I shouted. 'Reason is the voice of sanity,' and rejoiced in a feeling of superiority over the brainless ants that crawl over the surface of this planet.

Then I stopped and stared at the chair with dilated eyes. Wait a minute! The woman had beckoned to me! But . . . but had she? Could she not have been beckoning to someone long dead? A mere re-enactment of a scene that had taken place in the dim past.

I breathed a deep sigh of relief and again took pleasure in my keen deductive powers. Sherlock Holmes would have undoubtedly booted that fool Watson down the stairs had I been around at the time. I could hardly wait for nightfall and the possible reappearance of the apparition, which I could now watch with detached interest, completely free from brain-sapping, reason-freezing fear.

I went downstairs and cooked a meal of six fried eggs, three sausages and boiled mushrooms. Nothing like brainwork to give a man an appetite.

*

Not a sight or sign of her did I see for three weeks.

It has been my unhappy experience that you can never rely on women, be they dead or alive, time-images or just whispers in a dark room. When you expect them, they never turn up; when you least want them – there they are, standing on the doorstep, armed with a nightbag and a seductive smile.

I sat up in bed and stared at that chair for night after night, and it remained as empty as a Russian church on May Day. I gave her every encouragement: 'Come on, you silly cow. Don't be shy. Show yourself.'

Finally, although I did not actually give up, I began to lose interest. Rather like a lover whose advances are not so much repelled as ignored. If a fire is not fed, it eventually dies down and becomes a mass of smouldering embers.

At the end of the third week I was forced to realize my mistaken assumption. We all think that ghosts can materialize only during the hours of darkness and that daytime is a kind of non-spook period, when the only spirits that are worthy of concern are kept in bottles.

At three o'clock in the afternoon, with the sunlight streaming through my nylon curtains, I walked into my bedroom – and there she was – seated in the chair and staring at me with those never-to-be-forgotten eyes. I stopped and was quite unable to subdue a sudden wave of fear. Then I remembered she was only a time-image; no more real than an old movie projected on a screen, long after the actors were dead.

I said: 'So there you are!' and sat down on the bed.

I decided she was – had been – a most beautiful woman. The long white face would defy the cruel fingers of time until late middle-age, and then there would be a graceful wilting; a gradual transformation. I do not know how long we sat and looked at each other – only, of course, she was not looking at me – but presently her arm came up and the hand beckoned, inviting me – or someone – to come forward and possibly be suitably rewarded for walking a few, faltering steps.

I laughed. It was really remarkable to feel so fearless; to view this apparition as merely an object for investigation. I said:

'I wonder, little lady, who he was? I take it you are beckoning to a man. Shameless hussy. Did he obey? He'd have been a fool not to, despite those glittering eyes.'

The beckoning went on. Arm bending, fingers almost clenching, then opening – the continuous gesture was becoming a little boring. I decided to experiment. I got up and walked towards the fireplace, then looked back over one shoulder. Her head had turned and the eyes were still watching me – and the left hand – the non-beckoning one – was out-stretched, as though she were appealing to me not to go away, and fear came riding in on a wave of anger. I shouted: 'Go away, damn you. I won't be badgered by a patch of coloured air. Go . . . o . . . o . . . o . . . o . . .'

She vanished. Left an empty chair and a man who cried out, 'I didn't mean it. Come back. Please come back.'

The summer died and autumn turned green leaves to russet-brown, then sent a chill north wind to chase them along country lanes and urban pavements. And during all that time the chair remained empty.

Gradually I came to accept the awful truth. I had fallen in love with a shadow. A beckoning figure that had as much reality as the Mona Lisa, Venus de Milo, or – and I kept harping back to this theme – a beautiful heroine in an old film.

Do not think for one moment that I surrendered to this humiliating passion without putting up a soul-shaking fight. While I lay in bed, day after day, week after week, eating little, unwashed, unshaven, watching an empty chair, I cursed myself and the long dead woman, and tried to climb back on to the throne of reason.

One night I moved into a spare room, determined not to look upon that cursed chair for at least three weeks, confident that it needed only will power to set me free again. But in less than ten minutes I was tormented by the thought that she might have returned, was sitting in a darkened room, beckoning, beckoning . . . and I would not be there. I unlocked the door, ran into the room that had been my haven in a world gone mad and sank down before the empty chair. My voice went screaming back along the misty avenue of time:

'Come back. Drive me mad – but come back.'

At the end of the third month, tired of appealing to a recalcitrant shade who refused to put in an appearance, I decided on a course of action that was long overdue. I went back to the second-hand furniture shop.

The old man came out of the shadows and peered at me over a pair of rimless spectacles.

'How can I serve the gentleman?'

The mere sight of his silly goatlike face, his frail, bent body, made the smouldering rage that had been fed by months of humiliation blaze up into a searing flame. I spat the question at him: 'The chair. Where did you get it?'

He shrugged, a helpless gesture that brought him to the threshold of death. 'I have sold so many chairs, Sir. I cannot remember where they all came from.'

I thrust my face forward until it was a bare six inches from his own. I saw the weak, watery eyes, the flabby, wrinkled skin and I hated him with a hatred that passed all understanding.

'You said it came from a house with an unfortunate history.'

He sighed, then turned away and began to walk between an agglomeration of rubbish that littered the floor, and I had the ridiculous idea that if I took my eyes from him for so much as a single second, he would turn into a lamp standard or just disappear. His plaintive voice manufactured words:

'All houses have an unfortunate history, as the gentleman must be aware. Tragedy walks in every room.'

I took three long paces forward and grabbed his shoulder, then swung him round. He did not appear to be frightened or even surprised at my aggressive action.

'Don't play with words. You know the chair I mean. Where did it come from?'

He eased his shoulder from my grip and stared wistfully out of the window. I had to strain my ears to catch the whispered words.

'It was pulled down as the gentleman will find out if he but walks to Bedford Park. Now a thousand little brick boxes cover its graveyard.'

I said softly, appealingly, 'The chair was in this shop. You must have seen her.'

His eyes were faintly mocking when he looked up.

'I am a very old man. She had no power over me. I would suggest the gentleman go to the Twilight Home. There is an old lady there. A Miss Pirbright. She may remember.'

The Twilight Home For Distressed Ladies – I was not aware that such places still existed – was an old house that loomed up from behind a curtain of high walls. I pressed the brass bell button and, trembling with excitement, although I had not the faintest idea what questions I was to ask or the kind of reception I would receive, waited for the grim, green door to open.

I was soon confronted by a tall coloured girl attired in a spotless white overall, whose face resembled a beautiful brown-tinted mask. She smiled gently and asked, 'You wish to see someone, sir?'

I cleared my throat. 'Yes, a Miss Pirbright.'

Her smile deepened. 'Won't you come in?'

I followed her along a path that was bordered on either side by flowering shrubs, then up a flight of steps and into the house. When we entered a spacious hall, she stopped and looked at me.

'Are you a relative, sir?'

'No – an old friend.'

She nodded slowly. 'I see. It is a very long time since Miss Pirbright received a visitor and she's very old. Over ninety, I believe. And – well – she's rather muddled. So do not be surprised is she does not recognize you.'

I would have been much more surprised if she had, so did not comment, but followed the nurse down a long passage and out into an enclosed verandah. Here a number of ancient ladies sat in deep armchairs, some staring blankly out of the windows, others reading or knitting, while a few – a pitiful few – talked with thin, querulous voices.

Miss Pirbright was tucked away in a far corner.

Extremely old age can be beautiful. It can also be pathetic, frightening or repulsive. Miss Pirbright was all three: a bundle of skin and bones wrapped in a tartan shrawl, a wrinkled monkey-face surmounted by a mist of sparse white hair. The nurse gently shook one boney shoulder and all but shouted: 'Miss Pirbright . . . Miss Pirbright. You have a visitor.'

The head came up and a harsh voice pronounced a single word. 'What?'

'A visitor for you. Isn't that nice?'

The faded blue eyes examined me with faint interest, then the voice found another word. 'Visitor?'

The nurse smiled at me ruefully. 'It's not one of her best days, I'm afraid. Don't tire her. I'll be back in a little while.'

I sat down on a nearby chair and tried to control my rising anger, for how could I possibly get information from this animated corpse, without shaking it until the toothless gums rattled? But I tried.

'Miss Pirbright,' I said imitating the nurse's shout, 'Did you once live in an old house in Bedford Park?'

I watched the tiny, clawlike hands pluck at the shrawl fringe, and when it seemed as if there was to be no answer, repeated the last two words several times. 'Bedford Park . . . Bedford Park . . .'

Her head nodded violently and the fingers became as tiny snakes writhing in a nest of wool.

'Aye, the house . . . house . . . sunlight and wallpaper and Miss Emily in the window.'

'Miss Emily!' The name was a verbal gem and I grabbed it, rolled it across my brain, toyed with it, all but set it to music. 'Tell me about Miss Emily.'

The old head came up and the eyes were filled with gentle reproach.

'Everybody knows Miss Emily. Beautiful as a spring morning, she is. Aye. Going to marry Mr Ascot, she is . . .' Again the violent nodding, the writhing fingers. 'Was . . . was . . . only, he never . . . never . . .'

'Never what?' I prompted. 'What was it that Mr Ascot did not do?'

Now there was a shocked expression on the wrinkled face, as though I had spoken an unmentionable word, or unearthed a secret that had been locked away in that dying brain for seventy years.

'He never came . . . not when he should. Miss Emily didn't cry. Just walked from church and went back to the house. Aye, sat in chair and waited.'

I shuddered. A man who has spent a lifetime looking for gold and has suddenly stumbled into an untapped mine, could not have experienced the joy that momentarily robbed me of speech. At length I was able to repeat the one word: 'Chair!'

The old brain had found another memory trail.

'Chair – aye. Old it were, the covering all tattered and after – he never came – not when he should – Miss Emily covered it herself. Clever she was with a needle. Never know it weren't done by an expert. "That be fine work, Miss Emily," I said. And she laughed and laughed . . . until she cry.'

So that was why the brocade was not very faded. It was not more than fifty – sixty – seventy years old? It was difficult to know the exact period the old woman was talking about, but it would seem to be somewhere back in her distant youth. I took a deep breath and dared to ask the final question.

'Miss Pirbright . . . did . . . did . . . Miss Emily ever sit in the chair and – beckon?'

I was not prepared for the look of terror that suddenly transformed the old face into a grimacing mask. The tiny mouth gaped and I could see a shrivelled tongue twisted up like a scrap of rotting leather, and a horrible sound came from the contorting throat as though a scream were being strangled at birth. I patted her back, muttered soothing words, but she jerked away, took two shuddering breaths, then asked in a shrieking whisper:

'How d . . . o . . . o yer know she beckon. Beckon . . .'

Before I could improvise a suitable answer, she went on as though I were not there, lost in some private nightmare that my question had brought back to life.

'I came into the room . . . moonlight it was . . . and Miss Emily was seated in that chair. I knew she'd done something dreadful . . . face as white as death . . . and God forgive me . . . I didn't want to move . . . just stand there and gasp . . . not scream . . . not then . . . and she beckoned to me . . . hand up . . . fingers bending . . . bending . . . bending . . .'

The harsh voice died away and I growled: 'Go on. What happened?'

'I . . . went to her . . . eyes glittering like lighted candles . . . smell of almonds . . . bottle on floor . . . she said . . . said . . . I die in his arms!'

That was all I could get from the old crone and presently the nurse returned and was none too pleased to find her in a state of near-collapse. But I walked down the bush-lined path on cushioned feet. I had solved the mystery. Miss Emily had committed suicide after being left at the altar. The truth was so farcical, so story-bookish, my ridiculous passion had died like a hothouse plant exposed to a winter's frost.

I was free.

I entered the house and ran upstairs to my bedroom.

Miss Emily – I had her name off pat now – was seated in the chair; pale, beautiful face turned towards me, eyes glittering, arm raised, beckoning – begging a young Miss Pirbright to come forward and hear her final nonsensical words. I stood by the door and laughed. Laughed until the tears ran down my face, stamped, pounded clenched fist against trembling legs, then screamed my contemptuous rage.

'If you had been there yesterday, my fine lady, I would have come to you. But not now. To die for love! You should have hated him. Died for hate. That would have been worth while. Hate ... hate ...'

I walked slowly towards her and the beckoning arm was more insistent now; sawing the air, jerking, the fingers opening and closing as though they were trying to grab a handful of departing life. I looked down into the pale face, once more confident, fearless, knowing exactly what must be done. I spoke gently as befits an intelligent man, dealing with an unusual situation. 'Time-image you may be. But I can't have you sitting there beckoning away for the rest of my life. The one sure way of bursting a bubble is to prick it.' And without wasting further time or words, I turned about and – sat on her.

It should have worked. It really should. A time-image can have no substance and once a sane, intelligent, fearless man has planted his posterior into its lap, there should absolutely nothing. But, oh, most merciful God, in whose existence I have never believed, why were there solid legs beneath mine, and why did two arms crawl round my chest ... and two cold hands seek my throat ... and hot breath sear my neck? I kicked and screamed ... tore at the confining arms and gradually – so very slowly – she melted. Became cold rubber, slimy flannel, tainted mist – then nothing. A bad dream dispersed by the first light of a summer morning.

I got up. Grabbed that damned, thrice accursed chair and smashed it against the nearest wall. I tore the brocade, pulled out the stuffing, broke the wooden frame . . . and then . . . a skull rolled across the floor . . . a skeleton hand caressed my knee . . .

No . . . no . . . there's no need for that. No need for strait-jackets, syringes or any of the other instruments of torture you've got stacked away. I'm quite calm now. But you do realize how she did it, don't you? Having killed him, she must have flattened him . . . or maybe dried him out. Then stripped the chair down to its frame . . . and folded the body up. Ha . . . ha . . . ha . . . damn clever when you think of it.

Fold legs under thighs, shove him down into the chair, torso and head fit very nicely into the back, arms into arms – get it? Then she replaced all the stuffing, re-covered the chair with a nice piece of new brocade . . . then . . . then died in his arms.

But having done all that, why does she still sit there, on that plain wooden chair and keep staring at me . . . beckoning . . . BECKONING . . .?